A DECEPTION
AT THORNECREST

ALSO BY ASHLEY WEAVER

Murder at the Brightwell

Death Wears a Mask

A Most Novel Revenge

Intrigue in Capri (ebook short)

The Essence of Malice

An Act of Villainy

A Dangerous Engagement

Ashley Weaver

MINOTAUR BOOKS
NEW YORK

This is a work of fiction. All of the characters, organizations, and events portrayed in this novel are either products of the author's imagination or are used fictitiously.

First published in the United States by Minotaur Books, an imprint of St. Martin's Publishing Group

www.minotaurbooks.com

Library of Congress Cataloging-in-Publication Data

Names: Weaver, Ashley, author.
Title: A deception at Thornecrest / Ashley Weaver.
Description: First edition. | New York : Minotaur Books, 2020. | Series: An Amory Ames mystery ; 7
Identifiers: LCCN 2020016410 | ISBN 9781250159793 (hardcover) | ISBN 9781250159809 (ebook)
Subjects: GSAFD: Mystery fiction.
Classification: LCC PS3623.E3828 D45 2020 | DDC 813/.6—dc23
LC record available at https://lccn.loc.gov/2020016410

Our books may be purchased in bulk for promotional, educational, or business use. Please contact your local bookseller or the Macmillan Corporate and Premium Sales Department at 1-800-221-7945, extension 5442, or by email at MacmillanSpecialMarkets@macmillan.com.

First Edition: 2020

10 9 8 7 6 5 4 3 2 1

For the women of the Novel Ladies Book Club:
Amanda Phillips, Courtney LaBoeuf, Denise Edmondson,
Sabrina Street, and Victoria Cienfuegos.
Here's to fourteen years and counting!

A DECEPTION
AT THORNECREST

1

THORNECREST
ALLINGCROSS, KENT
APRIL 1934

IT WAS ON a sunny spring morning in the eighth month of my pregnancy that a woman arrived on my doorstep claiming to be married to my husband.

The day started out much like any other, with no hint that I would soon be involved in a melodrama worthy of any of the radio plays with which I had lately been amusing myself. I arose early and breakfasted heartily before going to the morning room to complete my correspondence. My husband, Milo, was in London for the weekend, tending to some business with our solicitor, and I was taking advantage of the solitude to catch up on my letter writing.

Things had been quiet at Thornecrest, our country house, over the past few months, and, for once, I didn't mind the slow pace. My pregnancy had been progressing well, and we were expecting our first child in a month. Many of the anxieties I had felt in the initial stages of my pregnancy had begun to subside as we neared the birth. Perhaps it was the growing bond with my child. Or perhaps it was simply the knowledge that the baby's arrival was inevitable, whether I was prepared or not.

I was composing a letter to my cousin Laurel, who was on holiday in Greece, expressing just such a sentiment.

I am growing more and more excited the closer I come to the baby's arrival. I had worried that I might be anxious, but I am feeling rather calm and confident about it all. Perhaps when one realizes that life is about to be irrevocably altered, there is little choice but to embrace the change with open arms.

Little did I realize how apt this sentiment would prove to be.

A brief clearing of the throat drew my attention from my letter. I looked up to see Grimes, our butler, standing in the morning room doorway.

"Excuse me, Mrs. Ames," he said.

"Yes, what is it?"

He hesitated, and that was the moment I knew that something must be amiss. The butler was normally the epitome of unflappable professionalism, but I could tell he was doing his utmost to remain composed. That didn't seem to bode well for whatever he was about to say next, and I felt a brief surge of alarm that something might have happened to Milo before Grimes's next words put me more at ease.

"There is a young woman here . . ." The words trailed off, and I waited for him to continue, wondering at his uncharacteristic reticence.

"She gives her name as . . . Mrs. Ames," he said at last.

I frowned. Certainly it wasn't my mother. Grimes was acquainted with her, and he wouldn't be acting so strangely if it were she. Despite her somewhat aggressive personality, she was not the sort of person to ruffle Grimes's feathers. No, it must be someone else.

But there was no other Mrs. Ames. Though my maiden name and my married name were, coincidentally, the same, neither Milo nor I had another female relation with the same surname. Unless it was some distant relative of whom I was unaware.

"Does she say if she's a relative of mine or of Mr. Ames's?" I asked, to prod him forward.

He seemed to be marshalling himself for some unpleasant task, and then he came out with it.

"She claims to be Mrs. Milo Ames, madam."

I blinked. Surely he had misspoken. He did not correct himself, however, and I realized that he meant what he said.

"Mrs. . . . Milo Ames," I repeated after a moment of heavy silence.

"Yes, she's come looking for Mr. Ames . . . her husband."

This was growing more bizarre by the moment.

"There must be some mistake," I said. It was the only logical conclusion.

"Undoubtedly," he replied. I could tell, however, that he was not convinced. Grimes had never especially cared for Milo, and he didn't put forth much effort to hide the fact. Even now that Milo was making great strides toward putting his past behind him, Grimes remained staunchly disapproving. Perhaps it was because Grimes had always been loyal to Milo's father, and Milo and the elder Mr. Ames had never seen eye to eye.

In any event, there was nothing to be done about this mysterious situation but to face it head-on.

"You'd better show her in," I said. "I'm sure we shall sort this all out."

He nodded. "Very good, madam."

I rose from my seat at the writing desk and smoothed my hair, telling myself that I should remain calm. I didn't want to jump to conclusions. While it was true that my husband had something of a colorful reputation, I didn't think that bigamy would be much to his taste. After all, one marriage had often seemed to require much more effort than he cared to exert.

Nevertheless, I was a bit flustered by the idea that someone else was claiming to be married to him. It was all so strange.

A moment later Grimes returned to the room, followed by a young lady.

"Ah . . . Mrs. Ames, madam."

"Thank you, Grimes."

I knew he was curious, but he was too proper to linger in hopes of overhearing something; he turned and left, closing the door softly behind him.

I turned my gaze to my visitor. The girl was young and very pretty, with pale blond hair and cornflower-blue eyes. She was also distressed. Though she tried to hide it, I could tell that she was in a state of barely suppressed agitation. Her gloved hands were clenched at her sides, her face was ashen, and she was breathing much more quickly than the walk from the front hall to the morning room would normally dictate.

I was quite sure that Grimes had not told her what she was walking into, and I tried to decide the best way to broach the subject.

"Good morning," I said, deciding upon the conventional greeting.

"Who are you?" she asked bluntly. There wasn't any aggression in her tone, and I took it that she had been expecting to see Milo . . . or whoever she thought her "Mr. Ames" was.

"I'm Mrs. Ames," I said.

This caught her off guard. She looked a bit uncertain then, and I considered how I should proceed. One wasn't exactly taught the proper etiquette for such situations, after all.

"Mrs. Ames?" she repeated at last.

I nodded.

"Who . . . who is your husband?"

"My husband's name is Milo," I said.

She grew a shade paler, if possible, and it seemed to me that she swayed ever so slightly on her feet. I took a step toward her, but she collected herself and met my gaze before looking me over. It was, I thought, the first time she had looked closely at me, and her eyes stayed for a moment on my rounded stomach.

"You're going to have a baby," she said in the dazed tone of someone who has been met with a terrible shock.

"Yes." For some reason, I felt almost guilty admitting it.

She burst into tears.

Good heavens, this was going poorly.

After the briefest of pauses I hurried to her side, trying to decide how best to comfort her. Displays of great emotion had always been vexing to me, and this situation was particularly bewildering.

"He told... He said that he loved..." Her words broke off into a sob, her face buried in her hands.

I was at a total loss, but I was now certain that it wasn't Milo who had seduced this young woman. He wouldn't have made such a rash declaration.

I gently took her arm and led her toward the white Louis XIV sofa before the fireplace. She sank into it, still crying into her hands, and I looked around for a handkerchief. It was, I feared, too late to spare her gloves, but she might at least have a proper place to wipe her nose.

I discovered a clean handkerchief in the drawer of my writing desk and brought it to her.

She took it, still crying, but it seemed as though she was beginning to get control of her emotions.

I lowered myself into the chair beside her and waited for her to speak.

"I've made such a fool of myself by coming here," she said at last.

"Why don't you start from the beginning?"

She sniffed, wiping her eyes on the corners of the handkerchief, and then looked up at me.

"I met him in Brighton. I was taking a little holiday there. I'm a typist for a small company in London, but I had a few days off and a bit of savings, so I thought that I could benefit from the sun and sea air. It was very quiet since it was the off-season, but I enjoyed that. I'm not much of one for crowds of people."

I nodded encouragingly.

"And then, one day, I was walking along and there he was. The most handsome gentleman I had ever seen in my life."

Though I did not believe this young woman had married my husband, the description was accurate enough. Milo was remarkably good-looking, a fact that never failed to attract the attention of women wherever we went.

Of course, he was not the only handsome gentleman in England, and it was a stretch of the imagination to believe it was he who had bumped into this young woman on a beach in Brighton. Milo didn't even particularly care for beaches; they wreaked havoc on his Italian leather shoes.

"When did this happen?" I asked.

"It was the last week of January," she answered promptly.

Despite knowing that it could not possibly be my Milo to whom she was referring, my traitorous mind cast itself back to see if I could remember his whereabouts at that time.

He had been gone, I realized. He had been tending to some business affairs regarding a nightclub in which he had invested. Though I was quite certain he had been in London at the time, I supposed he might very well have gone south to Brighton instead. Not that I believed he would do such a thing.

"Would you like some tea?" I asked suddenly. I ought to have offered before now, but the truth of it was that I wasn't as concerned with my duties as hostess as I was with delaying her story. For some reason, my unease was building, and I needed a few moments to collect my thoughts.

But she shook her head. "I don't care for any, thank you."

And so there was nothing I could do but say, "Then please continue."

"I'm afraid I was gaping at him," she said. "He looked just like a cinema star. I knew he was going to walk right past me, so I thought that I would look at him for as long as possible. But he stopped in front of me. I stared at him for a moment, and then he leaned down and picked something up out of the sand. 'You've dropped your glove,' he said. I hadn't even realized that I had let it go. He held it out to me, and when I reached to take it, our fingers touched."

I found myself caught up in her romantic story, but the sudden recollection that she was allegedly telling it about my husband took some of the fun out of it.

"And so you formed an attachment?" I said, hoping to spare myself some of the details. I still didn't believe it was Milo, but it was all so strange. What I wished more than anything was that he would suddenly appear in the doorway and straighten all of this out.

"He remarked how cold my fingers were, and would I fancy a warm cup of tea? So we went to the teahouse. We talked for hours. And after that, we spent a great deal of time together over the next week. When it was nearly time for me to return to my job, I didn't know how I was going to bear it."

I thought back to being young and in love, to the undulating waves of bliss and confusion and anguish. Everything had always seemed so very urgent, as though the end of the world would come if romance were thwarted. The future had been alive with possibilities. And then suddenly one was married for six years and heavily pregnant. How quickly life goes by.

". . . and he said he didn't want to say goodbye either. And so we decided that we would be married."

"Just like that?" I asked, rather surprised at the swiftness of it all. Even at my most romantic, I could not envisage marrying a man I had known for only a few days.

She nodded. "We . . . we spent one more day together." One more night, their wedding night, was what she meant. I could tell that from the way she blushed and avoided meeting my eyes.

So this man, whoever he was, had taken her to bed under her assumption that he was her husband, though he had clearly been using a false name. What a wicked trick to play on a young, innocent girl.

"And then?"

"Then I had to return to my job, and he told me that he would follow me to London shortly. But . . . but he didn't. I've been waiting for so long, and I began to wonder if something terrible had happened to him, so I thought I'd better see if I could locate him myself."

"Did he give you this address?" I asked, wondering how far the charlatan had taken his ruse.

She shook her head. "I found his name in the London Directory. There was a listing for a flat and . . . and a big house in Berkeley Square. I . . . I thought it must be some mistake, for he had told me he didn't have a place to live in London. But he had mentioned that his people came from Kent. And then I found out that he had this property, so I decided to come here. I . . . I didn't know about you, of course."

"Of course," I said gently.

We sat for a moment, both of us, I am sure, contemplating how we might proceed from here. It seemed clear that either there was another handsome Milo Ames who hailed from Kent and had failed, for reasons unknown, to reunite with his new bride in London or that someone was using Milo's name, for what purpose I couldn't imagine.

The simplest way to deal with things, I knew, would be to have Milo come home directly. I ought to see if he could be reached at Mr. Ludlow's office.

It seemed the young lady was thinking the same thing, for she looked up at me. "When do you expect him back?"

"In a few days, but I should like to clear things up before then."

She nodded.

"He said his name was Milo Ames?" I asked.

She nodded again. "Yes."

"And he was from Kent."

"Yes."

"I assume someone must be using my husband's name. What did the man look like?"

I thought I detected a bit of sympathy in her expression as I asked the question. I'm sure she thought I was some sort of deluded cuckquean, left pregnant and alone while my husband ran about seducing other women.

A year or two ago, I might have believed it myself. But, though Milo had done his share of outrageous things in the past, he had left most of his wild ways behind him. Even in the wildest of times, I didn't think that he would have seduced a young woman under such outrageously false pretenses. He had never had any difficulties winning women without wedding them. Myself excluded, of course.

"As I said, he looks rather like a cinema star: tall and very dashing, with black hair and the bluest eyes you ever saw."

Tall and dark. Black hair, blue eyes. Though Milo was certainly not the only gentleman who might fit this bill, it did fit him.

A thought occurred to me. "Do you have a photograph, perhaps from your wedding?"

It seemed to me that she flushed slightly, and she dropped her gaze. "I . . . I have one, but I left it in London. I didn't . . . foresee needing it."

"Of course. Well, I'm certain there must be some explanation for all of this. Rest assured, we shall get it sorted out in no time."

"Yes, I . . . thank you, Mrs. . . . Mrs. . . ." She couldn't quite bring herself to call me by the name she had thought now belonged to her.

"Why don't you call me Amory," I said. "It will make things easier."

She drew in a relieved breath. "And please call me Imogen."

"Very well. Now that that's settled, perhaps we ought to come up with some sort of plan. The first thing we need to do, of course, is speak to Milo about all of this. He's in London now, but I should be able to contact him and tell him to come home."

She looked aghast at the suggestion. Her face grew a shade paler before my eyes. "Perhaps . . . perhaps it would be better if you were to speak to him without me."

I could see that she didn't relish the idea of some kind of dramatic scene. Despite my suggestion she had been deceived, she still thought we were talking about the same man. The only way to rectify that would be to have her meet Milo. I felt bad that Imogen was soon to learn she had been led astray by some rotten imposter.

"I can certainly speak to him alone first," I said. "But I think you'll find that my husband is not the man you met. What you have told me is a very serious matter. I must believe that there has been some kind of mistake, that someone is claiming to be Mr. Ames for some unknown purpose."

She nodded, though I could see that there was some little hint of doubt in her clear blue eyes.

An idea struck me suddenly. She might not have a photograph, but I did. I got up and crossed to the fireplace. There was a photograph of Milo and me there in a small gilt frame. We could clear up at least the question of his identity immediately.

I picked it up and walked to her. I expected, as I handed it to her, to see a look of confusion cross her face. But, instead, she looked up at me, her expression both miserable and pitying. "Yes. That's him."

2

I FELT A little surge of surprise followed by a sinking feeling in my stomach. I had been so sure this was all some sort of mistake, a case of stolen identity or some such thing. But it seemed rather improbable that someone might have stolen both Milo's name and his face.

There was, of course, the possibility that this young woman was operating some sort of scheme. Perhaps she had seen our picture in the gossip columns, read of our past marriage troubles, and assumed that I would pay her off to end the matter. It seemed the only possible solution.

But I looked at her, and, try as I might, I could not bring myself to believe that there was anything sinister in her motivations. One could feign sorrow and distress and even tears, but there was something in her whole attitude that made me believe that, whatever the true situation, she had been deeply affected by the experience.

Inwardly, I sighed. What a mess all of this was. I needed Milo to come home at once.

Until then, there was nothing that could be done. Although, I supposed I could at least help this young woman in the meantime.

"Where are you staying, dear?" I asked.

"I . . . I hadn't thought about it."

I realized belatedly that she had no doubt intended to stay here when she met up with her erstwhile husband. How very awkward this was becoming.

"You must stay here," I offered, though some part of me was very much hoping she would decline. Whatever the truth behind this situation was, things were bound to get even more uncomfortable than they were now. Granted, Thornecrest was large enough to accommodate a great many people without pushing them into one another's company, but the fact remained that I was not particularly looking forward to playing hostess under the circumstances.

"Oh, no!" she said quickly. "I couldn't. Is there, perhaps, a hotel nearby?"

"There's an inn in the village, the Primrose Inn. And there's an elderly lady, Mrs. Cotton, who lives in the blue house next to the apothecary shop. She offers short-term room and board." I rattled off the list of available lodgings a bit too quickly, perhaps, but I was very much relieved. I liked to consider myself a hospitable woman, but there were limits, after all.

"That will do nicely. Until . . . until things are resolved, I'll register under my own name: Prescott."

This was another relief. What a thoughtful girl. I could only imagine the talk that would spread amongst the villagers if she were to register as Mrs. Milo Ames.

"I'll have my driver take you there," I offered.

"Oh, no. I can walk."

"Are you quite sure?"

"Yes. I . . . I need some time to think."

I imagined that both of us would be doing a good deal of thinking over the next few days.

"I'll ring you when Milo gets back."

She nodded, her expression miserable. "You've been very kind. I'm so sorry to have come here and caused so much trouble."

"You haven't caused any trouble," I assured her, though we both knew that this wasn't precisely the truth.

"I . . . I just can't understand it," she said softly.

"I know, dear. But don't worry. We'll sort it all out."

She took her leave then, and I rang for Grimes.

"Yes, madam?" he asked when he arrived in the doorway. I was certain that he must be curious about my encounter with the other Mrs. Milo Ames, but his expression gave nothing away.

"Will you please see if you can locate Mr. Ames and tell him to come home as soon as possible?"

THE WAIT FOR Milo's return would no doubt be a long one, so I was glad that I had an afternoon engagement to keep me occupied. The Springtide Festival was to be held next weekend, and I was a member of the committee of ladies who were overseeing the preparations.

The annual village event was held on the grounds of Bedford Priory, the home of Lady Alma Bedford, one of our local eccentrics. The youngest child of the Earl of Endsley, she had purchased and restored the Priory, the property of which abutted Thornecrest, nearly thirty years ago, after her father's death. Now nearing fifty, she was a striking woman with strong features, short iron-gray hair, and sharp, dark eyes. She had a direct but not unfriendly manner and spent all her time and a good deal of her fortune on her stables.

If there was anyone in Kent who was as enthusiastic about horses as Milo, it was Lady Alma. She had never married but referred to her horses as her children. She seldom wore anything other than riding clothes and was often seen galloping about the countryside in all manner of inclement weather.

The first festival, a small gathering to celebrate the beginning of warmer weather with friends, food, and horse racing, had been her idea. With the initial backing of her wealth and her forceful personality, it had occurred annually ever since, growing in size and significance. We now had a fully formed committee with an allotment of local charitable funds to support the enterprise.

The Springtide Festival was a source of great excitement and pleasure in Allingcross, a chance for the locals to pit their best horses against one another in a race and hedge-jumping course, to eat and be merry, and to be outdoors and enjoy the sunshine now that winter was passing.

Though the event was held on the grounds of Bedford Priory, the ladies of the committee met at the vicarage. The vicar's wife, Mrs. Elaine Busby, was confined to a wheelchair after a dreadful automobile accident that had injured her and claimed the life of her daughter fifteen years before. She moved about quite easily in her chair, but Lady Alma thought it best that we meet at the vicarage and had tactfully argued that it was in a more central location than the Priory.

We had managed to get most of the planning done at prior meetings, and this was our final gathering before the festival. For most of the meeting, we simply enjoyed tea and idle chatter, drawing around to business matters only after the last of the biscuits had been consumed.

"The vendors are settled, and all of the food has been taken care of, I think?" Lady Alma looked at Mrs. Busby, who was overseeing that aspect of the planning.

She nodded. "It's all settled. We'll have the usual tea tent, which will serve refreshments periodically, as well as the various vendors who have chosen to set up booths with items for sale. I've spoken to everyone again this week. And then, of course, there will be tea following the races."

They talked for a few minutes then about what sorts of food would be available—cakes; sausage; puddings; tarts; apple, cherry, and pear jellies and jams from local orchards—and my mind wandered. Truth be told, I was glad to be little more than a nominal member of the committee this year. Now that my pregnancy was nearing its end, it seemed that the strain of every task was multiplied.

"There are several new locals with wares for sale this year," Mrs. Unger said as the conversation drifted to the other festival events.

"I know several ladies have spoken of entering the pickling competition," Mrs. Norris put in.

"My husband will be offering pony rides to the children," Mrs. Hampton reminded us. "And I believe Mabel will be telling fortunes."

The door to the sitting room opened just then, and a young woman stepped into the doorway. It was Marena Hodges, one of the village girls. Her shoulder-length dark hair was windblown, and her cheeks were flushed from the cool breeze. Even the thick woolen jumper and mud-flecked leather boots she wore did nothing to diminish her prettiness and the elegance of her bearing.

"Oh, excuse me," she said, casting her amber-colored eyes over the assembled guests before settling them on Mrs. Busby. "I didn't realize that you had company, Aunt Elaine."

"It's quite all right, dear. You're welcome to join us, if you like. We're discussing the festival."

A smile flickered across the girl's face, and there was some mixture of amusement and complacency in it. Her eyes, though they moved about the room, had a faraway look in them, as though her mind were elsewhere.

"That's kind of you, but, if you ladies will excuse me," she said, "I've a few things to attend to. You know I shall be only too glad to help you on the day of the festival, of course."

"I suppose I should be going as well," Lady Alma said, rising from her chair with her habitual swiftness. I was reminded rather of one of her geldings clearing a hedge. "I like to visit my darlings before dinner."

This was the committee's cue to adjourn. One by one, the assembled women took their leave, until it was just Mrs. Busby and me alone in the little sitting room. For some reason, I felt disinclined to go. Perhaps it was only that rising from chairs was getting more difficult with each passing day.

But it was also true that there was something comforting about the warm little parlor. For as long as I could remember, I had always felt at peace when visiting the vicarage. I supposed it had as much to do with the Busbys themselves as with the homely atmosphere of this room.

Mrs. Busby, with her silvery hair, warm brown eyes, and gentle spirit, was the picture of a grandmother any child would be glad to have.

"You look tired, Mrs. Ames," she said as I worked to summon the effort to begin to rise from my chair. "Would you care for another cup of tea?"

I was prepared to refuse but thought better of it. I wouldn't mind a few more minutes of company. After all, it was a good distraction from all the thoughts swirling through my head.

"That would be lovely. Thank you."

Mrs. Busby refilled my teacup. Despite the limitations of her chair, she moved easily and with natural grace.

"I suppose you'll be glad when the baby has arrived," she said, stirring sugar into her own cup of tea. "I know the last month or two is always a great strain."

I nodded, my hand straying to my stomach. "Though I must say, I shall miss feeling him so close to me."

"Yes, that is a special time." She looked wistful for a moment, and I felt a little as though I had made a faux pas. The Busbys had lost their only child, a daughter called Sara, in the accident that had confined Mrs. Busby to her wheelchair. Though I had not known them then, people often spoke of the way in which the vicar and his wife had borne the tragedy with strength and dignity. Their lives had changed immensely since the accident, but I had never known them to be discouraged. Nevertheless, I had noticed the way Mrs. Busby smiled, with just the faintest hint of sadness, when she interacted with the children of the village.

The sound of music filtered into the room, a rousing jazz piece. Marena had apparently turned on the radio in the room above us.

"I'm not sure if you've heard that Marena has been staying with us for the past few months?" Mrs. Busby asked.

"I heard something to that effect," I answered honestly. Though I tried very hard not to participate in village gossip, it was nearly impossible not to glean bits and pieces of news.

Though she called her "Aunt Elaine," Marena was not really Mrs.

Busby's niece. Marena's mother, Mrs. Jane Hodges, was a rather grim local woman who lived in a cottage isolated from the village and had always seemed a good deal more concerned with the bees she kept than with her daughter.

In consequence, Marena had spent a good deal of time at the vicarage in her younger days and had been great friends with Sara. She had, in fact, been in the automobile with Mrs. Busby and Sara on the day of the accident.

After Sara's death, Marena and the Busbys had remained very close, and Marena often spent time at the vicarage, doing her best to help Mrs. Busby adjust to life in a wheelchair.

"She and her mother have had another falling out." She sighed. "I don't know what to think of that woman. She doesn't realize that the harder she pushes Marena, the farther away she's going to drive her. It all started with Marena's young man, Bertie. I knew that the more Mrs. Hodges objected, the stronger Marena's attachment would be. That's the way with young people, isn't it? She should have just let the matter run its course."

I wondered if that was why Marena had seemed so starry-eyed. She had been walking out as of late with Bertie Phipps, a young man who lived not far from Thornecrest. He'd often helped both Milo and Lady Alma at their stables, and I thought he seemed intelligent and keen to make something of himself. Perhaps the two of them had been building castles in the air together. Marena had always been a dreamy sort of girl.

"Well," Mrs. Busby said brightly. "I just hope that the festival goes well. Mrs. Hodges will be there selling her honey, so perhaps she and Marena will be able to sort out some of their differences."

"Yes, perhaps they will," I answered vaguely.

Though I was sympathetic to Marena's situation, I was very much preoccupied with my own family difficulties.

". . . and with Marena's new position at the inn, it's been easier for her to stay here, but still . . ."

I nodded, but my thoughts had shifted back to Milo. I wondered if he was on the train yet. Grimes had reached Milo and confirmed that he would arrive home that evening. It had occurred to me more than once that I ought to have rung up Milo myself, but I didn't want to talk to him about the matter over the telephone.

As my thoughts switched to Milo, so, it seemed, did Mrs. Busby's.

"And what of Mr. Ames?" she asked. "How is he feeling about the arrival of the baby?"

She had always been very careful when she spoke to me about Milo, tiptoeing around mentions of him as someone might of a person with some dreadful disease. Sin being the prevailing ailment in his case.

"I think he's very much looking forward to it," I said.

"I'm glad. I saw him in the village this morning, but it was from a distance, and I didn't have the chance to speak with him."

Milo had been in London for two days, so it must have been another morning, but I didn't bother to correct her. My mind was still preoccupied by her question and my answer to it. Milo had given every indication that he was ready to be a father.

Unless, that is, he had married another woman in Brighton.

I AT LAST bid Mrs. Busby farewell and returned to Thornecrest where I ate dinner alone and then went to my room to read, studiously avoiding looking at the clock.

I tried not to worry about the situation with Imogen, but it was very hard not to. The truth of it was, Milo and I had had a somewhat rocky relationship for much of our marriage. It was only in the past two years that things had begun to grow better between us. While I really didn't believe that he would have committed bigamy, I couldn't help but feel that there was something amiss here, for I couldn't quite discount Imogen's teary-eyed sincerity.

He arrived home quite late. I was sitting in our bedroom, my eyes trained on the same page of a book that they had been rereading for ten minutes.

"Hello, darling," he said, his gaze sweeping over me in that way he had of late of assessing my condition whenever he saw me. "Is everything all right?"

"Yes. That is . . . I'm not quite sure."

"Do you feel unwell?"

"No, no. I'm quite well."

"Grimes said that you weren't ill, but I was concerned, just the same."

Though perhaps it wasn't quite nice of me, I had been counting on that reaction to a certain extent. Under normal circumstances, he would've taken his time about coming home; he certainly would've waited for the morning train rather than returning at this hour.

"I'm sorry if I worried you," I said, a tad facetiously.

"Well, I'm glad to be home anyway. The flat always seems so empty without you."

He came and sat down on the bed, pulling at his necktie with a sigh. "So what was the reason for the summons? Did you miss me?"

"You didn't happen to marry another woman in January, did you?" I asked lightly.

He turned to look over his shoulder at me. "I beg your pardon?"

I gave him the faintest smile. "It's a simple enough question."

"What on earth are you talking about?"

I tried to gauge his reaction, to see if there was anything telling in it. There wasn't the faintest glimmer of guilt or even unease in his bright blue eyes, but I knew from experience that this was not conclusive proof of innocence.

I continued in a casual tone. "A very pretty young woman named Imogen Prescott came here today and said she married you three months ago in Brighton."

He laughed.

I searched his face, still trying to detect any sign of deception. It was very difficult to tell with Milo, for he was excellent at hiding his thoughts and, as a general rule, suffered little remorse for his misdeeds. But I was fairly certain that he was genuinely amused at the suggestion, and a bit of the weight I had felt on my chest since this afternoon seemed to lift.

Since I had said nothing, he seemed to realize that I was in earnest, and his brows rose. "You're serious."

"Quite serious. She identified a photograph of you."

His answer was swift and unequivocal. "Then she's lying."

"You're quite sure?"

He looked at me as though I had said something very silly indeed. "Yes, darling. I'm quite sure I did not marry a young woman in Brighton in January."

I let out a little sigh. "I had rather hoped you'd say that."

"You don't mean to say you believed her?"

"I didn't know what to believe," I admitted. "It didn't seem likely to me, but she was very convincing."

"Whatever she was, you ought to have known better than to think I would commit bigamy, of all things. One wife is more than enough to contend with."

I gave a little laugh. "Somehow I thought you might consider it from that angle."

"And, of course, I wouldn't want another wife when I've got you," he added belatedly.

"Oh, how you flatter me."

"What else did this young woman have to say?"

I related to him the details of Imogen's visit. He listened with his usual unreadable expression; nothing ever really shocked him.

"I suppose someone's been using your name," I said when I had finished.

"That does seem a possible explanation, though I don't know why anyone would want to go to all that trouble."

"Obviously someone was toying with that girl." I felt a surge of indignation. "They gave her a false name, convinced her that they were married, and now she's been . . . compromised."

"It seems a bit far-fetched. It's more likely that it's some sort of ruse.

It sounds as though she came here hoping to get money out of you. Perhaps she thought you'd pay her to go away without ever saying anything to me."

"The thought had occurred to me," I admitted. "But there was something very genuine about her. She doesn't seem to be that sort of person. Once you've met her, you'll see what I mean."

"Oh, I doubt very much that I'll ever meet her. I shouldn't be at all surprised if she has mysteriously disappeared from the inn by tomorrow. She's probably already back in London by now." He reached across the bed and patted my leg before rising. "She may have looked young and innocent, but there are a lot of excellent liars in the world, my sweet."

He went then to bathe and dress for bed, and I went back to my book. I found, however, that I still couldn't seem to concentrate.

I had the uneasy sensation that there was trouble on the horizon.

THOUGH I KNEW it would be best to straighten things out as soon as possible, I put off ringing the inn for Imogen the next morning. Perhaps I was not quite ready for the emotional upheaval I knew it was likely to cause.

Milo, still appearing unperturbed and, indeed, mostly disinterested in the whole matter, had gone off to the stables to see to his horses. A keen equestrian, when he wasn't darting off to London or the Continent, he was often gone to livestock auctions or horse shows or out riding for long stretches.

Not that I minded. Truth be told, I was rather glad at the moment not to have him underfoot. Though I truly believed that he was blameless in the whole matter, I still felt unaccountably irritated with him in the way one does when one dreams a spouse has done something untoward and one can't quite shake the feeling of annoyance upon waking.

I considered going out walking in the direction of the village to see if I could encounter Imogen casually in the streets or shops near the inn, but I didn't feel quite up to a strenuous jaunt this morning. Besides, there was no reason to rush.

I supposed I was just feeling a bit out of sorts. Pregnancy had forced me to slow my usual pace, and I wasn't used to being at such loose ends.

Looking around the sitting room, I spotted several items that could use tidying. I had finished knitting a blanket and bonnet for the baby, and there was also a stack of children's books with colorful illustrations that Milo had purchased in London.

I had just put everything into my knitting basket to carry to the nursery when Winnelda, my maid, appeared in the doorway.

"Oh, madam, let me do that for you!" she said, rushing toward me and taking the basket from my hands before I could protest. "You shouldn't be carrying things, you know. Not at this delicate stage."

"I'm perfectly capable of doing it," I said. I submitted rather than argue, though I didn't feel at all delicate and was perfectly capable of managing a basket of that size. I was very much looking forward to the baby's arrival, for it seemed that I couldn't do anything without being fussed over.

"Are you feeling all right, madam?" Winnelda asked, eyeing me as she prepared to take the basket from the room. Ever since discovering I was going to have a baby, she had watched me with all the care the proprietor of a china shop might exhibit when dealing with a piece of Royal Worcester bone china. As she was the eldest of six sisters, I thought she ought to know I wasn't in danger of breaking into pieces at the slightest provocation just because I was with child.

"I'm feeling very well, Winnelda," I said, for what was surely the thousandth time in the last five months.

"Would you like something more to eat?"

"No, thank you. I've just had a very large breakfast."

She looked at me a bit skeptically. Her mother, she had informed me, had gained a good deal of weight when pregnant with each of Winnelda's sisters, and I was not living up to the standard. Though I was fairly tall and naturally slim, Winnelda seemed to think it unusual that I had not grown more rotund.

I turned, prepared to leave the room.

"From the back you still can't tell . . ." she said sadly. "Maybe if you eat more eggs. And put some extra butter on your toast."

I had been eating quite enough for an entire family, so I wasn't at all concerned. Nor was my doctor, who felt that I was in excellent health.

"I'll keep that in mind," I said. I escaped the room then, deciding that a walk would do me good after all.

I collected a jacket and made my way out the French doors in the morning room. The air was cool but refreshing, and I drew in a deep breath as I walked across the grass, which was still damp with morning dew. Spring had begun to make its first marks upon the landscape, and green was sprouting all around me: the verdant lawns, the leaves on the trees, the last of the snowdrops giving way to the daffodils. It was always lovely to see the first signs of new life emerging in the countryside.

Fitting, too, I supposed, that new life would be joining my household as well.

Without thinking too much about it, I wandered in the direction of the stables.

Milo didn't enter his horses in the Springtide Festival races. He didn't think it sporting to pit his Thoroughbreds and show horses against the local animals. It was a snobbish sentiment, perhaps, but I had to agree that it would be difficult for anyone in the county to defeat Milo's horses.

I reached the stable door and stepped inside. Things were quiet and neat, everything in its place. In contrast to his nonchalant approach to most things in life, Milo, like the stern captain of a Royal Navy vessel, ran a tight ship in his stables. He had no patience for shoddy or incompetent work, and his somewhat tyrannical approach to the matter had left more than one browbeaten stable hand in his wake.

I walked alongside the stalls, looking at the horses. The smell of fresh hay hung in the air, and there were the soft sounds of horses rustling and nickering. The biggest stall belonged to Xerxes, the prize of Milo's stables. He was a coal-black Arabian with the devil's own temper, notorious for biting and kicking stable hands, and no one but Milo had ever been able to ride him.

He snorted when he saw me, tossing his jet-colored mane in a show of ill temper. "You needn't worry, Xerxes," I said. "I haven't the faintest intention of bothering you."

He stamped a foot in response, but I ignored him and moved on to the next stall. This was where my horse, Paloma, was housed. She was a sleek chestnut mare with white forelegs and face.

"Hello, old girl," I said as she came to greet me. I rubbed a hand down her nose and wished that I had thought to bring an apple or carrot with me. For obvious reasons, I had not been able to ride in some time, and I missed our jaunts across the fields together.

I heard Xerxes snort again, loudly, but paid little attention until a voice sounded behind me. "Oh, good morning, Mrs. Ames."

I turned to see Bertie Phipps, Marena Hodges's young man. I hadn't heard him approaching. He was a tall, handsomely built boy with a shock of darkish blond hair that he was constantly sweeping back from his forehead. He was dressed in shirtsleeves and grass-stained, mud-flecked trousers and holding a harness in one of his hands.

"Good morning, Bertie," I said. "How are you?"

"Very well, Mrs. Ames. And yourself?" He flushed a little as he said this, his eyes landing on my stomach and flittering guiltily away.

"I'm quite well, thank you," I replied, ignoring this reaction. "You're helping Mr. Ames with the horses, I see."

"Yes, ma'am. A good day to exercise them, he says. I'm always glad to give them a turn about the pasture."

I looked at the specks of mud on his trousers. "Don't tell me you attempted to ride Xerxes."

He shook his head. "Not yet. But one day. It was Hades that threw me. Went over a hedge when I wasn't expecting it."

"You weren't harmed?"

"Oh, no. I know the right way to fall. Lady Alma says each fall is a horseman's badge of honor."

Bertie also spent a good deal of time at Lady Alma's stables. Lady Alma often gave him odd jobs to do, just as Milo did. It had been a dream of Bertie's to own a horse of his own, and he had saved every penny he could toward that end. Only recently, he had accomplished his goal and purchased a horse he called Molly. Milo had told me Bertie was very much looking forward to riding her in the Springtide Festival race.

"Well, I'm glad you're all right," I said.

"None the worse for wear, excepting my clothes, of course. It's a bit muddy now that the snow's melted, but I don't mind mud if it means the sun is shining."

"Yes, the weather is rather lovely, isn't it? I saw Marena yesterday. I thought she must have been out for a walk with you."

His smile faltered. "We . . . we haven't been seeing so much of each other lately," he said, the slightest flush creeping up on his cheeks.

I realized that I had made some sort of error; that was what I got for assuming.

"Oh," I said faintly. "I'm sorry."

"It'll be all right. We love each other, and that's what matters in the end. We'll settle things." He offered me an unconvincing smile.

"There you are, Phipps," Milo said, striding into the stables, his spotless jodhpurs, shining black boots, and crisply pressed white shirt in marked contrast to Bertie's soiled attire.

"I've sent Geoffrey off with Hades, so you can take Gwendolyn. She's never been one for hedges."

"Right away, Mr. Ames," he said. He turned, tipping his head to me, the lock of blond hair flopping forward. "Good day, Mrs. Ames."

"Good day, Bertie."

He left the stables and Milo turned to me. "Do you think you should be out here?"

"Why shouldn't I?"

"Horses can be unpredictable. I shouldn't like to see anything happen to you."

I sighed. I supposed I was simply going to have to put up with being treated like a porcelain doll until the baby arrived. "I don't intend to throw myself in the way of any trampling horses."

He smiled. "I'm glad to hear it."

I glanced at the door just in time to see the departing figure of Bertie Phipps disappearing into the sunlight. "Have he and Marena Hodges parted ways?"

Milo shrugged. "I haven't the faintest idea."

I was not at all surprised that Milo had failed to keep up with the shifting sands of village romance.

It was curious. Marena had looked so radiant yesterday. Certainly there had been nothing to mark her as a woman who had recently had her heart broken. I suspected the end of the romance had been more her idea than Bertie's.

"Were you looking for me, darling?" Milo asked, recalling my attention.

"Not particularly. Winnelda was stifling me, and I felt the need to escape."

"You'd think in a hundred odd rooms you might have evaded her."

He was right, of course. Thornecrest was large enough that one could avoid human contact indefinitely if one had a mind to do so. But rooms full of antiques, however lovely, were no substitute for fresh air.

"I needed to breathe," I said simply.

He studied me, then neatly summed up what I was feeling in that easy way of his. "You're worried about that girl."

I nodded. "Among other things."

"You rang the inn?"

"No. I've been avoiding it."

"You'll likely find she's gone when you do. I'd wager we'll not see her again."

"Perhaps not," I answered. I didn't know whether to hope he was right or wrong. A part of me supposed it would be better if that were the case, if Imogen had been hoping to get something from me with her lie and, having failed, would not come back. Another treacherous part of me hoped that there was some sort of mischief afoot.

While I was enjoying this first phase of motherhood, I had to admit that the past few months had also held something akin to tedium. Despite my increasing maternal feelings, my streak of adventure had not been quelled. And things had been exceedingly quiet since we had returned home from New York in November.

"Come, darling," Milo said, sliding an arm around me. "I'll frighten Winnelda away and you can keep me company while I answer some correspondence. I've been neglecting responding to some letters; you know how I hate it."

"All right."

We walked back toward the house in companionable silence. I glanced at Milo as we went. He looked relaxed and happy. He usually appeared that way after he'd spent time with his horses. I felt some of my own tension leave me, as though his contentment was contagious. His arm was still around me, and the solid warmth of him against my side was comforting.

I was growing accustomed to it, I realized—of finding comfort in his presence. Our marriage had not always been this way; in the past we had been at odds nearly as often as we were in tune. I was immeasurably glad that, with a baby on the way, we were closer than we had ever been.

We entered the house through the front door and were greeted by Grimes. For the second time in as many days, his normally imperturbable countenance had slipped ever so slightly, and I could tell something was wrong.

"What is it, Grimes?" I asked as Milo helped me off with my jacket.

"There is a . . . gentleman asking to see Mr. Ames."

"Who is it?" Milo asked.

Grimes hesitated. "He refuses to give his name."

How very odd. I didn't know what to think. Everything was normally so quiet here at Thornecrest, and now we were having all manner of excitement.

Milo let out a short, irritated breath. "It's probably one of those Americans with the nightclub. They all seem averse to revealing their identities."

Since Milo had thrown in his lot with American bootleggers to open a nightclub in London, I didn't think he had much room for complaint on their unconventional and secretive behaviors.

"Where is the fellow?" he asked.

"He's in the morning room, sir. He . . . declined to leave until he had spoken with you."

"Thank you, Grimes."

"I'll come with you," I said. "You know I enjoy meeting your underworld friends."

Milo gave me a look but did not protest as I followed him toward the morning room. He motioned for me to precede him as we reached the door, and I caught sight of the gentleman standing before the fireplace and looking up at the painting on the wall.

He turned at the sound of our approach, and I blinked. The strange young man standing in our sitting room looked so much like Milo that I thought for a fraction of a moment Milo had done some feat of magic and entered the room before me without my noticing.

Milo, it seemed, must have noticed the resemblance as well, for he dispensed with any formalities. "Who the devil are you?" he demanded.

The young man smiled Milo's smile. "My name is Darien Ames. I'm your long-lost brother."

4

I'M FAIRLY CERTAIN I must have gaped at him, so startled was I by this announcement. A brother? Surely not. And yet, the proof seemed to be before my eyes as I studied him. He was a bit younger than Milo, but it was uncanny how much he looked like him.

He smiled at me, and a dimple appeared in one cheek. "Mrs. Ames, I presume?"

"Yes," I said slowly. I was still uncertain as to how to proceed.

"I'm pleased to meet you. I've seen your pictures in the society columns. You're even lovelier in person, if possible."

"Thank you," I said vaguely.

I turned to look at Milo for some cue as to how I should react.

Milo was never better at hiding his emotions than when there was something significant to conceal, and this incident was no exception. To look at him, one would think our visitor was no more noteworthy than a traveling salesman come to try to ply us with his goods.

"I don't have a brother," he said flatly.

If the young man was discouraged by this less-than-warm welcome, he gave no sign of it. It seemed Milo wasn't the only one who could hold his countenance.

"You do, in fact." His tone was light. "An illegitimate half brother, at least. Our father had a relationship with my mother for several years, until he tired of her and left her with nothing but a broken heart, a baby to care for, and a stain on her reputation. He was a blackguard, through and through."

"I don't know if what you're saying is true, but if you're trying to make me angry by insulting my father, you'll have to try much harder."

The smallest smile flickered across the young man's face, and I was struck again by how much he looked like Milo. From a distance, I imagined they would be nearly indistinguishable.

The realization came to me suddenly. This was no doubt the man who had married Imogen, the man that Mrs. Busby had seen in the village when Milo had been in London.

Things were falling into place. It seemed Imogen had married a Mr. Ames after all.

"You didn't like our father either then," he said. "It seems we have something in common besides our looks, despite having been raised in different households."

Milo's face was still impassive, but I knew his gambler's brain was running things through, trying to determine what the best course of action might be in dealing with this young man. I thought that perhaps I should say something, but for once all my years of society training failed me, and I was at a loss.

"What do you want?" Milo asked at last.

"Who says I want anything?"

"Then what are you doing here?"

The young man gave a dry laugh. "I take it you're not going to welcome me home."

"This isn't your home," Milo replied.

Darien glanced around the room, his insolent gaze taking in the antique furniture and expensive décor, all of it furnished by Milo's father. There was nothing overtly mercenary in his expression, but I wouldn't have been surprised if a request for money was forthcoming.

"No," he said at last. "I know it's not, but I did hope that you'd be happy to see me."

I might have felt sympathy for him at those words, but there was something in his tone that expressly rejected the sentiment.

"How do I know you're even telling the truth?" Milo said.

"For pity's sake, Milo," I broke in, finding my voice at last. "Look at him."

Milo glanced at me, his expression making it clear that my interference was not exactly welcome.

"If you don't mind, darling, I'd like to have a talk with Darien alone."

I hesitated. I didn't like being excluded from the conversation. And, what was more, I was fairly certain the two men could do with a buffer between them. Whatever the situation, I felt that neither of them was in the frame of mind to hold a civil conversation.

I could tell by looking at Milo, however, that he wasn't likely to take my wishes into account at the moment. And, in all fairness, it made sense that they might want to discuss this matter in private.

I suppose my hesitation was obvious, for Darien flashed me a smile. "Don't worry. We shan't kill each other in your absence."

"That remains to be seen," Milo said, his eyes on his brother.

Darien's smile widened.

"I . . . shall I send in some tea?" It was a silly thing to say, perhaps, but tea had mediated more precarious situations than this.

Milo glanced again at the young man who claimed to be his brother. "I think something stronger may be in order."

"My sentiments exactly," he replied.

I nodded. There was a sideboard in the corner of the room with all the liquor they might require, so it seemed there was nothing else for me to do but take my leave.

With one last glance at the two men, I turned and left the room.

I HAVE NEVER been very good at waiting. Alas, aside from putting my ear to the keyhole—a task that my growing stomach would make physically difficult if I were even so inclined—there was little that I could do.

And so I went to the sitting room and began working on my knitting. Keeping my hands busy did not, however, stop my mind from turning over all the possibilities produced by this latest turn of events.

I had no doubts that this young man was Milo's brother. Their looks convinced me of that, but even if they had not been so similar in appearance, there were mannerisms I had noticed in Darien's face, even in the space of a few moments—the tilt of that flashing smile and the impudent flick of the brow—that could not have been replicated by chance.

Milo's father had never remarried after the death of his wife; by all accounts he had loved her deeply and been much affected by her passing. Nevertheless, I supposed it would be naïve to believe that he had never sought out another source of female companionship. Yes, it was entirely probable that the young man was telling the truth on that score.

But even this brought up several more questions. Why had Darien chosen now to make this appearance on our doorstep? Had it something to do with Imogen? As far as she went, why had he chosen to marry her using Milo's name? And if they had married in Brighton and agreed to meet in London, what had brought both of them to Thornecrest at the same time?

The whole thing was a muddle, each question leading directly to another more complex one, and I felt a sudden surge of annoyance that I had allowed myself to be dismissed from the conversation. Surprise half brother or no, I ought to have stayed and heard what there was to be said.

Time ticked slowly by. I finished the infant sock I was working on and began to knit its mate.

At last Milo came into the sitting room. I set my knitting aside, studying his face for clues as to how the meeting had gone. It was difficult to tell, though I could detect a faint hardness about his mouth and a certain set to his shoulders that told me that it hadn't ended in handshakes and welcoming pats on the shoulder.

"Has he gone?" I asked.

"Yes."

"But he's coming back." Surely things couldn't be settled between them in one brief conversation.

"Yes, there are a great many matters to discuss."

"What happened?" I asked.

"He does appear to be my half brother." His voice betrayed nothing of how he felt about this revelation. Perhaps he didn't know yet how he felt. "He had a few documents in his possession that bear him out: letters, a photograph of my father with his mother."

"Are you . . . surprised?"

"It's unexpected, of course, but nothing my father might have done would much surprise me. In any event, we never took much interest in each other's personal lives, aside from the reprimands he would occasionally give me for being too public in my behaviors. He might have had any number of mistresses."

I didn't know exactly what Milo was thinking, but I knew this must be an extreme shift from the way he had seen things. He had been the only child of parents who were deceased, the last of the Thornecrest Ameses, and now there was this young man, a brother he had not expected and did not especially want.

"Are you all right?" I asked softly.

He looked over at me. "Of course."

In the past, I might not have pressed, but we were much more comfortable together now than we had been in the early days of our marriage. I had learned that it was possible to get behind that impassive façade of his.

"Surely you must have some thoughts about all of this."

"Certainly I do, but I'm afraid they're not for your delicate ears, my love." There was an edge in his voice now, the irritation he felt at all of this coming to the surface.

Milo very much liked to be in command of things, was accustomed to matters bowing to his will and his money, and this situation was something entirely beyond his control. A brother was not going to dematerialize no matter what one thought about him.

"I know it's quite a surprise," I said, "but that doesn't mean it need be unpleasant."

"I have a bastard brother who's used my name to convince a woman to marry him. You don't think that's a bit of a problem?"

I sighed. "Of course. Did you speak to him about Imogen?"

"I did. He claims they were never married."

"He denies it?" I was trying to keep my temper down. Milo had enough to process at the moment without my adding fuel to the fire.

"He said he only discovered upon his mother's death, a year ago, that I existed. Since then he has been meaning to come and introduce himself, following our movements in the society columns, apparently. In the meantime, however, he began a romance with Imogen. He didn't mean it to be long-lasting and decided on a whim to use my name instead of his own."

"He didn't mean it to be long-lasting, but he meant for her to think they were wed?" I repeated, incredulous. "Does he realize that the marriage is likely legally binding? If he signed the marriage certificate, they are wed no matter what name he used."

"It would come down to a question of fraud for an annulment, I suppose," Milo said. "But he claims there was no ceremony, only that they stood on the beach and declared their love for each other." His tone let me know what he thought of this display of sentiment. I felt another pang of sympathy for Imogen.

"She said they were married," I pressed.

He shrugged. "Perhaps she said that because she was desperate to find him. There's little doubt they consummated their relationship. If she did so on the assumption that they would soon be married, it must have come as an unpleasant surprise to discover that he had gone missing."

"Whatever the case, he has treated her abominably," I said with feeling.

"Certainly," Milo agreed.

I rubbed a hand across my face. "What a dreadful mess."

There was a moment of silence, both of us lost in thought, and then I voiced my next question. "What brought him here? Did he ask you for money?"

Milo looked at me. "No. I offered it to him, in fact, and he laughed in my face. He said he didn't come here for money, that he merely wanted to make his . . . existence known to me."

This surprised me. I didn't know Darien, of course, but, from his actions thus far, he had struck me as the sort of man who was out to get what he could from life, with little regard for the consequences. I would have thought he might have taken Milo's money gladly. What surprised me even more was that Milo had offered it.

"I didn't suppose you'd give money to him," I said.

"It's not his fault my father abandoned his family. He deserves something for that."

"That's very generous of you."

His expression darkened. "Generosity was not my aim, but the offer was substantial enough. I wonder that he refused it."

I knew it was typical of Milo to turn to his wealth for answers. Money had solved a great deal of the problems in his life, and he was suspicious of things that didn't bend to its influence.

Truth be told, however, I agreed with him. Darien's refusal to take money didn't make me feel as though he was trustworthy. Quite the contrary. If he wouldn't take what Milo had offered him up front, I wondered if there was something else that he was playing at. There were too many facets to this puzzle. Something was going on that we weren't yet aware of.

"Where is he staying?"

"At the inn, I suppose. I certainly didn't invite him to stay here."

"Imogen is at the inn," I said, rising from my chair. "I should go and see her. I think it best that someone break the news to her before she sees Darien there and assumes that they're going to have a happy reunion."

"That's not your worry, darling," he said.

"I know, but I feel sorry for her. Under other circumstances, she might have been my sister-in-law."

Milo swore under his breath.

I went to him and put my hands on his chest, looking up at him. "It's all going to be all right, you know."

He offered me a smile, one hand moving to cup my face. "Yes, of course."

He leaned to brush a kiss across my lips and then he left, no doubt to place a telephone call to our solicitor's office.

A moment later Winnelda came hurrying into the drawing room.

"Oh, madam," she said breathlessly. "That young man . . . Who . . . who was he?"

"He's Mr. Ames's brother," I said. There was no reason to keep it a secret. Everyone was going to know about it soon enough.

"I didn't know Mr. Ames had a brother."

"Yes, Mr. Ames didn't know it either."

"He . . . smiled at me as he left. I think he even winked! Very improper, of course. But he's ever so good looking, isn't he?"

I felt an immediate tinge of alarm. If Darien was going to be a frequent visitor, I was going to make sure he stayed away from Winnelda. It would prove most inconvenient for all of us if he was to trifle with her. What he had done to Imogen made it abundantly clear he was not to be trusted.

"He's very good looking," I agreed. "But I think you had better steer clear of him. He . . . he isn't exactly . . ."

I hesitated, trying to think of how best to warn her without making Darien seem too appealing. Winnelda had always had romantic notions, and I didn't want to increase his allure by casting him as the prodigal son.

"Oh, I know just what you mean, madam. It's never wise to get involved with a gentleman that handsome." She paused. "That is, it's different for you and Mr. Ames. You know how to handle him. That is . . ."

She seemed to feel that she was digging herself deeper and deeper and decided that it was best to change the subject.

"Well, as I said, he's very improper. And I don't approve of that sort of thing."

"No," I agreed. "His behavior thus far hasn't been that of a gentleman."

"Perhaps he will behave better now that he's come home," she suggested.

Come home. Things weren't going to be that simple.

I sighed; this was all much more excitement than I had bargained for.

NOT HALF AN hour later, our car pulled up before the Primrose Inn. I asked Markham, our driver, to wait for me as I made my way inside. It was a fairly standard place as far as village inns went, a small but tidy lobby with a worn rug and furniture that had seen better days.

There was a girl at the desk that I didn't recognize, fair and freckled with pale blue eyes that were, at the moment, fixed on the magazine that lay on the counter in front of her. I was relieved that I didn't know her, for I thought the task at hand would arouse considerably less interest than if it were someone familiar.

I walked up to her. Glancing down, I saw it was a gossip rag that held her attention. So much for my hoping that she would show discretion. I would have to be careful not to give her fodder for any gossip of her own.

"Good afternoon," I said brightly when she failed to greet me.

"Afternoon," she said, pulling her eyes from the page to look at me. "Do you want a room?" She asked this in a singularly discouraging manner.

"Thank you, no. I wonder if you could tell me in which room Miss Imogen Prescott is staying."

"I don't know the name."

"Perhaps you could check the register?" I suggested.

The girl gave a little sigh and moved over to the register lying on the counter. She put a finger to the page and moved it slowly downward as she read over the names. It was very leisurely business, and I wondered if she was doing it expressly to annoy me. Her eyes had moved much more quickly over the pages of her gossip magazine.

"No one here by the name," she said at last.

"Are you quite certain?"

"Yes." Her gaze met mine, a touch defiantly.

It seemed that Imogen must have decided to lodge at Mrs. Cotton's rooming house, my alternate suggestion.

"Hello, Mrs. Ames."

I turned to see Marena Hodges coming out of a little room that led off the foyer—an office, I thought.

"Oh. Hello." I had forgotten that Marena Hodges worked here. Mrs. Busby had mentioned as much to me at the vicarage, I remembered suddenly, but I had been daydreaming. Now I had to think of a way in which to extricate myself without giving away too much information. It was a miracle that gossip wasn't already flying all across the village, and I didn't want to be the one who started it. I could only hope that Imogen and Darien didn't suddenly appear at the same time.

"I'm looking for a friend, but I think she must have taken a room with Mrs. Cotton," I said quickly.

To my relief, neither she nor the freckled girl, who had slid her magazine beneath the desk when Marena appeared, seemed curious about my friend.

"I suppose I'll see you at the festival?" Marena said.

"Yes. I'm quite looking forward to it."

I was just preparing to turn and leave when I heard the front door of the inn open behind me and caught sight of Marena's face. It had lit up like a chandelier.

For some reason, I felt a sinking feeling in my chest.

This instinct was quickly confirmed by her next words, words uttered in the breathy, exhilarated voice of one newly in love. "Hello, Darien."

5

EVEN IF SHE had not used his name, it was clear from the way Marena was looking at him that they had met before. Indeed, from the pretty blush that suffused her cheeks, I suspected they had done more than that.

It occurred to me to wonder how long Darien had been in Allingcross. It couldn't have been much more than a week; it was nearly impossible to keep things quiet for that long in a village this size.

That seemed an extraordinarily short amount of time in which to have courted Marena. Then again, I was well acquainted with the swiftly lethal aim of the Ames charm. From the rate he acquired female admirers, it seemed Darien possessed it in spades.

"Mrs. Ames," he said, his gaze moving from Marena to me. "It's lovely to see you again so soon."

"Yes. I . . ." I tried to think of a reason why I might have come directly to the inn where he was staying. I had even beaten him here from Thornecrest, I realized. He must have stopped off somewhere else.

I couldn't, of course, say that I had come to the wrong place, hoping to warn Imogen. "I . . . I was hoping that I could speak with you."

It was something of a lame excuse, but it was the best I could come up with at the moment. Besides, it wasn't entirely untrue. Perhaps it would be good for me to talk to him, to determine for myself what his motives might be. He might be less guarded with me than he was sure to be with Milo.

"I'd enjoy nothing more than to speak with you," he said, the picture of courtesy. "I have luncheon plans with Marena, but perhaps . . ."

His voice trailed off as the front door of the inn opened again. We turned to see Bertie Phipps entering the lobby. If he had come to renew his suit to Marena, the timing seemed particularly bad.

"Hello," he said, a bit uncertainly upon spotting all of us standing there. He had changed out of his dirty riding clothes, but he still appeared somewhat rumpled and windblown. I assumed he had ridden his bicycle from Thornecrest, for there was a sheen of sweat across his sun-flushed face.

"Hello," Marena and I said at the same time. Darien, for his part, had swept his gaze across Bertie and summarily dismissed him, turning back to Marena. Evidently, he had determined that this young man was of no interest to him, and certainly no threat.

I had to admit that a side-by-side comparison of the two men, at this precise moment, was rather in Darien's favor. While Bertie was a bit taller and broader of shoulder, Darien's slim elegance was shown to its best with his black suit, which, though not expensive, was impeccably tailored. The dark fabric complemented his coloring, and his eyes, like Milo's, were very blue beneath sooty lashes.

It would be easy to see how Marena might have been swept off her feet by this young man, especially as she had always been somewhat inclined to romanticism. Bertie Phipps was handsome in a solid, wholesome sort of way, but he hadn't the Prince Charming appeal that Darien possessed.

"I came to see if you'd go out walking with me, Marena," Bertie said. "I've some sandwiches and apples we might share."

This caught Darien's attention. He turned to look at Bertie again as Marena stood motionless behind the desk.

There was a moment of silence. I had the unsettled feeling that something rather dire was happening, and I wished suddenly that I had asked Milo to accompany me. If things took an unpleasant turn, I was not about to throw myself between two brawling gentlemen.

Bertie had brawn on his side, but I thought that Darien would be quick. And there was something else. A hint of something dangerous about him, I realized. A ruthless flash in his blue eyes that told me he was more than capable of doing whatever was required for him to get his way.

It was Marena who found her voice first. "I'm afraid I can't right now, Bertie. I have other matters to attend to."

"Oh, come on. Just for a few minutes. Jenny here can watch the desk, can't you, Jen?"

The girl behind the desk said nothing, her gossip magazine becoming less interesting by the moment.

"I believe the lady has made herself plain," Darien said.

Bertie's gaze shifted to Darien. It was, I think, the first time that Bertie had paid him much attention. Until then he had likely thought Darien was merely a patron of the inn. I saw the change in his expression, the frown that flickered across his brow as he realized that Darien was something more.

"I'll talk to you later, Bertie," Marena said, a bit too cheerily. "I'll ring you up."

"Don't make the poor fellow promises you don't intend to keep," Darien told her.

Bertie's ears were growing red and his chest puffed out. He was still looking at Darien. "I don't think that's much concern of yours, mate."

"I'd say it is," Darien replied. I could see something of Milo's personality in the calmness of his reply, but unlike Milo, who was always master of himself, I could sense Darien was barely keeping his temper in check. His eyes had darkened and the muscles in his jaw had tightened. "You see, I've made Marena my business."

Bertie looked at him, then to Marena and back again. His entire face had taken on a crimson hue, and his fists were clenched at his sides.

I wondered if I should speak up, try to defuse the situation, but something told me it had already gone beyond that.

"You can't do this, Marena," Bertie said, his eyes boring into hers. "Not after what we've been to each other."

"Bertie, I think you'd better leave." Marena said this clearly and calmly, but I could tell that her self-possession was a front, for her hand upon the desk was trembling.

"What's this fellow to you, anyhow? You don't even know him."

"She knows me well enough," Darien said. "We've become very well acquainted over the past few days."

Suddenly, without warning, Bertie turned and, lunging forward, punched Darien in the face. Marena screamed, and Jenny jumped back farther behind the desk as though she was next in line to be assaulted, her freckles standing out in sharp relief against the sudden whiteness of her face.

To Darien's credit, he didn't fall. Instead, he staggered backward, catching himself on the edge of the front desk.

Blood streamed from his nose and lip, staining the cuff of his shirt as he wiped it away and pulled himself upright.

"I'll kill you for this," he said coldly. I was surprised at the dignity—and the sincerity—with which he managed to imbue the words with his face streaked with blood.

Bertie was unfazed and unrepentant. "Go ahead and try it," he said.

Darien's eyes flashed, and I was momentarily worried that the fighting was about to begin in earnest, but then Marena came around the desk, inserting herself between the two of them.

"Get out, Bertie," she said, her eyes blazing with fury. "Get out before I call the police!"

"But, Marena," he pleaded. "I . . . didn't mean . . ."

"Go!" she cried. "Now!"

With one last bewildered look around him, almost as though he were waking from some strange dream, Bertie Phipps turned and left the inn.

Marena turned to Darien, clutching his arm. "Oh, darling. Are you all right?" she asked.

He had pulled a handkerchief from his pocket and was quelling the blood with it. "I'm fine."

I couldn't help but think, absurdly, that it would be such a shame were his nose to be damaged. I should hate for it to ruin the perfect symmetry of his features.

"Shall we ring for the doctor?" I asked.

"No," Darien said.

"But, darling . . ." Marena countered. "Don't you think . . ."

"I said no," he repeated, loudly; she flinched.

I decided then that there was nothing else to be done on my part. Darien clearly didn't want my help, and I was certain he wouldn't be in the mood to discuss the situation with Milo when he was currently bleeding onto his white shirt.

"I'll just be going now," I said. "Perhaps we may talk another day?"

"I shall look forward to it," he said with a gallantry that belied the indignity of the bloody handkerchief pressed to his face.

"Let's go get you cleaned up," Marena said, leading him away.

I bid farewell to Jenny, who was certain to find her magazine dull after the events she had just witnessed, and left the inn, glad to be back in the fresh air. This was rather more drama than I had been prepared for. After all, an ill-timed meeting between Darien and Imogen was unlikely to have ended in fisticuffs.

Good heavens. What a mess all of this was becoming.

I FOUND SUDDENLY that I hadn't the energy to visit Mrs. Cotton's rooming house in search of Imogen. Perhaps, instead, we could have her come back to Thornecrest. Whatever the case, I knew the discussion couldn't be put off for long. It would be dreadful if she were to encounter Darien in the village, especially in the company of Marena Hodges; I could only imagine what sort of scene might ensue.

As Markham was driving me back to the house, we passed the festival grounds on the border of Bedford Priory. The local workmen had been there, putting up the tents, and everything was looking quite cheerful and festive.

It was then that I noticed the solitary figure of Mrs. Busby in her wheelchair. She sat, apparently alone, in the middle of the field.

"Pull over, will you, Markham?" I asked.

He drew to a stop alongside the gate in the fence that edged the festival grounds and came to open my door.

I got out and went through the gate and across the field, grateful that the grass was dry. Hopefully we wouldn't get much rain before the festival.

"Hello, Mrs. Busby," I said as I approached her.

She looked up from the notebook in her lap where she was jotting things down, last-minute festival plans, no doubt. "Oh, Amory. Whatever are you doing here?"

"I was driving past and saw you. I thought I would see if you needed help of any sort." It was a bit useless of me to ask, as I wasn't able to do much in my condition. But I hated to see her out here alone. Someone must have wheeled her here, of course, but I didn't know where they might be now.

"How sweet you are, dear. The vicar is here somewhere," she said, glancing absently about. "I suppose he must be behind one of the tents. He's been running about doing my bidding. So accommodating he always is. Oh, here he is now."

The vicar came from behind one of the tents in the distance. Mrs. Busby waved at him, and he approached us with a smile. He was a stout man with a genial face that had probably been handsome in his younger years. He had thin gray hair and bright blue eyes and a ready smile. I had always liked the man and the feeling of genuine goodwill I always felt in his presence.

"Mrs. Ames! How good to see you."

He clasped my hand tightly in his. The only drawback to him was his damp and clammy handshake. Milo had once unkindly, though accurately, described it as grasping a large piece of lukewarm raw meat.

"How have you been, my dear?" One always had the impression that, beneath his friendly blue gaze, he was truly interested in the answer to this customary question.

"I'm very well, thank you."

"Good, good. I hope you shall be feeling well enough to attend the festival?"

He made no direct reference to my pregnancy, but I appreciated the subtle way in which he inquired after my health.

"I hope so. I've been rather looking forward to it." I felt a bit bad for telling a borderline fib to the vicar. In truth, I found I wasn't much looking forward to the Springtide Festival. While I usually enjoyed the merriment as much as anyone, I was tired as of late and my feet tended to hurt if I remained on them too long. As it was the event of the spring in the village, however, I was certainly planning to attend and enjoy myself as much as possible.

"Were you after something particular in the village, dear?" Mrs. Busby asked me suddenly. "You should send someone to fetch it for you."

"Oh, I just had a small errand to run."

"The weather is lovely for it," the vicar said, looking up at the sky. "Hopefully the Almighty will see fit to grace us with a day as nice as this for the festival."

"Yes, I do hope so," I said, using this mention of the festival to move things along to the subject on my mind. "I just saw Bertie Phipps. I know he's looking forward to riding his new horse in the races."

Something flickered across both of their faces so quickly that I wasn't entirely sure I had seen it at all. Whatever it was, I expected it was to do with Bertie and not the mention of the race.

"Did you?" Mrs. Busby asked. "I'm sure he'll enjoy racing."

"You haven't spoken to him lately, then?" I asked casually. "I had thought he was often at the vicarage."

"Oh, as to that, I . . . I'm not really sure I've seen him much as of late." She was feigning interest in something in the distance in that way people who are bad at lying have of avoiding the truth.

"I believe that he and Marena have parted ways," I said. I didn't know if this was gossip I should be repeating, but I didn't suppose it would be a secret much longer. Not after Bertie had hit Darien in the inn. Besides, it was clear the Busbys knew something.

"Yes, I think you're right," Mrs. Busby said, seemingly seizing upon the excuse that I had offered her. "Now that you mention it, I think Marena may have hinted at it."

There was something strange going on here. Was it possible they knew about Darien and didn't wish to tell me? But no. She had mistaken Darien for Milo, so she couldn't be aware of his existence yet. Perhaps she knew only that Marena had found a new love interest.

I thought I might as well let them know I was in possession of the details. "In fact, I'm afraid that Bertie had a rival, and he . . . struck him in a confrontation just now."

If either of them was shocked by this bit of news, they didn't show it. Perhaps they had seen too much of sin to be much startled by a minor incident of physical violence.

The vicar tutted, as one might over a schoolboy tussle. "I'm sorry to hear that. I hope the young men resolved things."

"As to that, I think there are emotions yet to be resolved," I said.

"Well, these things pass quickly with young people," he replied.

Mrs. Busby nodded. "Yes, I have often seen that to be the case. Well, I do hate to rush off, Amory, but I'm afraid I still have a few more things to tend to."

"Yes, of course. Are you certain there is nothing I can do to help?"

"No, no, dear. Go home and put your feet up." She reached out and patted my arm. "Take care of yourself, and we'll see you at the festival."

I turned back toward the car, wondering why they had both been acting so strangely. There was more to this situation than met the eye.

6

AS MUCH AS I dreaded it, I knew it was time to sort things out with Imogen. As soon as I returned home, I rang Mrs. Cotton's rooming house. The maid there was about as efficient as Jenny at the inn had been, and it took several moments for me to be connected with Imogen.

"Mr. Ames has returned," I said, when at last she was on the other line. "Would now be a convenient time for you to come and see us?"

"I . . . Yes, that would be all right." She sounded uneasy, and I couldn't exactly blame her.

"I'll send the car for you," I told her, and this time she accepted.

I rang off, and, after instructing Grimes to notify Markham, who I had asked to wait outside, that she would be awaiting her ride, I went upstairs to change into a more comfortable pair of shoes. Then I went back to the drawing room to find Milo was there smoking a cigarette. He rose and ground it out in the silver ashtray on the table as I entered the room.

I related to him the fact that Darien had taken up with Marena Hodges. I left out the altercation with Bertie, however. There was no need to make Milo angrier with his brother than he already was.

I was quite cross with Darien myself. Though I had never advocated violence, I couldn't help but feel sympathetic to Bertie's urge to punch him.

I still wondered why Darien had come here. It seemed strange to me that he should have arrived at the same time Imogen did, especially when he had meant to leave her behind. What was more, he said that he had been in Allingcross for a few days, long enough to meet and court Marena. Why hadn't he come to see us directly upon arriving?

"And I've sent Markham to pick up Imogen," I concluded to Milo. "Someone needs to break the news to her that Darien isn't . . . that he doesn't intend to . . . Well, I think someone should tell her what sort of man he is."

"So she's still in the village, is she?"

I sighed. "I'm afraid so." I sincerely wished Milo had been correct in his assumption that she would abscond without notice.

"Then I suppose the least we can do is warn her off."

I knew all of this must be intensely irritating to him, even more so than it was to me. While he had always lived a life primarily focused on his own pleasure, there was, implanted deep within him, a sense of familial obligation. Whatever responsibilities he shirked, whatever flights of fancy he pursued, he had always made sure that Thornecrest was well cared for, that the easy respectability of the Ames name remained intact. Heritage mattered to him, and now he was suddenly saddled with a troublesome relation who he could neither comfortably embrace nor cast aside.

"I'll be very glad when all of this is sorted out," I said as I took a seat near the window.

"Let's just hope she isn't up the pole."

"Milo! You needn't be vulgar." Though it had also occurred to me that Imogen could potentially be expecting a child, that certainly wasn't the politest way in which to couch the question.

He shrugged. "I'm simply pointing out that it would cause even more trouble for her, especially if she returns to London pregnant and claiming her 'husband' has gone missing. No one's going to believe a story like that."

He was right, of course. There was sure to be a scandal if Imogen was pregnant and Darien refused to marry her. This was the sort of thing that could ruin a young girl's life.

"Well, we'll just have to hope that she's not . . . in the family way."

Milo shot me a look that said he thought I was silly for avoiding the word when I was in the condition myself, but propriety had been so deeply ingrained in me that I found it difficult to rid myself of it.

"I rang Ludlow," he said, switching the subject to our London solicitor.

"What did he say about Darien?"

"Nothing. I didn't tell him about Darien, just set up a meeting tomorrow morning. I want to talk to him about it in person. I would like to know if he knew anything of this. Surely he would have told me when my father died."

"Yes," I agreed. "And there certainly would've been some mention of a legacy if your father had left one to Darien."

"On that note, I'm quite sure," Milo replied. "There was no mention of another child in my father's will."

I thought it shabby of Milo's father to have completely disowned one of his sons, illegitimate or not, but I already knew that the deceased Mr. Ames had been neither a kind nor a sentimental man. I supposed it was no use casting further aspersions upon the dead.

"In any event, there's no legal way for Darien to try to get anything."

"I'm sure he realizes that," I said. "Besides, you said he refused your money."

"He did, but I still don't trust him. There's always the chance he refused what I offered in hopes of catching a bigger fish."

"Perhaps that's what all this mess with Imogen is," I mused. "Maybe he thinks that if he creates enough scandal, you'll pay him a large sum to distance himself from the family."

Milo quirked a brow at me, and I realized the absurdity of this hypothesis. If Darien had paid any attention to the gossip columns, he would know that scandal was the last thing that would worry Milo.

I was a different matter. I had never enjoyed the way our names were bandied about in the press, and I liked it even less now that we were going to have a child. I didn't want him or her to go to school one day and be reminded of his parents' past misdeeds. Or of his uncle's unsavory reputation.

"I'm going to take the evening train to London and stay at the flat tonight," Milo said. "Will you be all right?"

"Yes, certainly. The sooner things are sorted out the better." I sighed. "This is all so vexing."

"Better than the alternative, I suppose?"

"The alternative?"

He smiled. "That I had secretly married someone else in Brighton."

I gave a little laugh. It seemed silly now that I had even so much as considered the possibility. "Imogen was very convincing," I said, only half teasing.

"You didn't really believe her?"

My first instinct was to make a joke of the matter. That was always the most comfortable thing to do whenever we got too close to discussing our feelings. Perhaps it was a ridiculous way to go about a marriage. It had certainly given us more than our share of troubles in the past. Nevertheless, it was a difficult habit to break. This time, however, I thought I should tell him the truth.

"Perhaps some small part of me did wonder—only very briefly—if there might have been some sort of . . . dalliance with the young lady," I admitted at last. "After all, she's young and very pretty, and I'm . . . quite pregnant."

He didn't look affronted, as I thought he might. I supposed he knew better than I did what his reputation had been, even after we married.

He had begun to earn my trust over the past two years, but that didn't entirely wipe away what had come before. We had never really discussed the rumors, the speculation of the gossip columns when he was photographed with other women. There had always been excuses, and I had tried to brush aside my doubts.

Perhaps it was just that I hadn't wanted to know. I didn't want to know now. He had been working to prove himself to me, and I didn't want to go back to that time when my love for him had been marred with questions. I had believed in him in the face of Imogen's story, and I knew that the tiniest of doubts that had surfaced had been nothing more than a shadow from a past we had overcome together.

He came to me, his hands taking mine.

"Amory."

I looked up at him, met his gaze. It was usually difficult to tell what he was thinking, but there was something very transparent in his eyes at this moment.

"There is no one else," he said. "And you've never been more beautiful than you are now."

He lifted my hand to his lips and kissed it.

The words were touching, but I was acutely aware of the extent of his flattery. "That's sweet of you, Milo, but I'm not exactly ravishing in my current state."

"I beg to differ." His arms slid around me. "I quite like these extra curves. Perhaps we ought to keep you pregnant."

"I thought I said for you to stop being vulgar, Milo," I chided him with mock severity.

He leaned to kiss my neck. "Being vulgar is quite my favorite pastime."

I laughed and moved my hands over his shoulders as his mouth found mine. The kiss deepened, and he pulled me closer, at least as close as he could with my large, round stomach between us.

There was a clearing of a throat in the doorway.

We looked up to see Grimes standing there, his face impassive. It seemed we were always being caught in moments like these, though it was usually poor Winnelda who was set to stammering and blushing. Grimes betrayed no such embarrassment. He merely stood stiffly with his eyes averted, waiting for us to behave ourselves.

"Yes, what is it?" Milo asked. He hadn't released me, and I stepped out of his embrace to make Grimes more comfortable.

"Excuse me, sir. Miss Imogen has arrived," Grimes said, an almost imperceptible change in his tone letting us know that he declined to refer to her as "Mrs. Ames."

Grimes had always felt like an ally to me in Milo's more disreputable days, and I knew that even though Milo had proven himself to me, it would take a bit of time for him to win over Grimes.

"Thank you, Grimes. You may send her in."

"Very good, sir."

He turned and left the room. I turned to smooth my hair and check my lipstick in the mirror. "Grimes must think you're quite wanton for kissing me in my condition."

"I'm sure prim and proper Grimes is well aware how it was you got in this condition."

I might have laughed at this bit of indecorum, but there were footsteps outside the door, and then Imogen came slowly into the room. Her eyes moved quickly from me to Milo, and the smallest frown flickered across her face. Then her gaze came back to me, almost imploring.

I went over to her. "Do come in, Imogen," I said gently. "This is my husband, Milo. As I'm sure you've realized, this isn't the man that you met in Brighton."

"No," she said faintly, her eyes still searching his face, an understandable confusion on her features. "He looks so much like him, but . . . but he isn't."

"Why don't you sit down, dear," I suggested. I went to her and took her arm, leading her to a chair. She looked as though she was perilously close to tears, but she didn't give in to them at once. I saw her look again at Milo, as though hoping that her gaze had deceived her.

"I'm sure this must all be very confusing," I said. "But there's an explanation for it. We've only just learned about it, and I thought it would be best if you came here rather than talking about it over the telephone."

Milo, who had thus far said nothing, moved to the sideboard and poured a bit of brandy into a glass. He brought it over to Imogen and handed it to her. She was on the edge of refusal, but then she thought better of it and took the glass from his hand, taking a sip of the contents.

"Thank you," she said, the color coming back to her cheeks.

"Now," Milo said, seating himself on the sofa that was across from her. "It's come to our attention that you've been involved with a man named Ames."

She nodded.

"I'm afraid it was my brother."

A frown flickered across her face. "But . . . but he told me his name was . . . that is . . . Is your Christian name Milo?"

He nodded. "The gentleman—and I use the word in the loosest sense—who you met is called Darien."

"But I don't understand. Why did he tell me . . . ?"

Milo glanced at me, and I understood at once. He wanted me to tell her. Perhaps he thought it would be easier coming from a woman.

"Darien is Milo's half brother," I explained. "Milo was actually unaware of his existence until this morning. It seems that Darien only recently learned about his connection to our family. I . . . well, we believe that he thought to use the name as a . . . an alias of sorts."

All the color drained from her face again. "So he was only toying with me," she said. "I thought that I had married the man of my dreams, and now . . ."

"He . . . led us to believe you were not legally wed," I said gently.

A blush rose up to overtake the paleness of her face as she realized it was now common knowledge that whatever sort of "honeymoon" they had enjoyed had not been within the bounds of matrimony. "He said . . . I thought . . . we were going to marry in London."

She burst into tears then, and there was nothing that the brandy could do to help it. I took the glass from her and set it on the table, patting her back and muttering whatever soothing things I could think of.

I glanced over her head at Milo, who looked more impatient than sympathetic. He had never been much moved by tears.

"Have you a handkerchief, Milo?" I asked pointedly.

He pulled one from his pocket and rose to hand it to me. "I'll just leave you ladies to discuss things," he said.

I shot him a look, which he ignored, and he walked from the room.

I handed the handkerchief to Imogen, who wiped her eyes and blew her nose. Then she crumpled it in her hands, her gaze trained on the little ball of fabric. "I know what you must think of me . . ."

"No," I said, reaching out to pat her arm. "He deceived you. The fault lies in him, not in you."

"I ought to have known it was too good to be true," she said sadly. "I just feel so . . . so stupid."

I felt another surge of anger at Darien.

"I'm terribly sorry, dear."

She sniffed. "Well, better I found out now than later, I suppose."

I hesitated. Though I didn't like to intrude on her privacy, the question needed to be asked. "There is one more thing . . ."

She looked up at me. "Yes?"

"It's rather a delicate question, but it's important. You don't suppose you . . . might be in a similar condition to mine?" I asked gently.

She looked at me, her eyes wide, and then looked away as color suffused her face once again. She shook her head. "No."

"You're fairly certain?" I pressed. I didn't mean to embarrass the girl, but if there was going to be difficulty, perhaps I could find some way to help her through it.

She managed to meet my gaze. "I'm sure."

I nodded, breathing out a sigh of relief. That was one less thing we needed to worry about.

"Can I get you anything?" I asked, wishing I could find some way to help.

"No. Thank you. I've already caused you a good deal of trouble."

"Not at all. Please know that you're always welcome here."

"Thank you." She rose. "I should be going now. I . . . need some time to think about things."

"Yes, of course. What will you do now?"

"Go back to London, I suppose," she said. "Though perhaps not for a day or two. I've already paid Mrs. Cotton for the week, and I could use the time to . . . sort out how to proceed."

"Are you all alone in London?" I asked, hoping she would have someone to support her when she returned home after this difficult errand.

"No," she said. "I live with my sister."

"You didn't ask her to accompany you?" I asked.

She flushed and shook her head. "She doesn't know I'm here. I didn't want her to know about this."

I could understand that, for the entire thing must be very embarrassing to her. Darien had certainly made a mess of things.

"You will let me know if there's anything I can do?" I asked, sensing that she was eager to take her leave.

"Yes. Thank you, Amory."

Imogen left the house, and I was left with a vaguely dissatisfied feeling. There was, I supposed, not much I could do, but I still wished there was some way I could help.

I went looking for Milo and found him in his study, a comfortable, masculine room with dark wood paneling and heavy furniture, gathering some paperwork to take with him to visit Mr. Ludlow.

"I don't know what we're going to do about all of this," I said, perching myself on one of the leather chairs near his desk.

"I don't know that we have to do anything about it," he said without looking up, sliding a sheaf of documents into an attaché case.

I was not surprised by his lack of interest in the matter. Problems of the heart were not of any importance to him, and I supposed he would like to wash his hands of the whole mess. It wasn't going to be that easy, however. Darien was his brother, and, like it or not, one couldn't so easily sweep family aside.

"If he's going to associate himself with our family, use the Ames name, then I think that we might . . ."

"It's not really any of our concern. Darien and Imogen are both adults."

"But . . ."

"I'm sorry the girl was hurt, but, after all, it's not the first time a woman has been seduced by a man under false pretenses. It happens all the time. Frankly, she should have been more careful."

"That isn't fair."

"No," he said, looking up from his paperwork. "It's not, but it's the way things are."

I sighed.

"You can't fix everyone's problems, darling."

Perhaps not, but that didn't mean I was going to stop trying.

MILO LEFT TO catch the train to London, and I was left to my own devices. Naturally, my mind was still on the situation with Imogen and Darien, and I found my thoughts wandering to his newest dalliance. Someone ought to warn Marena about Darien, but I had the feeling it would do very little good.

"Winnelda," I said as I prepared for bed. "Have you heard any of the village gossip about Marena Hodges and Bertie Phipps?"

If she thought the question strange, she didn't show it. Winnelda was always happy to share the interesting tidbits she had learned.

She nodded. "I've heard a few things, here and there. I know May who does the cleaning at the vicarage. She sometimes overhears a little when she's there."

I'm sure she does, I thought. It occurred to me that this might be a very useful source of information.

Before I could press Winnelda further, however, she continued. "May said she wasn't surprised Miss Marena broke things off with Bertie. She said Miss Marena's always been the sort to prefer a sophisticated gentleman."

And she had found one—or at least a good imitation of one—in Darien, I thought grimly.

"May's a bit of a snob, though," Winnelda went on. "She agrees that

Miss Marena ought to have a toff. I think Bertie Phipps is a very nice young man, whatever she says. But, anyway, Miss Marena broke things off with Bertie a fortnight ago. May says they were arguing a good bit leading up to it."

"Oh?" I asked. May had certainly heard more than "a little."

"Yes, they didn't quarrel in the vicarage, but she would see them through the windows, walking along the lanes. She said she could tell they were rowing, though she never heard the cause."

"I see." So, if they had parted ways two weeks ago, at least Darien was not to blame for that. He had caused enough trouble already.

"There was some funny business about it, though," Winnelda went on. She said this in a reflective tone that gave me pause.

"What do you mean?"

"I'm not entirely sure, and neither is May. But things were going so well with Bertie. Everyone thought they were going to be married. May heard them discussing moving to London one day. And then suddenly they were quarreling, and Bertie was gone. May says Mr. and Mrs. Busby seem to avoid talking about him as well."

"Perhaps it's just that Marena has broken things off with him, and the Busbys don't want to make her uncomfortable by mentioning it."

"That's what I thought. May said it seems to be more than that. She said it's as though he had done something wrong."

I thought about my encounter with the Busbys. I had had a similar impression, as though they were uncomfortable at the mention of Bertie Phipps. But what did I know of it? Perhaps he had said something hurtful to Marena over the breaking off of their relationship. Perhaps he had even behaved in an untoward manner and that was why they had quarreled.

"Did May say what she thought it might be?"

"She didn't know, but she somehow had the impression Bertie had stolen something."

This surprised me. Bertie had always seemed to me to be a very upstanding, hardworking young man. I found it difficult to believe he would resort to theft.

"Money, you mean?"

"May wasn't sure, exactly. She just heard the vicar and Mrs. Busby discussing something missing from the vicar's study. They didn't even mention Bertie's name. It was just the impression May had, that they were talking about him."

It was all very curious.

"I don't suppose you need worry about it, though, madam," Winnelda said. "You've got enough to think about with the baby coming."

Perhaps she and Milo were right, though I was loath to admit it. None of this was really any of my business, after all. And I did have more important matters to consider.

I was just going to do my best to put it all out of my mind.

7

DARIEN MADE HIMSELF scarce in the remaining days leading up to the festival, and I didn't know whether to be relieved or alarmed that we had heard nothing from him. I supposed he was busy wooing Marena Hodges, and I only hoped the village was large enough to keep him from encountering Imogen.

It was also possible he had decided to leave town. Half of me hoped that he had, but the other half still had aspirations that the brothers might develop some sort of relationship. I knew that Milo had always viewed himself as being alone in the world since his father's death—indeed, since long before then—and the idea that he might be able to gain a familial relationship was heartening.

Of course, now, with the baby due to arrive shortly, was not the most ideal of times for upheaval in any of our lives. But was there ever an ideal time for such things? Perhaps we would be able to sort it all out before the newest Ames made his or her arrival into the world.

Milo's trip to London had done little to enlighten us about Darien's history. Mr. Ludlow confirmed his ignorance of Darien's existence. It seemed that Milo's father had indeed washed his hands of Darien and his mother, never looking back after he left them.

I suspected that Milo was also considering making some sort of settlement for his brother, though I was sure Mr. Ludlow had assured him he was under no obligation to do so. As I had known it would, the bond of blood was proving difficult for Milo to ignore. Or perhaps Milo just thought that giving Darien enough money would get rid of him.

Whatever the case, nothing much had been resolved by the time the festival arrived. I was doing my best, however, to keep from dwelling on any of it.

As for Bertie, aside from a sheepish glance in my direction when he returned to work with Milo's horses, he made no reference to his altercation with Darien. I decided to let the matter rest. I was certain the young people could work out their own matters of the heart without my interference.

The day of the festival was lovely, the spring weather for once deciding to cooperate. The sun shone brightly, unimpeded save for the few fluffy white clouds that the light breeze blew across the sky, and the morning temperature held the promise of a mild day.

I turned away from the window and took one last look in my bedroom mirror. Springtime was in full bloom, and I along with it. Despite Winnelda's claims that I was still too thin, I felt very round and healthy.

I had chosen a flattering pale blue silk dress for the day and my most comfortable pair of low-heeled leather shoes. I also wore a straw hat decorated with a blue ribbon and white roses.

Though the weather promised to be fair, there was a cool breeze, so I selected a loose jacket in a complementary shade of darker blue over my dress. All the better to hide my "condition," I supposed, though it wasn't as if everyone didn't already know there was a baby on the way. But I realized it was going to take some time before the sentiments of the older generations regarding impending motherhood would become more modern.

The baby moved, apparently agreeing, and I pressed my hand to my stomach. "It's a lovely day, little one. I'm glad you'll be here soon to see the springtime."

Milo drove us from Thornecrest in his Le Mans. He had always enjoyed careening about the winding village roads, startling birds and skimming hedgerows, but I had noticed that he drove more carefully these days. I could only suppose that it was in deference to my condition, and it was yet another change to which I would have to grow accustomed.

He parked the car in the shade of an elm tree not far from the festival grounds, and we walked along the path, which led to a slight rise of land that allowed us to look down at the festival spread before us. We paused for a moment, taking in the cheery sight.

The tents looked bright and clean, scattered across the green in the morning sunlight. Colorful flags and banners fluttered in the wind, and flower garlands bedecked the different stalls where vendors sold their wares. The smell of sausage and popcorn and fresh pastries wafted through the air, making my mouth water. I was eager to try all of the delicacies. In addition to the items for sale, I knew the afternoon tea, hosted by the ladies of the planning committee, would offer myriad delectable treats.

It made a pretty picture, and the sound of music and the laughter of children and adults alike floated up to us. I thought how nice it would be to bring my own child to the festival in years to come.

"Ready for merrymaking?" Milo asked me.

"I am indeed," I replied, taking his arm as we began making our way toward the festival grounds.

We were early, but the crowds were beginning to form. It seemed as though half the village had arrived already, and we exchanged greetings with several villagers as we reached the outskirts of the festival. There was a celebratory mood in the air, and everyone seemed bright-eyed and jolly.

I noticed that the clothes of the attendees were as brightly colored as the festival flags. Several of the women had brought out their spring florals, and most of the men had shed their tweeds in favor of lighter linen and seersucker.

Even Milo, whose sartorial choices tended toward darker colors, wore a pale blue jacket with light-colored trousers. He went hatless as he was often wont to do in fair weather, and his hair gleamed blue-black in the sunlight.

We crossed the green and made our way into the maze of tables and tents. In addition to edible wares, there were vendors selling an impressive array of local items. I spotted finely crafted wooden furniture, whittled decorative pieces and intricately carved walking sticks, homemade soaps, and quilts and beautifully knitted blankets among the wares for sale. I made a mental note to purchase some items for the baby before we left for the day.

A tent was set up for the competitions. As we passed by it, I saw that already a table full of a variety of pickled vegetables in gleaming jars and a table of pies and cakes were awaiting judging later in the day.

In another section of the grounds, there were games set up where one might win a variety of prizes. Several young men in smart clothes and straw boaters were attempting to claim trophies for their ladies, who cheered and clapped their gloved hands at the antics of their suitors.

Children ran here and there in packs, playing and laughing in delight as they spied the various amusements. I reflected again how glad I would be to share this happy tradition with our child.

There was, amid the hubbub and gaiety, a sense of anticipation in the air. In the village, the Springtide Festival marked the symbolic beginning of spring. And today felt like spring. The air was light and warm, as though with the promise of blue skies and blooms in the days to come.

I spotted Lady Alma in the crowd as we wandered leisurely through the grounds. It was not difficult to do, as she was dressed in tan trousers tucked into boots and a blazer of bright red tweed. As usual, one had the impression that she might leap onto the back of a horse and gallop away at any moment.

She was talking animatedly to Mr. Yates, a local farmer, but then she looked up and spotted us. She said something to the man and then strode in our direction.

"Ames, glad to see you," she said without preamble when she reached us. "I've just acquired a mare I want to breed with that brute of yours."

Though this subject was a bit less-than-polite conversation, I knew the two of them were accustomed to discussing such matters whenever they were together. They played their horses against each other like other people played chess.

"Good morning, Lady Alma," Milo replied. "I'm afraid I've more pressing matters of breeding near at hand, but we can certainly discuss it in the future."

This uncouth reference to my pregnancy earned Milo an elbow to the ribs, and he suppressed a smile.

"Come by anytime," said Lady Alma. "My mare is called Medusa. She's black as sin, twice as mean, and three times as fast. Sired by Damocles. Nearly won the Derby, you remember?"

"Yes, he was a fine horse. I'd heard he'd sired a foal a year or two back. High-tempered, is she?"

She nodded. "A nasty beast, to be sure. Bites and kicks with no provocation. Most of my grooms won't go near her. But she's a beauty and runs like the wind."

"There was a lot of talk about the potential sale when she was born, and then I heard nothing more about it." Though he didn't sound particularly interested in the matter, I suspected Milo was irritated he had missed out on the sale.

Lady Alma seemed to have intuited as much, for she gave him a sly smile. "One has to stay on top of these things, Ames. The owner died, and I talked his heir into selling her. Cost me a pretty penny, I can tell you, but I think she'll be worth it. Bred with your Xerxes, I can't imagine a finer racer. I'll pay you a handsome stud fee."

I blinked but hid my surprise, reminding myself that such plain speaking was common among horse breeders.

"I'll come by one day next week to discuss it with you," Milo said.

This transaction concluded to her satisfaction, Lady Alma's gaze finally came to me. "And how are you, Mrs. Ames?"

I was always a bit amused by the way in which the daughter of an earl was so careless of social niceties. In a way, I appreciated that she followed her own rules. I knew all too well how tedious the traditions of society could be, and there was something admirable about Lady Alma's disregard for them.

"I'm very well, thank you, Lady Alma. And you?"

"Excellent, excellent. This is my favorite time of year." She ran her eyes over me as she likely did her horses. "You look well. A bit rounder, I think, than when we last met at the vicarage. Won't be long before there's another fine addition to the Ames stables, eh?"

"I . . . ah . . . I suppose so, in a manner of speaking."

"It's an excellent time for offspring," she said. "I look forward to hearing news of the new arrival at Thornecrest."

"Thank you."

"Oh, there's old Henson," she said suddenly. "I need to speak to him. Excuse me, will you?"

And then she was gone.

I looked at Milo, who smiled broadly. "If Lady Alma says this is an excellent time for offspring, you're fortunate indeed."

"I'm doubly lucky, really," I replied as I began to walk away. "I didn't even have to pay a stud fee."

He stared after me for a moment before laughing heartily and striding forward to catch up with me.

AS THE MORNING wore on, Milo and I continued our amble through the festival grounds, taking our time enjoying what the various booths and stalls had to offer. As we walked, we enjoyed huffkins, the dimpled pastries filled with stewed cherries and topped with a dollop of fresh cream.

Though Milo was much more at home in the smoky confines of nightclubs and gambling parlors, he seemed to be enjoying the simple country amusements as well as the sunshine and fresh air. He looked particularly at ease this morning—his eyes bright, his smile flashing often—as we walked along, greeting the various villagers. Milo, despite his somewhat reckless reputation, was well-liked among the people of the village. The women found him handsome and charming, as women generally did, and the men found him knowledgeable and ready to converse on everything from horses to the state of their hops crop.

I was glad that he seemed to be enjoying himself, though I knew that the matter of what to do about Darien must still be on his mind.

I wondered if his contentment had something to do with the festival itself, and I realized suddenly that I had never thought to ask him about his early experiences here.

"Did you look forward to the festival as a child?" I asked.

"Before I was sent off to school, it was one of my favorite amusements. Almost as good as Christmas."

I smiled. "Madame Nanette would bring you here, I suppose," I said, referring to his childhood nanny, the woman who had raised him when his mother died.

"Yes. She would bring me and would then spend the rest of the day trying to find me, as I ran wild with the pack."

I could picture it very well. Milo had never been a docile sort of a person. Even in the one childhood photograph I had seen of him, there had been a spark of mischief in his eyes.

"She always caught up with me at the races, though."

I knew that, for many people, the races were the highlight of the festival, and I suspected that there was still a bit of the excited boy that was waiting for the sound of the starting pistol in Milo.

We stopped walking then, as we had reached the edge of the festival grounds. Before us, in the distance, stood Bedford Priory. As its name denoted, the manor was an Elizabethan priory that Lady Alma had purchased thirty years before.

Despite being preceded by four brothers and the weight of entailment, she had been left a handsome inheritance by her father, the late earl, and she had set about modernizing the Priory's interior and building the finest set of stables, excepting Milo's, in the county.

A copse of trees hid the stables from our view at this vantage point, but one could make out the pastureland and the neat lines of her pasture fences.

"She's done a fine job with the Priory," Milo said. "It would no doubt have fallen into ruin without her, and now it's one of the finest manors this side of London."

High praise indeed from my husband.

We turned back toward the festival and began making our way through again. Though I had sampled the huffkins and a slice of Folkestone pudding pie, I was now inclined toward Canterbury tart. Whatever Winnelda said, I was eating more now than I ever had in my life. It seemed our baby had a very healthy appetite.

A moment later we encountered the vicar and Mrs. Busby. She wore a cheery yellow dress with a lace shawl draped across her lap and he stood behind her wheelchair, his genial face beaming at us.

"Mr. and Mrs. Ames, good morning," he said.

"Good morning. The festival seems to be a great success. We're having a lovely time."

"Everything's going so well," said Mrs. Busby exultantly. "I'm so happy. It's always such a relief when one's plans come to fruition, isn't it?"

"Your hard work is seeing its rewards."

"And nature has decided to cooperate," Mr. Busby said. "It seems the Almighty indeed smiled upon us."

"Yes," I agreed. "The weather couldn't have been lovelier."

"I suppose you're looking forward to the races, Mr. Ames?" Mr. Busby said, turning to Milo. As I had often done in the past, I admired his knack for knowing just the right way to draw people into conversation. It was a useful skill for a vicar, I imagined.

"Indeed," Milo agreed. "It's always interesting to see what sort of horseflesh the locals are breeding."

"Mr. Yates has a young mare that looks particularly promising."

"I thought the same. She's got spirit and an excellent gait."

The two went on talking about horses, and Mrs. Busby leaned toward me, lowering her voice. "Have you seen Marena yet this morning?"

"No," I said. "I'm afraid I haven't."

Mrs. Busby frowned. "She said last night that she planned to be here early and was already gone from the vicarage when the vicar and I left, but I haven't seen her either."

My suspicious mind wondered if she had met with Darien. I thought they would probably avoid the festival, if that was the case.

"I do worry about her sometimes," Mrs. Busby said. "In many ways, she has been like a daughter to me." That sad, faraway look came into her eyes as she said it, and I knew she was thinking about the daughter she had lost. Then she shook off her melancholy and offered me a bright smile. "I'm sure she is about somewhere."

"Well, my dear," said the vicar, breaking into our conversation. "Shall we take some time to investigate the pastries at that booth across the way?"

"If you say so, Edward," she said with a smile.

"You must try the huffkins," I said.

"We shall."

He tipped his hat to us. "Good day, Mr. and Mrs. Ames. I'm sure our paths shall cross again before the day is out."

"Good day, vicar," I answered. We stepped aside as he began to push her chair, moving it with practiced ease across the smoothest patches of ground.

"I'm happy everything has gone well," I said, looking after them. "Mrs. Busby puts so much effort into things."

"They do seem to enjoy doing all they can for the villagers," Milo agreed. "An admirable trait in a vicar."

I turned to look at them again and saw that Bertie Phipps had appeared. He was hatless and dressed in riding clothes, his sleeves rolled up to reveal his brawny forearms. I thought it lucky that Darien had not suffered worse than a bloodied lip when he punched him.

I was about to turn away, when something caught my notice. Mrs. Busby was preoccupied talking to a vendor, and the vicar stood slightly behind her. Bertie noticed and approached Mr. Busby, hesitantly at first, then with more boldness.

Given what Winnelda had told me, I watched the exchange with interest.

To my surprise, it seemed that there was a moment of terse conversation. Clearly, Mr. Busby and Bertie disagreed about something. I still found it difficult to believe that Bertie would've stolen anything; perhaps that was what he was saying now, that he was innocent.

I glanced at Mrs. Busby. She was still talking with the huffkins woman and didn't seem to have noticed what was going on behind her.

My gaze moved back to the vicar just in time to see him shake his head as an envelope passed between him and Bertie. Bertie tucked it into the inside pocket of his jacket.

Curious.

Mrs. Busby turned then, and I saw her expression slip as she realized Bertie was there. She nodded to him, a bit coolly, I thought. The vicar's expression remained unreadable, though I could see that his shoulders had tensed, and his hands were holding tightly to the handles of Mrs. Busby's wheelchair.

Bertie mumbled something, gave a little nod, and turned away from them at last, his expression clouded. He moved quickly toward us, seemingly with no thought to where he was headed, and might have run directly into me had Milo not held out a hand to stop his progress.

"Be careful there, old chap."

Bertie stopped, looking from Milo to me and back again. "Oh, Mr. Ames, Mrs. Ames. I'm sorry. I wasn't looking where I was going."

"So I noticed," Milo said. "Is everything all right?"

Bertie flushed, looking away. "Yes. Fine."

"You're sure?" I asked softly.

He hesitated, and I thought for a moment he was going to say something about what had happened with the Busbys. But he only nodded. "I'm sure."

"Ready to ride Molly in the races?" Milo asked.

"Yes, sir. I'm looking forward to it." I was surprised that the usual enthusiasm was lacking in his tone. Whatever was on his mind must be something serious.

"We'll be cheering for you, of course," I said.

"Thank you, Mrs. Ames. I . . . I suppose I'd better go make sure Molly is ready."

"Of course. We'll see you later, Bertie," I told him cheerfully.

He walked a few steps from us and then turned back.

"Mr. Ames, what would you do if you knew a secret, and someone would get hurt no matter what you did with it?"

I looked at Milo, hoping he wouldn't give one of his standard flippant replies. To my relief, he seemed to realize as well as I did the weight with which Bertie had imbued the question. "I suppose I'd have to consider the options and choose to protect what mattered most."

Bertie nodded. Then he turned and disappeared into the crowd.

8

"WHAT DO YOU suppose that was all about?" I asked Milo.

"I don't know."

"Do you suppose we ought to ask him about it?"

"Darling," Milo said, taking my hand in his and bringing it to his lips. "You don't have to solve everyone's problems."

I sighed. "I suppose you're right."

And so I determined to forget the matter and enjoy the festival.

Bertie had not quite left my mind, however, when I encountered Marena in the crowd not an hour later. Milo had wandered away toward the racetrack as I browsed the selection of knitted and crocheted blankets available for purchase. I had chosen one in white and one in a pale yellow and turned to pay for them, when I saw Marena standing beside me. She looked very pretty today in a dress of pale rose-colored silk with leather shoes of a similar hue.

"Oh. Hello, Marena," I said.

"Oh, Mrs. Ames!" She flushed a little, and I realized that she was no doubt thinking about the last time I had seen her, at the inn during the altercation between her two suitors.

"I . . . I wonder if I might speak to you for a moment?" She glanced around us, making it clear that she didn't wish to be overheard.

"Of course." I handed the two blankets to the woman who was minding the stall. "I'll be back for these in just a moment, if that's all right?"

Then I followed Marena to a little space between two of the tents. When she turned to face me, she didn't meet my eyes. "I wanted to talk to you about . . . well, to apologize for what happened at the inn."

I had thought as much. Though it was really not my concern who she involved herself with, I was sure the altercation I had witnessed had been embarrassing for her. I also wondered if she was worried that I might mention something to the Busbys. I suspected she wouldn't have told them about Darien. Though I had mentioned to them that Bertie had a rival, I had kept the fact it was Milo's brother to myself.

That was no guarantee, however, that they didn't know. It was always amazing to me that anything could be kept quiet in a village of this size. But I supposed there were ways to keep secrets when they were important enough. No doubt there were a good many skeletons in the village cupboards that had yet to be discovered.

Before I could say anything, she plunged ahead. "Bertie acted ridiculously. I've never been so angry. I broke things off with him a few weeks ago, but he doesn't seem to understand that I meant it. He's a nice boy, but it just wasn't going to work between us. We want different things from life. And then Darien came along, and, well . . . I'm crazy about him. I've never met anyone like him."

I wasn't quite sure how to respond to this, as I agreed that Darien was certainly unique, though my opinion of his particular brand of originality was clearly not as positive as hers.

"I want to tell you that Milo and I don't know Darien," I said. "We didn't know of his existence until a few days ago."

She nodded. "He told me that Mr. Ames didn't know about him, that his arrival here was a surprise. He wanted me to know that he is . . . well, illegitimate. He said it would be best if I knew now rather than later. I told him, of course, that that doesn't matter to me. It's not his fault what his parents did, is it?"

"No, it's not. But what I mean to say is that we cannot vouch for him."

A slight frown flickered across her face, a cloud passing over the sunshine of her exuberance. "What do you mean?"

"I mean that we really know nothing of his background. And there is another matter . . ." I paused, weighing how much of it was none of my business and how much of it was my responsibility, as someone a bit older and wiser, to relate to her the dangers of involving oneself with a man one barely knew.

"There's the matter of another young woman with whom he was connected," I said, deciding she needed to know. It wouldn't do her any good to shield her from the truth. Indeed, the sooner she found everything out the better. On that score, Darien and I were in agreement.

If I thought she would be shocked by this information, however, I was to be surprised. "Imogen, you mean."

So he had told her that much, had he?

"He mentioned her to you?" I asked.

"Yes, Darien has told me all about his past. He said that he and Imogen had talked of getting married but that he realized he wasn't in love with her and couldn't go through with it."

She spoke with calm authority on the matter, as though she were in Darien's complete confidence. I found it difficult to believe he had told her the extent of his relationship with Imogen Prescott.

"It seems he falls in and out of love rather easily." I hoped this pointed remark would drive home the fact that she hadn't known him nearly long enough to believe they were ideally matched, but she merely smiled serenely.

"I think, when real love comes along, one knows it."

"You've only known him a week."

"I feel as though I've known him forever," she said wistfully.

I recognized that tone in her voice and felt that any influence I might have on her was negligible. Nevertheless, I pressed on. "That may be, but it's difficult to think clearly when one's feelings are so strong."

She smiled at me as though I had said something very silly. "I've always heard that you and Mr. Ames met and married quickly. Perhaps it runs in the family."

I had come up against one of the arguments that was most difficult to rebut. Inevitably, young women looked at Milo and assumed a whirlwind romance with a handsome and charming gentleman led to a life of bliss. This was not the case; there were a great many things I had not considered when pledging to spend the rest of my life with a man I barely knew.

It was difficult to tell them this, however, when I was currently so happy and contented. I wouldn't change my life with Milo, but the path to get here had certainly not been a bed of roses.

Whatever the case, one look at Marena's face told me it would be useless to argue the point with her at present. She was besotted, and I knew that nothing I could say about my own relationship—or about Darien—was going to dissuade her.

"Is Darien here today?" I asked, glancing around as though he might suddenly appear.

She shook her head. "I was with him this morning and told him that I would meet him later. He doesn't care much for juvenile frivolities."

I mastered the urge to roll my eyes, but only just.

"I saw Bertie talking to Mr. and Mrs. Busby a few minutes ago, so I suppose it's just as well that Darien isn't here to encounter him."

"Darien isn't afraid of Bertie," she said quickly, rising to her beloved's defense. "Bertie caught him off guard. It wasn't a fair fight. In fact, it was only at my urging that Darien decided to stay away from Bertie. He wanted to fight him to restore his honor."

I knew she meant this as an endorsement of Darien, but I found that Milo's brother, despite our short acquaintance, was already growing very tiresome.

"And, of course," she went on, "Mother is here, and I haven't told her about Darien yet."

That was one more reason to be grateful Milo's brother was not making an appearance at the festival.

I could only imagine what a meeting between Mrs. Hodges and Darien would be like. Mrs. Hodges was the grimmest woman I had ever come across, and I had encountered some grim figures in my day.

"I haven't told her that things are over between Bertie and me," Marena said, drawing me away from my reverie. "I . . . I thought it was best for the time being."

Mrs. Hodges had always been opposed to Marena's involvement with Bertie Phipps, so I was sure the news would have been welcome. That Bertie had been supplanted by a disreputable young stranger was probably the reason why Marena had yet to mention it to her mother.

"Well, I'm sure everything will work itself out in time," I said. I hoped that it was true.

"Yes, I'm sure you're right. Thank you for talking with me, Mrs. Ames. I feel much better about everything."

I only wished I did.

I stepped out from the space between the two tents and found Milo standing there. I wondered how much he had overheard.

"Oh, hello, Milo," I said.

"What were you and Marena talking about?"

I glanced over my shoulder, surprised to see that Marena had disappeared. She must have gone off in another direction, hoping to avoid Milo and the topic of Darien, I supposed.

"Oh, the fair and such."

He shot me a look that said he wasn't fooled. "Amory, have you been involving yourself in things you shouldn't?"

I ignored the question and returned to the booth where I completed the purchase of the baby blankets.

Then I turned back to Milo. "It was Marena who wanted to speak to me," I said. "But, in answer to your question, I do feel like Darien is our concern, whether or not you agree."

"Not for much longer. I'm going to make sure he leaves Allingcross."

"I don't know that he'll be easily persuaded."

"He will," Milo said with a confidence I found difficult to doubt. He had always been extremely adept at getting his way, and I couldn't help but feel this case wouldn't be any different.

I supposed Marena would be heartbroken were Darien to leave, but I couldn't help but feel it would be the best thing for her. Indeed, it would likely be the best thing for all of us.

"She's infatuated with him," I said. "I'm afraid it's much worse than we thought."

He shrugged. "What of it?"

"Milo, surely you see that he . . ."

"Yes, darling," he said, cutting me off with a dismissive wave of the hand. "But we needn't worry about him today. He's not here."

"Marena mentioned that he wasn't coming because he thought the entire thing juvenile."

"I rather suspect it was because I told him not to come."

I turned to look at him. Though it was not at all surprising he had been in contact with his brother without telling me, I found I was a bit annoyed he had kept it a secret.

"Why didn't you mention you'd spoken to him?" I asked casually.

Milo's expression told me he wasn't fooled by my show of indifference. "Don't be angry, darling. You didn't miss an emotional reunion between long-lost brothers. If such a thing is ever to occur, I'll be sure to let you know."

I quelled my irritation and the impulse to make a sharp retort. While a part of me was a bit hurt that this had occurred without me, I understood that the matter really was a private one best settled between Milo and Darien.

Though he lived life on a public scale, indifferent to the opinions of others, Milo was a maddeningly private person when it came to discussing his thoughts. It was a lucky thing I understood him as well as I did, for there had been very few occasions when he had confided his feelings to me.

To be fair, I, too, had often found it difficult to discuss my emotions with him in the past. We were improving on that score, but this latest revelation made it clear we still had a ways to go. And just because I understood Milo's instinctual desire to keep matters to himself didn't mean I appreciated having been kept in the dark that it had happened.

"When did this occur?" I asked.

"I went to see him at the inn yesterday afternoon. We had a drink and discussed a few things."

He was being purposefully vague, and I didn't intend to let it pass.

"What did he say, Milo? The particulars, if you please."

He smiled. "There really isn't much to tell, darling. We agreed that there was more to be discussed at a future date, and I told him it would be better for all concerned if he didn't appear at the festival today. He's going to come to Thornecrest the day after tomorrow. But let's not discuss Darien any more today, shall we?" Milo said. "We've better things to do."

I let out a little sigh. He was right, I supposed. While I had a good many more questions, there was no reason to let the matter of Darien and his rampant love affairs spoil the festival. There would be plenty of time to think about it later.

I tried to put the matter from my mind as Milo and I went to the livestock tent, more from my desire to look at the lambs, kids, and piglets than from any interest on Milo's part. Aside from the horses, there had been no livestock to speak of at Thornecrest for many years. I, on the other hand, was keen to coo at the baby animals. It seemed the maternal spirit was strong within me.

"Shall we add him to the menagerie?" Milo asked as I patted the head of an adorable little lamb.

"I'm not sure Emile would take to him," I said with a laugh. Emile was our pet monkey. Milo had acquired him in Paris in some sort of bet, the particulars of which I had yet to understand, and he had become a part of our household.

"He'd probably ride the thing across the drawing room the moment our backs were turned," Milo agreed.

I laughed at the mental image, but it halted as I looked across the tent and spotted Imogen standing near the edge of the crowd at one of the booths outside. She looked very pretty in a dress of pale green that complemented her fair coloring, but her unexpected presence at the festival was a bit jarring somehow. Truth be told, I had rather hoped that, after learning Darien had used a false identity to woo her, she would go back to London and forget all about him. It seemed, however, this was not the case. Even from this distance I could detect the forlorn aura that hung about her.

I wondered why she was still here in Allingcross. Did she seek to reconcile with Darien? I hoped not. From what I had seen, his involvement with Marena Hodges had gone too far, and, in all honesty, I suspected it would be difficult for Imogen to compete with Marena for his affections. Imogen was a lovely girl with her blond hair and clear blue eyes, but she lacked Marena's vibrant energy, the vitality that flashed in her eyes. I could see how Darien would be drawn to the dark-haired village beauty.

Besides, even on the off chance that he was to take Imogen back, I foresaw a future full of heartache and strife if she were to link herself to him. No, it was better for all concerned that the marriage had not been legal.

Not for the first time that day, I felt incredibly cross with Darien. It was wretched enough that he had abandoned Imogen after promising to marry her; now he was cavorting about with Marena Hodges when Imogen was still in the village. Had Imogen seen them together? It seemed likely enough. I pitied the poor girl and wished there was something I could do to help her. The very least I could do was advise her to go home and try to put the past behind her.

Milo's voice pulled me from my reverie. "I'm going to speak to Mr. Yates there for a moment," he said, catching sight of the farmer.

"All right." As he walked away, I reluctantly surrendered the lamb back to its mother and, exiting the livestock tent, started toward the place I had seen Imogen. A voice caught my attention before I could reach her.

"Hello, Mrs. Ames."

I turned to see Mrs. Hodges, Marena's mother. She had set up a booth to sell her honey, it seemed. She stood behind a table covered in a white cloth and arrayed with jars of all sizes, each glowing a warm golden brown in the sunlight.

"Good afternoon, Mrs. Hodges," I said. "How are you?"

"Well enough, I suppose." Her eyes ran over me. "You look as though you've had better days."

I put a hand on my stomach. "It won't be long now."

"So I see."

From another woman, this might have been a pleasant conversation starter. From Mrs. Hodges, it was more of a criticism. I supposed she didn't approve of my parading my stomach for all to see.

Marena's mother was a thoroughly unpleasant woman. She had none of her daughter's warmth, nor her beauty. Indeed, I had heard people comment that it seemed impossible that she might be the mother to so beautiful a girl. While the sentiment was not exactly kind, it was true that there was no resemblance between the strong-featured, hard-eyed woman and the vivacious girl who often drew appreciative glances from the men in the village.

For today's festive occasion, Mrs. Hodges was dressed all in somber gray, and it seemed her mood matched her ensemble. Her mouth was drawn into a grim line; it was apparent that she was not enjoying herself.

"I'd like very much to buy some honey from you," I said, feeling, for some unaccountable reason, the urge to appease her. Perhaps it was that I relished a challenge.

Whatever the case, my words did not seem to cheer her as I had hoped. "If you like. I've several varieties. The lavender honey is the most popular."

She nodded toward one of the jars. I had had Mrs. Hodges's lavender honey before and had to admit that it was delicious.

"All right, I . . ."

Out of the corner of my eye, I spotted Imogen hurrying out of a tent, her face very pale, and disappearing behind it. I wondered what all of that was about.

"I'll take a jar of the lavender," I said. "Perhaps I may come back and pick it up later? I'd rather not carry it."

"I suppose that would be all right," Mrs. Hodges grudgingly agreed.

I paid her for the jar and then went to the tent Imogen had vacated. It was the fortune-telling tent, a sign proclaiming it to be the domain of "The Great Griselda." A young woman stood outside dressed in colorful garb, a scarf tied around her head, with large hooped earrings and bangles at her wrists that jingled when she moved. It was Mabel, one of the village girls, but I played along and pretended not to know her.

"May I tell your fortune, mistress?" she asked in an accent of no discernible origin.

I wasn't normally one who ventured to look too far into the unknown, but it was all in good fun and would add a few more pence to the coffers of the Springtide Festival Committee. Besides, I was curious why Imogen had left the tent in such haste.

She led me into the tent, which had been draped with colorful fabrics. Two chairs sat at a table covered in a gold cloth, a crystal ball resting in the center. The Great Griselda motioned me to one seat and moved to the other.

She looked into the ball, squinting her eyes as though my future were clouded in mystery. At last she nodded and then spoke. "There will be a change to come in your life, my lady. One for the better."

"Indeed?" I encouraged her.

She nodded. "A small thing that will become very important." She sat back in her chair, looking pleased with herself.

With my bulging midsection, the glimpse into my future wasn't exactly revelatory, but it was sweet of her to give me such a pleasant fortune.

"Thank you," I said. "That was very enlightening. I wonder . . . The young woman who was here before me, what sort of fortune did you tell her?"

The young fortune-teller frowned, dropping her mystic guise and the accent along with it. "I don't know what she was in such a huff about. I thought she'd like her fortune. It's not as though I can really . . . That is . . ." She paused and reassumed her persona. "It's not as though the Great Griselda can change what the future holds."

"What did you tell her?" I asked.

"I merely told her that something from the past would arrive to change her future. That secrets would be revealed that would make all become clear."

It was standard stuff, the sort of vague prophecies than any imitation occultist would give. Why, then, would it have upset Imogen?

"Well, thank you very much, Mab . . . Griselda."

"You're very welcome, my lady," she said.

I got up from my seat, and she followed me out of the tent just as Milo approached from the direction of the livestock pens.

"Would your husband like his fortune told, my lady?" Mabel asked, watching him.

"I don't think so," I said. I knew Milo had no patience for such things.

She looked a bit disappointed. I couldn't help but wonder if the pretty young fortune-teller was just eager to have a few minutes alone with my husband. It wouldn't be the first time.

"There you are, darling. I wondered where you'd disappeared to," Milo said as he reached me.

"Having my future read," I said lightly.

"Well, I'll venture to predict your near future includes the sound of a pistol and the pounding of hooves."

I saw that the crowd had begun to move as one toward the field on the south side of the festival grounds.

It was time for the races.

 9 

MILO HAD SECURED us one of the little enclosures close to the track, and we waited with anticipation for the race to start. I was mostly just relieved to have a seat, even if it was merely one of the plain plank benches, as temporary as the makeshift racetrack itself.

The crowd was in a jovial mood. The air was filled with the sound of conversation, laughter, and the shout of spectators cheering on their favorites. Many of the faces I recognized from the village and the surrounding areas of the county. The Springtide Festival was not an exceptionally large gathering by racing standards. I had accompanied Milo to the Royal Ascot, the Cheltenham Festival, and many of the other great racing events in the country, and our little event was quite humble in comparison. Nevertheless, it was always met with great enthusiasm, and the locals took as much pride in their wins as any owner in England.

Lady Alma arrived in our enclosure, out of breath. "Thought I was going to miss it," she said. "I got caught up in conversation. Always an awkward thing trying to get away."

She took a seat on the other side of Milo, her gaze moving around the track as though calculating the odds of the horses she favored. Like Milo, Lady Alma refrained from running any of her Thoroughbreds, but she was always keen to place bets on the village racers and to keep an eye out for any potential breeding stock.

"Who's your favorite, Lady Alma?" Milo asked.

"Old Henson's filly, Jasmine," she said without hesitation.

"Is that so?" Milo asked. "The vicar and I both favor Yates's bay, Galahad."

"Galahad," she scoffed. "Jasmine will take the race by a length, mark my words."

"Would you care to wager on it?" he asked, flashing a smile.

She returned it with a grin of her own. "A hundred pounds."

Milo held out his hand and they shook. He had just increased my investment in the outcome considerably.

Milo could do as he pleased with his money, of course, but it always made me uneasy to see how easily he gambled it. Luckily for both of us, he almost always won. I wondered if he would be so fortunate today. If there was anyone who knew horses as well as he did, it was Lady Alma.

A few moments later we watched as the horses lined up at the gate. I shielded my eyes from the glare of the sun and studied them. There were a great deal of fine-looking horses, my amateur opinion confirmed by Milo's next comment: "Good stock all around this year."

I searched the line and realized suddenly what was missing. "Where's Bertie?" I asked.

"I was wondering the same thing," Milo answered.

"It's odd," Lady Alma mused. "I know how eager the boy was to show off his horse. Perhaps he's just late coming to the gate."

I stood, looking behind the starting line, hoping to catch sight of him approaching.

But no—the horses pranced, the gunshot sounded, and off they went. I watched the race, only half-focused on the outcome. It seemed whatever had been worrying Bertie had prevented him from racing. I felt sorry he had missed this opportunity to show both Molly and his skill as a horseman.

My attention was soon otherwise engaged, however, as the horses began to hit their stride. As Milo and Lady Alma had predicted, it was Jasmine and Galahad who pulled ahead as the horses made their way around the track.

Lady Alma shot to her feet, her gaze riveted on the track.

As they neared the final turn, I reached out and clutched Milo's arm, the fabric of his jacket bunching beneath my glove as I squeezed it in nervous anticipation. The corner of his mouth tipped up, though he didn't take his eyes from the racetrack.

The race continued, both of the horses outdistancing the rest. It was going to be close.

Unable to take the suspense sitting down any longer, I stood, and Milo stood with me. I tore my eyes from the racetrack to look at him and saw he was watching with a look of serene intensity. How he could be so calm at a time like this was beyond me. I had watched him at the roulette table often enough, however, to know that he was never ruffled by the vagaries of chance. He loved the thrill of it, of standing on the precipice between victory and loss, waiting to see which way the chips would fall. I, on the other hand, felt rather like I might lose my breakfast.

Jasmine and Galahad reached the final stretch neck and neck. They were both practically gleaming in the sunlight, their muscles rippling as they propelled themselves forward, inspired by some inborn sense of competition and the skillful urging of their riders.

"Come on, Jasmine," Lady Alma cried boisterously, her voice rising above the wild cheering of the crowd. "Come on!"

I was certain that Jasmine was going to win. She had edged ahead ever so slightly as they neared the finish line. Their legs were all a blur, but I could see the tip of her nose edge past Galahad.

And then, suddenly, Galahad shot forward in one final, triumphant burst of speed and shot across the finish line a nose ahead of Jasmine.

The crowd roared its approval at the tight race, and I cheered with them.

"We've won!" I cried, flinging myself into Milo's arms, or as nearly as I could with my stomach between us.

"Yes, we've won." He laughed, leaning to drop a kiss on my lips.

"Well done, Ames," Lady Alma said with characteristic good grace. She extended her gloveless hand to him as he released me. "When you come by to collect, we'll discuss that matter of your stallion."

"Indeed, we shall," Milo agreed.

He slipped an arm around me as the crowd began to disperse. "Well, darling, we're a hundred pounds richer. How shall we spend our ill-gotten gains?"

"Buy me something to eat," I said decisively.

IT TURNED OUT Milo's winnings were safe from my appetite. We went to the tea tent after the races for refreshments laid out by the local Ladies Charitable Society. The tea was hot and strong, and I added a liberal amount of sugar as I stacked a dainty plate with sandwiches and biscuits.

Everyone was in high spirits after the race, and there was laughter and chatter over the clink and clatter of china and silverware. A cool breeze was blowing, making the scalloped edges of the tent's awning quiver and dance. It was all so very cozy and idyllic.

Which made what was to come all the more startling.

Milo had gone off to discuss horses with some of the other gentlemen, and I nibbled on a biscuit as I made my own way around the tent, talking to various villagers and congratulating the members of the Springtide Festival Committee for the success of the festival.

Suddenly I spotted Mrs. Jane Hodges, Marena's mother, moving in my direction. I had had enough of her company at her honey booth, but I realized that it was too late to avoid her.

"Good afternoon, Mrs. Ames. I trust you'll collect your honey after tea is over?"

"Yes, certainly," I agreed. "Are you enjoying the festivities?"

She frowned. "I don't approve of horse racing. It only brings about gambling and all other manner of unsavory behavior."

"I don't suppose there's too much wickedness to be found here in Allingcross," I said lightly.

Her sharp eyes came up to meet mine, and I was surprised that the faintest hint of a smile showed on her lips. "Surely you, of all people, don't believe that, Mrs. Ames."

I wasn't sure whether she was referring to my past involvement with various murder investigations, which was common knowledge, or Milo's reputation, which was also much discussed in the village.

Before I had time to formulate a response, however, Marena approached us.

"There you are, Mother," she said brightly. "I've been looking for you."

"Looking for me? Nonsense. It's you who've been gallivanting about. I looked for you before the races and you were nowhere to be found."

"I was just where I said I'd be," Marena responded tersely.

"You most certainly were not," Mrs. Hodges sniffed, her gaze running up and down her daughter. "At least you've managed to keep yourself clean. I don't know why you wore those light-colored shoes outdoors."

"I'm not a child, Mother."

"If you'll just excuse me," I said, realizing the only way to extricate myself from the conversation was the direct approach. "I have a matter I need to discuss with Mrs. Busby."

They continued their hushed argument as I moved away from them, looking for Mrs. Busby. I really had no direct business with her, but I knew that even Mrs. Hodges could not disapprove of my leaving them to talk to the vicar's wife.

I noticed her at one of the tables in the corner. She sat speaking to Inspector Wilson, of the local police.

"How's the tea, Mrs. Ames?"

I turned to see the vicar approaching me with two full cups balanced on saucers. One for him and one for his wife.

"Very good," I told him. "Quite strong."

He smiled. "Oh, good. Last year they let Mrs. Hodges make the tea. Horrible, watery stuff." He shuddered. "Uncharitable of me to say so, perhaps, but I do need a good strong cup of tea in the afternoon."

I nodded my agreement. "I seem to tire much more easily these days."

"And all the days to come, I'm afraid. Parenthood is not for the faint of heart."

I smiled. "No, I don't imagine it is."

"For all that, it's life's greatest blessing. You're going to enjoy it immensely." Unlike his wife, the vicar was able to speak about children without sadness eclipsing his expression. I wondered if the faith incumbent in his profession had made it easier for him to accept a child's death, somehow. Or perhaps it had just made it easier for him to hide his sorrow behind that constantly cheery expression.

"I'm very much looking forward to it," I told him.

"I imagine you are. I think you—and Mr. Ames—will make wonderful parents." I couldn't help but wonder if the good vicar had fibbed just a bit on this last pronouncement. I knew a good many in the village had their doubts about Milo's suitability for fatherhood.

Happily, I didn't share their misgivings. Whatever his faults, I was certain Milo was going to be an excellent father. His own father's lack of interest in Milo's life would be the impetus for his involvement as a parent.

As for myself, in some ways, it was still strange to me to think that I would soon be a mother. Though I felt I had grown close to my baby in the time we had had together thus far, I still had my share of worries about motherhood. My own mother—both my parents, in fact—had always been somewhat distant, and I didn't want to be that way with my own child. I hoped I could manage it all.

"Thank you," I said to the vicar. "I certainly hope so."

He must have sensed the hint of worry in my tone, for he smiled kindly. "It all seems rather terrifying at first, I know. After all, life is so precious, and it's a great responsibility to have it in one's charge. But as soon as you hold your child in your arms for the first time, it will come naturally. There's nothing like it in the world." He looked down at his hands and the teacups he still held in them. "Well, I suppose I had better deliver Mrs. Busby's tea while it's still hot. She is a stickler about her tea."

I smiled. "Yes, of course. I'll come by and speak to her later. I wanted to tell her again how very well everything has turned out."

"That will mean a great deal. She takes pride in the festival. It's important to her."

"Her devotion to its success is always apparent."

He went off with his teacups, and I moved toward Milo, who I saw had just finished his conversation with the victorious Mr. Yates. His eyes scanned the gathering until they alighted on me, and he smiled. I was caught for a moment in the warmth of his gaze, the intimate connection we had across a space crowded with people.

Suddenly, there was the noise of some disturbance at one edge of the tent.

"Mr. Ames! Mr. Ames!" I heard a voice calling from outside. Milo and I both turned to see Peter, one of the stable boys, hurrying from the direction of the boundary line between Thornecrest and Bedford Priory, his eyes wide, his face white.

Milo moved toward him, and I quickly followed. We stepped out of the tent and reached him at nearly the same time.

"What is it?" Milo asked in a low voice. I glanced back at the tea tent. Conversation continued much as normal. Aside from a few people at the edge of the tent, who briefly looked up at Peter's arrival, it appeared we hadn't drawn much notice. Shouting was not unusual at the festival, after all.

There was definitely something unusual happening, however. Peter looked sick with fright or fear or some other dreadful emotion.

The boy was out of breath. He bent over, trying to suck in air, muttering something incoherent.

I stepped closer, placing a hand on his shoulder. "Slow down, dear," I told him gently. "Take a breath."

He drew in a ragged gasp, then another. "He . . . ground . . . need . . . help."

"What is it?" Milo asked again, his voice calm but insistent. "Is it one of the horses?"

Peter shook his head, drawing in another deep breath. "It's Bertie," he gasped at last. "He's fallen . . . off his horse . . . I . . . I think he's dead."

10

MILO FOLLOWED PETER off to the field in the direction of Thornecrest, and I went in search of the doctor. We hadn't called attention to the accident, not wanting to cause a stir amongst the festivalgoers. Besides, I still harbored hope that Peter was simply mistaken, that Bertie might have been unconscious and hurt. He had fallen from a horse that day I had spoken to him in the stables; perhaps another accident had occurred and he would be all right.

At last I located Dr. Jordan and told him what had happened. He hurried off, and I went back to the tea tent, looking out toward the fields but unable to see anything. I hoped that Milo and Peter would appear suddenly, helping a bruised but alive Bertie back so he could be properly tended to.

I saw Peter a few minutes later. He was walking a bit slower, and Milo wasn't with him.

I had hoped for the best, but as he drew nearer and I saw his face, I knew it was to be the worst instead.

"Mr. Ames said for you to send the police," he said in a low voice when he reached me.

"The police?" I repeated, though I knew with certainty what that meant.

Peter nodded, confirming it with his next words. "Bertie's dead." He was pale but composed. "A levelheaded lad," Milo had often called him; it was proving to be true.

I let out a breath, the shock of it hitting me, though I had half expected to hear the news. Poor Bertie. What a horrible thing to have happened.

A part of me wanted to go to the scene, but I knew that Milo would chide me for making the trek across the field in my condition. Besides, I had seen enough death as of late to last me a lifetime. The mysteries in which we had been involved in the past two years had had their share of distressing events, and I knew firsthand the impact of discovering a dead body.

I went with Peter toward the table where Inspector Wilson still sat with Mrs. Busby. He was a tall, thin man with silver-flecked hair and a thin mustache. I didn't know him well, and I hoped that he would be ready to take charge of the crisis.

"Excuse me," I said in a low voice when I reached them. "I do hate to interrupt, but I'm afraid there's been an accident."

I glanced at Mrs. Busby and saw how she paled at the words. She knew better than most what a dreadful impact that phrase could have.

"I'm afraid Bertie Phipps is . . . dead. He fell from his horse, between Thornecrest and Bedford Priory."

"Oh no," Mrs. Busby breathed, her hand fluttering to her chest.

"Peter here was the one who found him. He can show you the way. My husband and the doctor are already there." I was still speaking in a low voice, but I was fairly certain the women at the neighboring table had overheard, for there was already the sound of distressed whispers coming from behind me. It was not as though we could keep the matter a secret for long, of course, but arousing the sympathies of a crowd could be detrimental rather than useful.

To my relief, Inspector Wilson didn't have much to say on the matter. He gave me a swift nod that told me he had understood and turned and followed Peter from the tent.

I felt so helpless as I watched them leave. I wondered if there was someone from Bertie's family that I should notify, but I couldn't think of anyone. As far as I knew, he was very much alone in the world.

Except, perhaps, Marena, or Lady Alma. I wondered if I should try to locate them.

"Are you all right, dear?"

I looked down to see Mrs. Busby watching me worriedly.

"Yes, quite all right," I assured her. "It's just so shocking."

"Do sit down. You're quite pale."

"I . . . I was just thinking that someone ought to tell Lady Alma."

"Yes, the vicar can do that in a moment. Please sit down. It won't do for you to faint."

I didn't feel like I was going to faint, but I obeyed nevertheless, lowering myself into the seat beside her.

The vicar arrived at our table just then, no doubt having noticed the commotion, and I felt the sense of relief that comes with knowing someone else is going to take charge of the matter. One could always rely on a vicar in general and Mr. Busby in particular. Mrs. Busby explained to him in a low voice what had happened.

His face grew very grave. "I should find Marena."

Mrs. Busby gasped. "Oh, yes. I didn't think . . . Of course, you must find her and tell her before she hears it from someone else."

We were, however, too late.

Marena appeared suddenly at our table, out of breath, her face white. "Is it true? It's not true, is it? Someone told me that Bertie . . . that he was . . ."

I rose from my chair, hoping, selfishly, that someone would break the news to her before I needed to.

"Marena, dear," Mrs. Busby began gently.

Marena shook her head. "No," she said. "No. It's not true. I don't believe it. I won't believe it!" Her voice rose with each word until she was nearly shouting.

It was the vicar, with his usual adeptness, that calmed her rising hysteria. He gently took her arms and spoke to her in a calm but firm voice. "He's with the Lord now, Marena. No more harm can come to him."

She shook her head again, ever so slightly, as though she were trying to make sense of words spoken to her in some language she didn't speak.

And then she covered her face with her hands and began to cry.

Between the vicar and me, we managed to usher her into the chair I had vacated beside Mrs. Busby's wheelchair. Mrs. Busby leaned toward the girl, collecting her in her arms as best she could, and held her as her body shook with sobs.

IT SEEMED AGES as I waited for Milo to return to the tent. I thought of taking the car back to Thornecrest to wait for him there, but somehow I didn't want to leave the site of the festival just yet. Word had spread quickly about the tragedy, and there was a sense of sorrowful camaraderie in those who remained at the refreshment tent. We all seemed to be waiting to see what would happen next.

As there was nothing useful most of us could do, we sat drinking tea. I was certain my baby must be swimming in it by this point.

To my relief, Mr. and Mrs. Busby had escorted an ashen and dazed Marena back to the vicarage. She had taken the news of Bertie's death much harder than I expected. Though she had made it clear to me that she no longer had romantic feelings for him, it was clear something had lingered there. Her grief had been difficult to witness.

At last Milo appeared at the edge of the tent. I rose quickly from my chair and hurried toward him.

His clothes were muddy, and there was a spot of blood on his trousers. Bertie's blood, I assumed, though I hadn't imagined there would be blood from a fall. I felt a little wave of dizziness at the sight of it, and I was immensely glad that I hadn't gone to the site of the incident.

"Are you all right?" he asked, as though I was the one who had just spent over an hour at the site of a fatal accident.

"Of course. Are you?"

"Yes. I'm fine."

I looked into his eyes, trying to read something of what he felt there, but his gaze was veiled. This was not the first time Milo had dealt with death, but I thought there must be something a little harrowing in it, even for him.

Whatever he was feeling, he was clearly not in the mood to discuss it at present. Not that I blamed him; I felt numb and tired myself.

He seemed to sense this. "You look all in, darling. I'm terribly sorry I kept you waiting, but the doctor and Inspector Wilson have taken everything in hand. Come," he said, taking my arm. "I'll take you home."

We left the tea tent behind and made our way through the festival grounds, which had begun to clear. Though many of the vendors were still open for business and several people milled about, there was a heaviness that seemed to hang over the proceedings. It seemed even the children had lost their enthusiasm, for the ones I spotted moved at a much more subdued pace than they had earlier in the day.

The sun had begun to descend in the sky, bathing everything in a warm, golden glow. The breeze had grown cooler, but the cheerful flags and banners still swayed lazily, and the scent of flowers filled the evening air. It seemed the loveliness of it all almost mocked the somberness of what had happened.

To think how happy we had all been this morning, how cheerful Bertie must have been as he readied himself for the race. He was so proud of his horse, Molly. Not only that, I was surprised that she had thrown him; she was the gentlest of the horses, even more docile than Paloma, who had always been known for her even temper.

Something must have happened. Perhaps she had seen a hare or a fox in the field and bolted. I could think of no other reason why she might have thrown her rider.

What was more, Bertie had told me that he knew how to fall. How dreadful it was that his words had been so quickly disproved.

"That poor boy," I said aloud. "What a dreadful thing to happen."

"Yes."

I glanced at Milo, caught by something in his tone, but he wasn't looking at me. He seemed preoccupied.

"Are you . . . sure you're all right, Milo?" I asked again.

He looked at me then, offering a reassuring smile that chased all hint of the shadows from his eyes. "Yes, quite sure. Why?"

"I don't know. I know you liked Bertie."

"I did. It's a rotten thing to have happened."

"And I thought maybe it was rather a . . . grim scene."

"I've seen much worse."

He did have a point, though it wasn't something I wanted to think about at present.

We reached the car, and Milo opened my door and handed me in. I sank back against the leather seat and, leaning my head back and closing my eyes, breathed a sigh of relief. I hadn't realized how very tired I was until now. I couldn't wait to be back at Thornecrest.

Milo got in and started the car, and we turned toward home.

I watched the fields go by, bathed in the bright late-afternoon light, and caught sight of a few of Lady Alma's horses grazing.

A thought occurred to me suddenly.

"What happened to Molly? Has she been found?" Despite what had happened, I hoped no harm had come to Bertie's horse. He had doted on her and would have been devastated if she were injured.

"He wasn't riding Molly," Milo said. "It appears it was Medusa, Lady Alma's new horse, that threw him."

"Not Molly?"

"No. Molly was in the paddock."

I frowned, confused. "Why on earth would he be riding Medusa?"

"I don't know. A saddle was found not far from Bertie, and Medusa was wandering near the barn. She'd clearly been in a state, for she was wild-eyed and lathered. Her right foreleg was scratched as well, as though she'd scraped it on a fence when she jumped."

"Is she going to be all right?"

"I believe so. It took a good deal of effort to calm her, but I don't think there's any permanent damage."

I was glad to hear that, but something about the scenario didn't seem to make sense. It was all so strange.

"You don't suppose Bertie planned to ride her in the race?" I asked. "Everyone would have known that it wasn't his Molly."

"No," he said. "I don't think that's what he was planning. I can't imagine what might have induced him to ride her."

"It's so horrible that something like this happened. What are the odds of such an accident?"

He looked over at me, something flickering in his blue eyes. For a moment he said nothing, as though he was making some sort of decision. At last he spoke. "I don't think it was an accident."

I stared at him. "What do you mean? What else could it have been?" Even as I said the words, I knew what his reply would be.

"I think it was murder."

11

IT TOOK A moment to absorb this information. It seemed impossible that it might be happening again, that we might find ourselves at the scene of another violent death, but Milo very seldom jumped to conclusions. I knew, if he thought it was murder, that there was a very good chance he was right. No wonder he had been so reticent, so lost in thought.

It occurred to me that he had probably been debating whether or not to tell me about it. I was glad that he had chosen to, though I suspected it was more from the realization it could not be hidden long than from the desire to take me into his confidence where a crime was concerned.

"What makes you think so?" I asked, surprised at how calm I sounded. The prospect of a murder practically on our doorstep was horrifying.

"For one thing, it doesn't make sense that he would've been riding Medusa. He knew better than that. Lady Alma is more fanatical about her horses than I am."

"Perhaps he was overcome with temptation."

"Right before he was to ride his own horse in the race?"

What he said was true, but the fact remained that they had discovered Medusa loose and spooked. "But it seems he must have ridden her, doesn't it?"

"Either that or someone let her out after Bertie was dead in order to make it look like it."

Though I was always one to view matters with an eye for suspicion, I was skeptical. "That seems a bit far-fetched."

He smiled. "It seems our roles are reversed for once, darling. I'd like to believe I'm wrong, but you haven't heard the evidence."

"By all means, carry on."

"When I put her back in her stall, I noticed that one of the lower rails was broken. I looked closer and saw a bit of blood. It looked fairly fresh. I think Medusa was rearing up and scratched her leg on it. That's how she was hurt, not jumping a fence."

"You mean a stranger frightened her when they let her out."

"Something like that."

"And then the killer put the saddle near Bertie to make it look as though it had loosened and fallen off, taking Bertie with it," I said, following his train of thought.

"But Bertie wouldn't have been that careless. Besides, there's one more thing, irrefutable proof that Bertie wasn't riding Medusa: she didn't have a bit in. He wouldn't have ridden her without reins."

"No," I agreed, my mind racing. "But surely the killer must have realized that wouldn't make any sense."

"Well, perhaps they had intended to bridle her. Alas, Medusa clearly wasn't of a mind to cooperate. I'd wager she started rearing up and got out of her stall before the perpetrator could get close enough to accomplish it."

Another thought occurred to me, an unpleasant one. "If . . . if it wasn't a fall that killed Bertie, what did?"

"He was lying with a bloody rock near his head. Probably from that old stone wall that separates the Priory from Thornecrest. I'm fairly certain it must have been the murder weapon."

"But could someone hit him hard enough to kill him?" I felt a bit sick at the words and at the image they conjured up in my mind.

"It was a sharp rock. A good blow or two might have done it."

"But they couldn't have been sure it would work. It seems a haphazard way to kill someone?" I was trying to come up with any excuse I could as to why Milo might be mistaken. The possibility of murder seemed too horrible to contemplate.

Milo was undeterred, however. "If it was done in the heat of the moment, it might not have been intended to kill. When it did, however, the killer was forced to cover his tracks and decided to use Medusa to do it."

"It was risky, wasn't it? They might have been caught."

"Almost everyone at Bedford Priory was here at the festival. Lady Alma gave them all the day off. And that area of the field isn't visible from the festival grounds. The killer must have realized there was little chance of being seen."

I let out a breath that was closer to a sigh. It was all so strange and ghastly.

"What did Inspector Wilson say?" I asked. "Did you mention this to him?"

"I did. It seemed to me that he was already thinking along the same lines. The doctor also thought there was something strange about the wound."

"Like what?" I didn't really want to know, but I couldn't seem to stop myself from asking.

"He said he didn't see how he could have hit his head at that angle if the rock was lying on the ground and he'd fallen on it. He's going to examine the body more closely. There'll be an inquest, of course."

"Of course." My mind was racing. An inquest. And then an investigation into who might have wanted to kill poor Bertie Phipps.

I remembered his question to Milo the last time we had seen him. What did one do when a secret could hurt people? Had someone killed to keep that secret from coming to light?

How dreadful this all was.

What was worse was that I suddenly remembered the expression on Darien's face after Bertie had hit him and the words he had uttered: "I'll kill you for this."

SHOULD I TELL Milo what his brother had said? I grappled with the question as he helped me out of the car back at Thornecrest before driving off to park it.

I went straight to our bedroom, glad of a few moments of quiet solitude. I had given Winnelda the day off for the festival, but I expected her to burst upon the scene at any moment, asking about Bertie's death.

After turning on the bathtub faucets, I went back to my room and pulled one of my most comfortable nightdresses from the wardrobe. Though it was not yet six o'clock, I intended to bathe and get in bed, not leaving the comfort of my room until tomorrow.

Before I could retreat to the bathroom, however, Milo came in. His appearance necessitated my making a decision about the matter of Darien.

I wavered and then at last came out with it. "Milo, I think you should know. When Bertie hit Darien at the inn, Darien threatened to kill him."

I don't know what reaction I expected. Perhaps surprise or alarm. I ought to have known better. The only expression that crossed his features was annoyance.

"Did anyone hear him say it?"

I nodded. "Marena Hodges and another girl who works at the inn."

He let out an irritated breath. He said nothing for a moment, apparently thinking over the implications of what I had told him.

"It was probably an empty threat," I said at last. "After all, Bertie had just struck him. Anyone is bound to say such a thing in the heat of the moment."

"Perhaps. But when the person one has threatened to kill turns up dead a few days later, it's bound to look a bit suspicious, don't you think?"

I did indeed.

What was more, we knew nothing about Darien. Nothing about his past or his temperament. We certainly couldn't vouch for his character.

I felt a sudden little pang in my side and put a hand to my stomach.

Milo glanced over at me. "Are you all right, darling?"

"Yes, I'm fine."

"Are you sure?" He was watching me closely.

"Quite sure. I think the baby is just a bit excited this evening. It's been an eventful day, after all."

"I'm going to ring for the doctor."

I laughed. "Milo, don't be silly. There's nothing wrong. If we rang for the doctor every time this baby kicked me, he'd never have a chance to tend to anyone else."

I thought he was going to insist, but instead he came to me and placed a hand on my stomach. We were both still for a moment as the child moved. It was such a queer feeling to know that our baby was there, beneath the surface, waiting to make his entry into the world.

Milo smiled down at me. "She's certainly a lively little thing."

"Or he," I replied. Milo insisted we were going to have a daughter. My instincts on the matter had varied often enough that I had given up trying to guess.

"Perhaps she—or he—is intrigued by a mystery as much as we are," I suggested.

"Darling, even if Bertie was murdered, it doesn't mean we need to get involved."

I sighed, turning toward the bathroom. "Somehow I had a feeling you'd say that."

"You have to admit that now, just before the baby is born, is not an ideal time to entangle ourselves in another murder investigation."

I knew he was right, of course, but that didn't stop me from wondering who might have had reason to kill Bertie.

A part of me hoped that this was all some mistake. Perhaps, upon closer inspection, the doctor would discover that it had been an accident after all. Even as I tried to convince myself that such a thing was possible, I knew it was very unlikely.

As I went to turn off the water in the bathtub, my mind cast around for who else might be responsible for the murder. I didn't know the young man well enough to know much about his relationships with the villagers, other than Marena. But surely she couldn't be the only person with whom he'd had a close association.

He had no family in the village, I knew that much. Bertie's father had died when he was very young, and his mother had passed away shortly after I had moved to Thornecrest. Who else, then, might he have interacted with often enough to develop an enemy?

"What about the stable boys?" I called to Milo from the bathroom.

He came to the doorway. "What about them?"

"Do you think Bertie might have quarreled with any of them?"

I didn't like to believe that this might have come about from some misunderstanding between fellow employees, but such things had been known to happen.

"I see you're taking my objections to heart," Milo said dryly.

"It doesn't hurt to consider the options, in case we have anything that might be relevant to take to the police."

One of Milo's dark brows went up ever so slightly, denoting his skepticism, but he didn't argue with me. "I'll speak with Geoffrey," he said. "He'd know if anyone would."

I agreed that the stable master would be the best place to start. Though I was very curious about what he would have to say, I thought I would leave that aspect of things to Milo. It was never entirely satisfying to listen to someone else's recounting of an interview, but it made sense for Milo to be the one to speak with the stable hands; I didn't think they would confide in me as easily as they would in him. They were comfortable with Milo and knew what went on in the stables. Perhaps he could even find a way to learn something from Lady Alma's stable personnel.

"But I don't think it was any of them," Milo went on. "None of them had any reason to kill Bertie."

"Do you think it might have had something to do with the horses?" I asked. "A great many people were placing bets for the festival. Perhaps he got in with the wrong crowd."

"I doubt the stakes would've been high enough for such a thing, not among the local crowd. If they had, I'd have heard about it."

"Yes, I suppose that's true."

We were both silent for a moment, lost in our own thoughts.

"I saw the vicar giving him an envelope of some sort," I said suddenly. "In a surreptitious manner."

Milo was not impressed with this bit of information. "It might have been anything. After all, Bertie was often at the vicarage. Perhaps he left something there, and the vicar returned it in an envelope."

"Perhaps," I said, though this explanation wasn't entirely satisfactory. "You remember what Bertie said to you about knowing a secret? It was shortly after his encounter with the vicar."

"The two needn't be connected. Though the thought did occur to me that Bertie had mentioned a harmful secret."

At last we were on the same page.

"What if someone knew he was considering revealing it and decided he had to be silenced?" I suggested, trying to keep the excitement from my voice.

Milo considered this. "It's possible."

I wished now we had pressed Bertie when he asked the question. But there was no guarantee he would have revealed anything to us. And we had no way of knowing that he'd be dead a short time later.

Whose secrets might he have had access to? The first person that came to mind was Lady Alma. Was it possible that she had had something to do with his death? Casting my mind back, I could not recall having seen her at the festival before the races. In fact, she had arrived at the enclosure late and out of breath. That would have been about the time Bertie was killed.

Lady Alma and Bertie had had a close relationship, almost a friendship, though neither of them probably would have couched it in such terms. Might her feelings for Bertie have taken a turn in a more romantic direction? I quickly pushed this idea aside. Lady Alma had never shown any interest in men or marriage. She was rumored to have turned down several marriage proposals in her youth, choosing instead a life of solitary independence. From all I had seen, it had suited her well.

But it was still possible she might have had motive to kill him.

Though it wasn't nice, perhaps, I could picture it being the sort of murder Lady Alma would commit. She would have been brisk and efficient about it, eliminating the object of her scorn with a few well-placed blows.

"Do you think Lady Alma might have killed Bertie?" I asked. "Perhaps there was something she wanted to keep quiet, and Bertie found out about it."

"The same might be said for any number of people."

"Yes, I suppose so."

He studied me. "Have you some particular reason to suspect Lady Alma?"

I shook my head. "No. And I suppose she would have been able to get the bit in Medusa's mouth if anyone would. Nevertheless, we've learned not to rule people out, haven't we?"

"We have indeed," he said, coming to me. "But this time it's not our concern. I can already see that mind of yours spinning, and I don't want you to worry about it, darling."

"I'm not worrying, particularly. Just thinking."

He let out a sigh as he turned to leave me to my bath. "That's how it always starts."

THE DOCTOR CAME to visit the next morning after breakfast.

"I thought it best that I looked you over after your recent... excitement," he had explained when Grimes had shown him into the morning room.

"I feel perfectly fine."

"Yes, I'm sure you do. But it doesn't hurt to be cautious, now, does it?"

I was certain that Milo had put him up to this. Milo, though he gave every appearance of being completely sanguine about my condition, had been watching me like a hawk ever since he had discovered I was pregnant. As my husband had hastily departed for London after breakfast, I could not even shoot him angry looks as I gave way to the suggestion and led the doctor up to my bedroom.

It wasn't exactly comforting to know that, only a few hours ago, the doctor had been examining the dead body of Bertie Phipps. I suppose that was the sort of contrast that made up a doctor's life: the never-ending cycle of life and death.

The examination proved satisfactory; the baby was much less exuberant this morning than it had been the evening before but still sufficiently active to assure the doctor of its progress. I told him I had been eating and sleeping well and taking exercise.

At last he put his Pinard horn in his black bag and sat back in his chair. "Still planning to have the baby here, rather than in London?"

"I think so, yes."

My mother was quite adamant that I wasn't going to give birth in a hospital. "Filthy places," she had sneered. "Full of disease and all manner of unpleasant things. I gave birth to you in the comfort and cleanliness of my own house. If it was good enough for me, I think it should be good enough for you."

Milo, surprisingly enough, seemed to agree with her on this issue. "You've got the best care here that you could want," he had told me. "And Thornecrest is much more comfortable than the flat."

Dr. Jordan said he saw no reason why I shouldn't have the baby at home. In truth, I liked the idea of staying in my comfortable room much more than I did going to a strange place. But there was still some time to make my final decision.

"A good four weeks yet, I should imagine," he said. "I've known a good many first-time mothers to go past the expected date. Just try to rest and not overexcite yourself."

This was as good an opening as any.

"It was quite distressing about Bertie," I said, hoping he might have some sort of comment on the subject.

Dr. Jordan was not the sort of cheery country doctor one might hope for when probing for information. He had always been a bit stiff and formal, though certainly kind enough. I didn't hold out much hope that he was going to give me information about Bertie's unfortunate death.

"You'd do better not to think about it. A woman in your condition ought to think pleasant thoughts."

I clenched my teeth before I could retort on just what I thought of his apparent wilting violet philosophy concerning pregnant women.

"Mr. Ames had . . . blood on his clothes," I said, as though it had been very upsetting to me. "I suppose . . . I suppose it was Bertie's blood."

"It might have been the horse's," he said, neatly sidestepping my question.

"But poor Bertie hit his head, didn't he? On a sharp stone from the wall? My husband and Lady Alma have always kept that wall in such excellent repair. I don't know how that stone might have come loose."

He looked up at me, his gaze narrowing ever so slightly. I think he suspected what I was about and was trying to decide which tack to take.

Surely he must have known that Milo would have told me about the cause of Bertie's death. Then again, perhaps not. Perhaps he thought that Milo treated me with kid gloves, especially in my condition.

At last, he made his reply. "Bertie's death was most unfortunate, Mrs. Ames. But I don't think you should concern yourself with that. You've much happier things to think about. We want you in a good frame of mind when the delivery comes."

It seemed there was nothing for me to do but take the most direct approach.

"My husband tells me he has reason to believe that Bertie Phipps was murdered."

To the doctor's credit, his face revealed nothing. I suppose he had had a good deal of practice at concealing his thoughts over the years. A doctor needed tact, after all, and the ability to conceal a reaction to unpleasantness. And it was unpleasant to him, I was quite sure, to have the matter put so openly.

"As I said, Mrs. Ames. That's nothing you need to worry about."

I could see I wasn't going to get anything else out of him. It was disappointing, but I had known better than to expect much. An idea occurred to me, however, and I decided to try one more change of tactic.

"Lady Alma is very distressed, I suppose."

He looked at me rather closely, I thought, but I maintained an air of perfect innocence.

"Lady Alma was upset, yes."

"I believe she and Bertie were close."

The corner of his mouth twitched, a reaction that hovered somewhere on the strange border between amusement and disapproval. "It wasn't so much Bertie she was upset about."

I hesitated, confused, and then understood his meaning. "The horse, Medusa."

He nodded. "Oh, she was sorry Bertie was dead. But she was distraught about the horse, or as distraught as Lady Alma will allow herself to be. One never sees much emotion from her unless it's related to the horses. Wouldn't let any of the grooms near it. She wanted me to look at the blasted thing's leg. Me, a medical doctor. With a dead body lying there in the field."

So Lady Alma had appeared more concerned about the horse than she had about Bertie, had she? This was an interesting bit of information.

Granted, Lady Alma had never much lived by the normal rules of society, and one could not expect her to react accordingly. Bertie might have been like a favorite nephew to her, but she called her horses her children.

Dr. Jordan shook his head and then rose to his feet.

"I suppose that is all for now, Mrs. Ames. But just ring me up if you need me to come by. Otherwise, I'll stop in in a week or so to check on your progress."

"Thank you, Dr. Jordan."

He reached the door but stopped and turned to give me one last glance. "I know you've been privy to investigations into untimely deaths in the past, but I do hope you won't get involved in anything too . . . arduous over the next few days."

I smiled, dismissing his kindly warning. "Of course not, doctor. I wouldn't dream of it."

AFTER THE DOCTOR had gone, I went directly to Bedford Priory. I wanted to have a word with Lady Alma.

I was quite disappointed when I was told she had gone out riding and was not expected back for the better part of the morning. It was like her, of course, to escape tragedy on the back of a horse. I would just have to speak with her later.

I left my card for her and, returning to where Markham waited with the car, decided to proceed to the vicarage. Ostensibly, I was going to check on Marena. I wanted to offer my condolences. Of course, a part of me also wanted to see what Mr. and Mrs. Busby might have to say about the matter of Bertie's death. After all, the vicar and his wife were likely to have excellent insight.

Whatever Milo said, I knew I was not going to be able to rest until the matter was resolved. Though I had been exhausted the night before, I had had a difficult time falling asleep, a fact I would never have admitted to Dr. Jordan. Tossing and turning beside Milo, who slept as soundly as ever, I had gone over and over in my mind who, aside from Darien, might have had reason to kill Bertie.

There was Marena, of course. They had parted ways, but Bertie seemed to be standing in the way of her happiness with Darien. Might they have had a quarrel and she, in a fit of passion, hit him with that rock?

But no. She had been so devastated when she learned of his death. Surely she couldn't have been feigning her sorrow. In my heart, however, I knew the truth. Almost anyone was capable of hiding what they had done.

Though it was an uncomfortable thought, I also considered the vicar and Mrs. Busby. I couldn't picture either of them resorting to such a thing. Besides, it would have been almost impossible for Mrs. Busby to get across the field in her chair.

The vicar was another story. It was entirely possible that he might have followed Bertie and quarreled with him, hitting him over the head. Indeed, I remembered that he had not been at Mrs. Busby's side in the tea tent when I had first entered it. And there had been the matter of the tense conversation I had witnessed between him and Bertie and the envelope that had passed between them. What had been in it? Had they continued their discussion in the privacy of the field where the vicar had resorted to violence?

I shook off the thought. It was dreadful of me to even think such things about a man of the cloth. There must be some other answer.

I had to think that Bertie's comment about knowing a secret had been unrelated to the interaction with the vicar. It must have been something else he had seen or overheard that had put him in danger.

I arrived at the vicarage, and the maid showed me into the parlor. A few moments later she wheeled Mrs. Busby into the room. I smiled, perhaps a bit too brightly, trying to hide my guilt for wondering, however fleetingly, if she or her husband might have killed Bertie Phipps.

"Hello, Amory dear. I'm glad to see you." Her voice was pleasant, but she looked tired.

"I've come to see how Marena is doing. I know yesterday was a great shock."

"Yes indeed." She shook her head sadly. "She's taken it very badly, I'm afraid. I wonder if you would speak with her. I think it would do her good."

"Yes, of course," I replied. "I'll be only too happy to do what I can."

"Sometimes it's better, I think, to have someone a bit more distant to give advice. Perhaps that's one reason a vicar, in general, is so comforting in times of crisis. There is a different perspective one gains from talking to someone outside the sphere of family. But in Marena's case, of course, the vicar and I are very much like family to her."

"Family is often the strongest source of comfort." I couldn't help but think about Marena's mother. I didn't mention Mrs. Hodges, though it seemed that Mrs. Busby noticed the omission.

"Her mother was here, but I told her perhaps it would be best if she came back later. Marena was in such a state. I don't think it would have helped to see her. Mrs. Hodges isn't . . . precisely a sympathetic person." This bit of understatement was said with apparent sincerity and none of the usual malicious pleasure that edged the tones of village gossips. I could sense, however, that she wanted to discuss it.

"Yes," I agreed. "Mrs. Hodges has never seemed to me to be exceptionally . . . maternal."

She shook her head sadly. "She brought a basket of some of her honey and preserves for Marena. Her attempt at offering some comfort, I suppose. But she's not a warm woman. Even the way she spoke about Bertie's death was so very . . . casual. I knew it would have hurt Marena to hear it. 'I'm told she broke things off with him,' she said, 'so I don't know why she should appear so distressed.' As though the young man's death meant nothing. Why, even after what happened here, I am quite broken up about it. We'd known Bertie since he was a child, you know."

That phrase caught my attention. "What do you mean? What happened here?"

She blinked, as though suddenly realizing what she had said. "Oh, nothing. That is, I didn't mean to . . ." She sighed. "Well, we had a bit of unpleasantness with Bertie. I didn't intend to bring that up. I wouldn't speak ill of the dead, not for all the world."

"To be honest, I had heard a bit of gossip," I said lightly. "That is, someone mentioned that some items had gone missing from the vicarage and that Bertie was suspected."

Mrs. Busby flushed. "Whoever told you that?"

"I . . . heard it from one of my servants. You know how gossip spreads."

She sighed. "Yes, it's true. I'm afraid Mr. Busby found Bertie in his study one day. He didn't think much of it, but later he noticed some things had gone missing."

"What sort of things?"

"I'm not entirely sure," she said vaguely. "A few silver trinkets, I believe. The lock was broken on his desk, though there was nothing there but documents."

I was intrigued by this bit of information. Bertie had been rifling through the vicar's documents, had he? Was it possible he had learned something there that someone might not have wanted him to know?

"Were there any documents missing?" I asked casually.

"Oh, as to that, I couldn't say. I'm not even sure Mr. Busby could. He keeps everything, you know. He always means to put his records in order, but he's so very busy."

"Yes, of course."

The maid tapped at the door just then and came in with the tea tray.

"Did you bring something up to Miss Marena?" Mrs. Busby asked her.

"Yes, ma'am, but she wouldn't eat it."

Mrs. Busby sighed. "All right. We'll try again later."

The maid went out, and Mrs. Busby picked up the teapot, pouring for the both of us. "I knew it was a lost cause. She hasn't touched a bite and has been crying on and off since it happened. Poor dear. It was terribly upsetting for her, and then Inspector Wilson came here and made things worse."

"Inspector Wilson came here?" I asked. "What did he want?"

"He was asking questions about when she had last seen Bertie at the festival. I don't think he realized, you see, that there had been a falling-out between them. I suppose he thought they had been enjoying the festival together and assumed Bertie might have told her that he meant to ride Lady Alma's horse."

Mrs. Busby didn't know, then, that Bertie had been murdered. The inquest was tomorrow, so it would only be a matter of time before word spread across the village.

I realized, however, that my time for questioning people was limited. I would have to see what I could find out before the true manner of Bertie's death was made public and the suspects were more on their guard.

We drank our tea then and chatted of other things, though I had a difficult time making polite conversation when there was murder on my mind.

"Would you like to talk to Marena now?" she asked after a few moments.

"Yes, if you think she'll see me."

"I'm sure she will. Just go up the stairs at the end of the hall, dear. Her door is the first on the right."

I followed her directions, wondering as I went what I would say to Marena. It was a complicated situation. To be honest, I found it a bit surprising that she was as broken up as she was. After all, she had ended things with Bertie and seemed to be infatuated with Darien. That was not to say, of course, that she didn't still care for Bertie. But to take to her room and not eat seemed a bit of an extreme show of grief for losing a man one no longer loved. But perhaps she had decided that she loved him after all, now that it was too late.

I tapped softly at the door to which Mrs. Busby had directed me. "Marena, it's Amory Ames. May I come in?"

There was a long moment of silence in which I wondered if she was sleeping or declining to answer, and then there followed the sound of footsteps. The door opened. Marena greeted me, her face streaked with tears. "Oh, Mrs. Ames," she said. She looked out at me with red eyes. She had clearly been crying a great deal.

"Hello, dear. How are you?"

The tears welled in her eyes at the question. Perhaps it was silly of me to have asked it, but wasn't all expression of condolence rather useless when it came down to it? Still, one must observe the niceties, even when they were inadequate.

"Not very well," she said, dabbing at the tears with a handkerchief. She was keeping herself together, but just barely.

I thought somehow that Darien was unlikely to remain first in her heart now that Bertie had left a hole there. I had had my suspicions about her as a potential suspect, but it seemed to me that she was genuinely grieving. The sadness radiated from her.

"I loved him, you know," she said. "We didn't always get along. We . . . we had an argument and parted ways. And then I met Darien, and I got carried away, perhaps. Darien is so handsome and charming. But there is some part of me that is always going to love Bertie. We understood each other. We were meant to be together, and now . . ." She stopped, drawing in a deep breath to keep back a sob. "So I'm not at all well, as I'm sure you can see. I just can't believe that he's dead."

"Yes, I know it's been a great shock."

"I'm sorry. I've been dreadfully rude." She stepped aside from the door, pulling it open. "Do you . . . do you want to come in?"

"If I won't be intruding."

"No. I . . . I suppose I could use some company."

I followed her into the room. It was a small and plain but cheerfully furnished space with lace curtains, a floral bedspread, and a vase of flowers on the table before the window. There was a single wooden chair near a small desk, which had a few papers scattered across the top, and she offered it to me. She quickly tidied the papers and put them in a drawer and then went to sit on the edge of her bed.

"I haven't felt like seeing anyone," she said. "It's just that I need some time to think."

I nodded. That was certainly understandable.

"Bertie was always so very . . . alive. So strong and healthy. It seems impossible to me that he's just . . . gone."

"Did you see Bertie at the festival?" I asked gently, hoping to carefully edge my way into asking useful questions. If Marena thought this odd, she didn't show it.

"No. After I spoke with you, I was busy helping Aunt Elaine. It wasn't until I saw people talking excitedly that I realized something dreadful had happened. Then I heard what they were saying." Her voice caught.

I felt a pang of sympathy for her, learning about his death that way.

"I was cruel to him that day at the inn," she said softly. "I should have explained things better, should have . . ."

I reached out to pat her hand. "You shouldn't think about that now, dear. It's not going to do any good."

"I know, but I can't help thinking . . ." She looked up at me, tears shimmering in her eyes. "Will you . . . will you tell Darien? I can't bear to see him."

"He's supposed to come to Thornecrest tomorrow. I'll let him know that you're in need of some time."

She nodded. "Thank you."

"Is there anything else I can do?"

"Thank you, no. I suppose this is something I shall just have to face alone."

I said my goodbyes and left the vicarage a short time later. A part of me was unsettled. Why had Bertie broken into the vicar's desk drawers, if indeed he had done so? Had he found something in the documents, the secret he had been debating whether or not to reveal? Was Marena's grief truly genuine? Did Inspector Wilson believe that she, or one of the Busbys, was guilty of the crime?

Unfortunately, I was leaving the vicarage with more questions than answers.

"LADY ALMA IS in the drawing room, madam," Grimes said when I arrived home. "She's been here a quarter of an hour."

This was a bit of luck. I had been hoping she would ring me when she returned from her ride, but turning up at Thornecrest was even better.

"Thank you, Grimes. I'll go to the drawing room at once. Will you send some coffee?"

"It's already been prepared, madam. I will have it brought to you directly."

"Thank you." As I had often said, Grimes was a treasure.

I went to the drawing room and found Lady Alma pacing the floor. Her energy appeared as high as ever, but her face, when she turned to me, was drawn and grim.

"Good morning, Mrs. Ames. I came to see your husband, but Grimes tells me he's not in, so I said I'd wait for you."

It seemed, then, that she had not yet been home and received my card.

"Milo's gone off to London for the day, I'm afraid, but I was hoping to speak with you. Sit down, will you, Lady Alma? Can I offer you some coffee?"

"That would be very nice, thank you. I've been out riding all morning and could use with a bit of refreshment."

"Yes, I stopped at the Priory this morning and they told me you'd gone out."

The maid brought in the coffee just then and set it on the table as Lady Alma and I settled ourselves in our seats. At least, I settled myself; Lady Alma was shifting uncomfortably in her chair. I wondered for a moment if there was something amiss with the seat, but then I realized it was merely her restless energy.

"I wanted to offer you my condolences on Bertie's death. I know you were fond of him."

"It's a pity," she said. "A real pity."

"Yes. A tragedy."

I poured her a cup of coffee from the pot on the table and handed it to her.

She took it with a steady hand that belied her apparent agitation. Then, to my surprise, she reached into the pocket of her jacket and pulled out a silver flask, uncorking the lid and pouring a generous amount of the liquid into her coffee.

"Would you . . . care for a glass of something stronger?" I asked, gesturing toward the sideboard.

"That isn't necessary. Thank you."

She replaced the flask and then took a long drink of her coffee. When she set the cup back in the saucer with a little clank of china on china, I could see that she had nearly drained it.

Lady Alma was not a sentimental sort of woman, but I could see that, despite Dr. Jordan's assessment that she had been primarily concerned with her horse, she was troubled by Bertie's untimely death. Bertie had spent a good deal of time with Lady Alma in the past, and I had always thought she had looked on him with affection.

"I was very fond of that boy. He had the makings of an excellent horseman. And he was a kind, gentle young man."

We sat in silence for a moment, both of us lost in our own thoughts.

"I wondered when he wasn't at the race," she mused. "To think he was lying dead in my field." There was, as I had often noted, a startling brusqueness to her words, but I could hear the sadness that lay beneath it.

"It would have been quick, I suppose," I said, seizing upon what bit of comfort I thought I could offer. If Bertie had been struck hard enough to kill him, he wouldn't have been conscious long. It was a grim thought, but it was something to know that he wouldn't have suffered.

"Yes," Lady Alma agreed. "I doubt he knew what hit him."

It was an interesting choice of words. I wondered if she, too, suspected there was something amiss about his death. After all, Bertie had once told me that Lady Alma liked to say that the secret to avoiding injury was all in how one fell.

"It's so dreadful that rock should have been in just that place," I said, watching for her reaction. "To think that if he had fallen and hit his head anywhere else it might have been all right."

Her eyes came up to me, and I could see that there was a sharpness in them. Lady Alma was nobody's fool. "It's dreadful indeed."

"Is Medusa all right?" I asked. "I understand she was injured."

Her expression brightened ever so slightly. "Yes, she's all right. I was terribly worried about her, but I think her foreleg is going to heal nicely. I don't see that there will be any lasting difficulty."

I knew she had been worried about Medusa. I was glad the horse was going to be fine. I was glad, too, that the animal hadn't really been responsible for Bertie's death. I knew that would have been a difficult thing for Lady Alma to accept. Of course, she didn't know that yet. I wondered if I should tell her or wait for her to learn about the true cause of death at the inquest.

I decided not to mention it for the moment.

It turned out, however, that I was the one who was about to be surprised.

"I wanted to speak to Mr. Ames because it happened on the border of our properties," she said, setting her empty coffee cup on the edge of the table, "and I suppose we should decide together how best to go about things."

"Go about what things?" I asked, taking a sip of my coffee. Was she anticipating some sort of trouble about Bertie's death?

"The police and all that. But then it occurred to me that perhaps I should speak to you first. After all, you're the crime solver in the family, aren't you? Just because you're pregnant doesn't mean you can't be involved. Never thought women should be excluded from doing what they're good at just because of biology."

I frowned, at a complete loss. "I'm afraid I don't understand."

Once again that sharp gaze met mine, and I noticed she had suddenly gone completely still, almost like a tiger prepared to pounce. "Bertie's death wasn't an accident. Surely you realize that. I'm quite convinced that Marena's mother killed him."

"MRS. HODGES?" I repeated. "You think she's responsible?"

Lady Alma sat back in her chair. She seemed much more at ease now that she had come out with what she had meant to say. Or perhaps the brandy she had poured into her coffee had something to do with it. Whatever the case, there was a spark in her eye that seemed to me almost as vibrant as the moment she had stood watching the races at the festival.

"Bertie told me a week or so ago he had a secret, a secret that concerned Mrs. Jane Hodges. He wondered if he should tell someone."

My brows rose. So he had confided in Lady Alma the nature of his secret, had he? That certainly narrowed things down.

"Did he tell you what it was?" I asked.

She shook her head. "No. I tried to get it out of him, but he said he needed to think about it a bit longer before he decided what to do."

I had to admit, I found this source of the secret a bit surprising. Even disappointing, in some strange way. What sort of secret could Mrs. Hodges be hiding? The woman had always been sour and grim, and I had a hard time imagining that she had ever lived the sort of life that might create secrets worth killing for.

Then again, I had seen for myself the sort of violent acts that desperate people were capable of. Mrs. Hodges, I was sure, was no exception.

"I saw the scene myself," she went on. "That boy didn't hit his head on a rock in a fall. What nonsense. Every child knows better than to fall onto its head. And Bertie was a good and careful horseman. And, anyway, he wouldn't have ridden Medusa. He knew better."

"That may be so . . ." I began carefully, but she cut me off with a wave of her hand.

"Mark my words. The inquest will show tomorrow that he was killed."

"Even if that's so, it doesn't mean that Mrs. Hodges was responsible, secret or not."

"But, you see, I haven't told you the most striking fact as of yet." She paused, and I couldn't help but feel she was enjoying the intensity of her tale. "I saw her walking from the direction of that field after the races. She had been at her booth, selling honey, before the races started. She would've had no reason to be in that field."

"Perhaps she was merely taking a walk during the races," I suggested lamely. "After all, she doesn't much care for festivities."

"That might be the case. But why, then, did she leave the festival and then appear later in different clothes?"

I considered this. I hadn't noticed it at the time, but she was right. Mrs. Hodges had been wearing a different dress when I saw her in the tea tent. "You think she had blood on her clothes."

"The weather was fair and the ground dry. What other reason might she have had to change her clothes?"

It was fairly compelling circumstantial evidence, as far as it went. "Did you say anything to the police about this?"

"Not yet. That Inspector Wilson was rushing around, ordering people about. There wasn't time. Besides, he thought it was an accident like everyone else. I don't think the man would know a murder if it hit *him* on the head. It'll be the doctor that will find out what really happened. Jordan's always been a clever man."

I opened my mouth, not quite sure what to say. Should I tell her that Milo had similar suspicions? Somehow, I thought I should keep this information to myself for the time being. It didn't much matter, anyway, as Lady Alma was already rising to her feet.

"Pass this information along to your husband so it doesn't take him by surprise at the inquest. I thought you should both be aware of what's to come. I won't keep you longer. And, anyway, I need to change the poultice on Medusa's leg. Good day, Mrs. Ames."

And with that, she turned and walked briskly out of the room without waiting for my response.

I HAD A good deal to discuss with Milo that evening when he returned home from London. I managed to keep from mentioning Bertie's death during dinner, as I knew the servants would be curious about what we had to say. I thought it would be best to keep things as quiet as possible. It wouldn't do, after all, for word of what we knew to get back to the killer, whoever he might be.

I still had my doubts about Mrs. Hodges, but I certainly didn't intend to rule her out.

At last we were alone in the drawing room, drinking our after-dinner coffee as Milo smoked. I sat on the velvet divan near the fireplace and Milo sat in a chair by the open window, as I had been sensitive to his cigarette smoke as of late. Since I had overcome the morning sickness of the early stages of my pregnancy, few things had made me feel ill, but the strong scent of cigarettes did. In consequence, Milo had been smoking much less.

It was nice in the room with the window open, for the weather remained pleasant. We had a small fire crackling in the grate to ward off any chill, but the occasional cool evening breeze blew across the room, bringing with it the scent of the early lilacs outside.

I might have thought it a very romantic evening on another occasion, but tonight my mind was elsewhere.

"Lady Alma was here today," I told Milo, breaking into the comfortable silence.

"Was she?" Milo asked, rising from his chair to toss his cigarette out the window and pull it closed. "Was she still in a state about her horse?"

"No, about something else. She thinks Mrs. Hodges killed Bertie."

He turned to look at me. It was hard to tell what his reaction to this bit of news was, for he said nothing, waiting for me to continue.

I quickly related my conversation with Lady Alma that day and her certainty that Marena's mother was the killer.

"I find it hard to imagine that Mrs. Hodges would bash someone's head in," Milo said contemplatively. "Then again, she's always been an utter gorgon. Perhaps such a thing would be just to her taste."

"This is a serious matter, Milo."

"I'm being serious," he replied, though the corner of his mouth tipped up ever so slightly. "I wonder what kind of secret he knew about her?"

"One does wonder, doesn't one?" I replied. "I find it hard to believe that she has been able to hide anything major for all these years."

"What's more, how did Bertie come to know it?"

"Mrs. Busby mentioned that they caught Bertie in the vicar's office and that a lock on one of his drawers was broken, a drawer that contained confidential records."

"What kind of records?"

"As to that, she was very vague. She claimed the vicar wasn't entirely sure what might have been in the drawer. But I didn't have the opportunity to speak with him directly."

"Perhaps we might find a way to bring the matter up to him."

I smiled at him, glad he seemed inclined to let me investigate rather than protest my involvement as he usually did. "I do adore you when you say things like that."

His blue eyes flashed wickedly. "I adore you all the time, my darling, but I will take what admiration I can get from you."

I laughed. "You know perfectly well that I am putty in your hands."

It was his turn to laugh. "If that's the case, you are the most unmalleable putty I've ever come across."

"Well, perhaps not putty, exactly," I conceded. "But I'm awfully fond of you."

"Awfully fond, eh? You shouldn't make such extravagant declarations," he said dryly. "I'm likely to grow conceited."

He came over to me, and, placing his hands on the back of the divan on either side of me, he leaned down, his mouth very close to mine. "Have I told you how beautiful you are?" he asked in a low voice.

I looked up at him, my heart picking up the pace. It sometimes still startled me how very much I loved him, even after all this time. "Not tonight," I said, rubbing a hand along the lapel of his jacket.

"You're exquisite."

He leaned to brush a teasing kiss across my lips then pulled away, his mouth moving to my jaw and then just below my ear. "Of course, when I say 'we' might investigate, I mean me," he murmured against my skin. "You're not to wander about the village asking people questions, not in your condition."

"Milo!"

He kissed me again then, and, though I found it very annoying when he used his charms to silence my protests, I couldn't help but enjoy it. I slid my arms up around his neck and disregarded the matter for the time being. There would be time for this argument tomorrow.

I DID NOT go to the inquest the following morning. Milo said it wouldn't do for me to sit all day in a hot and crowded room, and I had to admit that I agreed with him. Walking around the village and short visits with suspects was one thing, but sitting for prolonged periods on an uncomfortable wooden chair in an airless room was quite another.

Besides, I could only imagine the sort of things the majority of villagers were to say if I appeared at an inquest heavily pregnant.

No, I was forced to rely on Milo's excellent memory to supply me with anything of interest. It seemed a very long time before I heard his footsteps in the hallway leading to the morning room where I sat knitting.

"Well?" I demanded as he came into the room.

"Good afternoon to you, too," he said with a smile.

I waved an impatient hand. "Don't give me nonsense. Give me the details of the inquest."

He let out a short laugh and came to brush a kiss across my lips. "My bloodthirsty darling, always so impatient for gruesome details."

I declined to encourage his teasing by giving him a response.

He sank into the chair across from me. "The verdict was murder, of course."

"Of course." I set my knitting aside, ready to give the matter my full attention.

"The doctor says he was hit with the rock several times. The first blow likely knocked him unconscious, and the rest were administered as he lay on the ground. His skull was crushed."

I grimaced.

"And one more thing: a chain was missing from around his neck. Marena Hodges said that he always wore it. It wasn't found anywhere near the body."

"Why should the killer want that?"

"An excellent question."

I thought suddenly of the envelope the vicar had given him. "Was there anything found in his inside jacket pocket?"

"No."

We sat for a moment in contemplative silence.

"I spoke to a few of the stable hands before I left this morning," he said at last. "That seems to be a dead end. None of them seemed to think that Bertie had any enemies, though more than one of them said that he'd seemed a bit distracted as of late."

"That was probably to do with Marena."

"Perhaps."

"Or with the secret he knew about her mother? It clearly bothered him, whatever it was."

"Mmm," he said noncommittally. He clearly wasn't entirely convinced, and I wondered why.

Grimes came into the sitting room just then. "Mr. Ludlow is on the telephone for you, sir."

"Thank you, Grimes," Milo said, rising from his chair. "If you'll excuse me, darling."

"Yes, of course," I said, still lost in thought.

He went to speak to our solicitor, and I continued to turn the matter of Bertie Phipps's murder over in my mind. Something was wrong with all of this, something I couldn't quite place. I supposed I would have to question Milo more closely about the inquest.

There was a tap at the door, and I looked up to see Grimes standing there. "Mr. Darien Ames has arrived, madam."

I wondered what the butler thought of all of this. He had been very loyal to the elder Mr. Ames. How did he feel about the appearance of a son the man had fathered on the wrong side of the blanket?

"Show him in, Grimes."

I knew Darien was coming to see Milo, that the two of them had much to discuss, but I wanted to be there to greet him. Milo would likely be detained speaking to Ludlow, and I would have a few moments alone with my errant brother-in-law.

It wasn't just idle curiosity that had me wanting to speak to my newfound relation. I had told Marena that I would pass along her message to him. I wondered if he had noticed her absence over the past day. Or perhaps he had found another woman in the interim. He did seem to move from one to the next with impressive speed.

"Hello, Darien," I said as Grimes showed him into the room.

"Good afternoon," he replied with a smile.

I studied him. It was uncanny how much he looked like Milo. It wasn't just the black hair and the smooth, handsome planes of his face. There was something about his expressions, even, that mirrored the ones with which I had become so familiar. I wondered if their father had made the same sort of expressions.

"Can I offer you some tea?" I asked.

"Yes. Thank you." He stepped forward then, and, in the light shining through the window, I realized that his eyes, though blue, were different from Milo's. Milo's eyes were a bright, clear azure, like the Mediterranean in the summer sun. Darien's were paler, stormier in color, hovering somewhere between wintry blue and an Atlantic gray. They were striking in contrast to his dark lashes. It was no wonder that women lost their heads—and apparently their good sense—over him, and I could tell at once that, if he remained in our lives, he was going to be difficult to keep out of trouble.

Milo had been the same in his day, of course. Indeed, there were still times when I was quite useless at preventing him from getting into situations he assumed, correctly, that his good looks would get him out of.

"Sugar or milk?"

"Neither, thank you."

"How are you finding Allingcross?" I asked him as I poured his tea. It was the sort of inane question one was expected to ask of a visitor, but I felt I had to start somewhere if we were going to become acquainted.

"It's . . . different from what I'm used to," he answered as he took the proffered cup and saucer. There was no derision in his tone, though I had almost expected it, and it occurred to me that he was much less acerbic today than he had been upon our first meeting. I wondered if it was because Milo wasn't here, and he felt no need to put up a front.

"What are you used to?" I asked him, curious about his history.

"The sea," he said. "Dover, Folkestone, Hastings. We moved around a bit, my mum and I, so she could find work, but we always stayed near the sea. She loved it."

"Milo said she has passed?"

"Yes. A year ago. Pneumonia."

"I'm sorry."

"It's a part of life, so they say." He took a sip of his tea.

Despite his carefree air, he couldn't hide the sadness that clouded his eyes. For all his bravado, it must have been difficult for him to be left alone in the world after her passing. Not only that, I could tell he had been very fond of his mother.

No doubt the sea had reminded him of her. I wondered if that was why he had been walking along the beach in Brighton that day when he encountered Imogen. Perhaps he had been lonely and drawn to seek companionship with the pretty young woman he met at the seaside. I realized I was making excuses for him, but I couldn't help but feel a bit more sympathy toward him than I had previously.

Milo came into the room just then. Apparently, he had been closer at hand than I had thought.

"Hello, Darien," he said. There was something in his tone that caught my attention, but I couldn't quite make out what it was.

"Milo." Darien rose from his chair to face his brother.

They made a stunning pair, the two of them standing side by side. It was a good thing, I reflected, that the two of them had not been brought up together. I thought the pair in combination might have proved too much for the women of London.

What a stir they would create the next time they were in town together. Of course, I realized I was getting ahead of myself. There was nothing to say that the two of them would ever be in London together. After all, their relationship wasn't exactly starting under the most auspicious of circumstances.

I did hope that they would be able to find a way to enjoy each other's company, however. Milo, though he would never admit such a thing, had no doubt felt the void of family connections in his life. It would do him good to have a brother.

"I heard there was some excitement at the festival," Darien said as he took a seat.

I was a bit surprised he had brought it up. Then again, perhaps it was his roundabout way of inquiring after Marena.

"Yes, Bertie Phipps was murdered," I said, watching his face. "The verdict was given at the inquest this morning."

I looked at his nose and the corner of his mouth, noticing there was no permanent damage from his altercation with Bertie.

He must have noticed my searching gaze, for he smiled. "If he went around hitting people, I imagine he had plenty of enemies."

"I spoke to Marena," I said, ignoring his quip. "She's very distressed about Bertie's death and said she needs some time before she sees you again."

He took the news as one might expect: with a show of amused indifference. "If that's what she wants."

I hadn't meant to bring it up, but irritation was beginning to rise again, and suddenly I felt that the question couldn't be avoided. "In the meantime, don't you think you should speak to Imogen?"

"I suppose I should. The sooner that's out of the way, the better."

I tried to tamp down my anger. He was treating the young woman abominably, but I had the feeling that he would not respond well to being lectured. He seemed to enjoy saying and doing things for the shock they would cause, so the best course of action seemed to be to remain unfazed by his brazen behavior.

"You don't mean to continue your relationship with her then?" I asked calmly.

Darien looked up. "I thought I had made that plain."

"It wasn't plain to her," I said, just barely keeping from clenching my teeth in an attempt to refrain from telling him what I really thought of his behavior.

He shrugged. "It was all a lark. She knew it as well as I did."

"She was very distraught when she came here."

He seemed to sense that I was getting angry and apparently decided that he had had enough of goading me toward it. "I appreciate that you're indignant on her behalf," he said with apparent sincerity, "but you've been taken in by her. Imogen comes off as a sweet, innocent girl, but that's not how she really is. If you'll pardon my saying it, I certainly wasn't the first young man she's had a *lark* with."

"That's enough," Milo said mildly.

Darien looked over at his brother. "Have I said something shocking? I would have thought any wife of yours would be accustomed to scandalous talk."

There was the faintest flicker of irritation in Milo's eyes for a brief instant, and then it was gone, replaced by that mask he so often used, the cool, expressionless one it was so difficult to see behind.

"There's no need to discuss your escapades with my wife," he said.

"You'll recall that she brought it up," Darien said lightly. "But as you wish, dear brother. I didn't come here to offend. After all, we're family."

Though the words sounded pleasant, I knew that they had been designed to irritate Milo further. This time Milo showed not even a glimmer of annoyance. Darien would have to work a bit harder if he wanted to push Milo to some sort of outburst; Milo was too skilled at hiding his emotions to give his brother that particular satisfaction.

There was a sudden tap on the door. We all turned to see Grimes standing in the doorway.

"Excuse me, Mr. Ames, but Inspector Wilson has just arrived. He's requested to see you at once. I told him you had company, but he says it's most urgent."

I suddenly had an uneasy feeling.

"Show him in," Milo said.

Grimes left, and I looked at Darien. He had affected an almost bored expression, but I thought there was a certain tension in his shoulders as Grimes returned a moment later with the inspector in tow.

"Good afternoon, Inspector," Milo said. "What can we do for you?"

The inspector looked more uneasy than any of us. Hat in hand, he glanced around the room, before his gaze came back to Milo. "Good afternoon, Mr. Ames. I'm afraid my errand isn't a pleasant one."

"Oh?"

He turned to look at me for a moment, as though he was expecting me to take my leave. I looked back at him, a genial expression on my face.

At last he seemed to realize that I wasn't going to leave the men to their discussion, and he cleared his throat. "I've come to talk to you about the death of Bertie Phipps."

Milo nodded. "I thought as much. Would you like to have a seat, Inspector?"

Inspector Wilson cast his eyes around at the expensively upholstered furniture and shook his head. "I'd just as soon stand, Mr. Ames. I won't be staying long."

"Very well."

Inspector Wilson cleared his throat. "As you know, the verdict of the inquest was murder."

Milo nodded.

"This afternoon, a witness came forward, someone who could place a suspect at the scene of the crime."

Lady Alma must have decided to go to the police then. I hadn't thought her evidence enough to make Mrs. Hodges a definite suspect, but perhaps Inspector Wilson felt differently.

A thought occurred to me. "But weren't we all at the scene of the crime, so to speak?" I asked. "After all, it happened not very far from the festival."

"That's true, Mrs. Ames, but I'm speaking a bit more specifically than that." He didn't elaborate but instead turned back to Milo. "Rumor has it that you've got a brother who's recently come to the village."

"I have a half brother, yes," Milo said. He admitted that much and nothing more, didn't even bother to indicate Darien, who was watching the conversation with interest.

Inspector Wilson, however, had turned to look at Darien. It was clear enough who he must be; that resemblance was unmistakable. "This is the young man in question, I take it?"

Darien rose from his seat then, giving the inspector an overly polite bow of his dark head. "Darien Ames, at your service."

"Mr. Ames, it's come to my attention that you were quarreling with Mr. Phipps not long before he was killed. In fact, the altercation came to blows. Is that true?"

Darien passed a hand across his jaw. "It came to a blow. Just one. Bertie Phipps hit me, but I declined to return the favor."

"But you threatened to kill him, didn't you?"

There seemed to be a shift in the atmosphere, and I realized that something serious was happening here, something that had nothing to do with Mrs. Hodges. I glanced at Milo, but his gaze was resting on Darien, his expression intent.

Darien shrugged, still maintaining his air of confidence. "I might have said something to that effect. One often does in the heat of the moment. I didn't mean anything by it."

"Were you at the festival yesterday?" Inspector Wilson asked.

"No. Marena . . . Miss Hodges said it would be better if I didn't come."

"And yet you were seen crossing the field where Bertie Phipps's body was found around the time when he must have been murdered."

Darien's voice rose. "Now wait a minute . . ."

"Be quiet, Darien," Milo said.

"Our witness told us as much this morning. A search of your room at the inn revealed a pair of boots with blood on them, an envelope of money with Albert Phipps's name on it, and a chain worn by Mr. Phipps that was missing from the body."

"What the devil . . ." Darien said.

There was the sound of footsteps as a second man came into the room, a sergeant in uniform.

Inspector Wilson's gaze came back to me. "I'm sorry to do this here, Mrs. Ames, but it can't be helped."

He stepped forward, and the sergeant moved forward with him.

"Mr. Darien Ames," Inspector Wilson said gravely. "I'm arresting you for the murder of Albert Phipps."

14

THERE WAS ONE momentary flash of something like fear in Darien's eyes, and then it was covered by that cheerful bravado.

"This is preposterous," he said with a smile. "There must be some mistake."

"I'm afraid not, sir," replied Inspector Wilson in a tone that was almost bored. No doubt he had heard countless criminals confess their innocence upon arrest, most of them guilty beyond all doubt.

But what about Darien? Was he guilty? I found it nearly impossible to believe. Granted, I knew very little about the young man, but my instincts told me he was not a killer. I had seen something in his expression in that brief moment, the alarm and dread of a child who suddenly realizes he is lost, and my heart went out to him.

"If you'll just come with us, sir," the sergeant said. "Please be aware that anything you say may be taken down and used in evidence."

He took hold of Darien's arm.

Darien turned to Milo, his eyes flashing. "Aren't you going to do anything?"

"What do you expect me to do?" Milo asked.

"I didn't kill him," he protested.

"Perhaps not. But you won't be hanged today. There will be a trial."

These rather cold words told him plainly what sort of help Milo was going to be, and so Darien turned to me.

His eyes locked on mine, and suddenly he looked much younger. "I didn't kill him, Amory. You must believe me."

And, heaven help me, in that moment, I did.

AFTER INSPECTOR WILSON and his sergeant had led the protesting Darien away, I turned to Milo. I was still half-dazed by what had happened.

"This is dreadful."

"Yes, I'm sure Darien thinks so, too," he replied, though he didn't sound especially affected by the scene we had just witnessed. Indeed, it was apparent to me that he wasn't feigning his calm. He had dropped the mask he had worn for Darien, but there was only indifference beneath it.

"What are you going to do?" I asked him, unconsciously echoing Darien's question.

His brows rose ever so slightly. "I'm not going to do anything. As I told him, there will be a trial. It's out of our hands."

I stared at him, not knowing what to make of this coldness toward his brother. "Surely you don't believe he killed Bertie."

"He seems a perfectly logical suspect to me."

"But . . . but we've discussed other suspects. What about Mrs. Hodges? What about the broken drawer in the vicar's desk and the envelope that apparently had money in it?"

"None of them threatened to kill Bertie. Darien did. And the envelope was found in his possession."

"He threatened Bertie, yes, but he didn't mean it. You know he didn't."

He looked at me, and there was something hard in his gaze. "I don't know anything about him, and neither do you. Just because he's my brother doesn't mean that he can't be a killer. Indeed, in the short time we've known him, he's given us a very good indication that he is cold-hearted and remorseless."

It was true that he had treated Imogen badly, but it wasn't a fair comparison.

"That's not the same thing, and you know it," I protested. "Just because he's a cad doesn't mean he's a murderer."

"It's the job of the police to sort it out."

"Milo, he's your brother," I said, appealing to his better nature.

I ought to have known better.

"I met him only a week ago. Do you suppose that the very thin thread that is our father's blood means anything to me?"

I studied him, wondering if he meant it. I knew how he felt about his father, how he had always felt about him. What was more, Milo had no hint of the sentimentalist in him.

I grasped at straws. "But you . . . you offered to give him money. Surely you thought he deserved something."

"The money I offered him came from my father. Our father owed him as much. I owe him nothing."

There was something very set about his expression that made me realize he didn't intend to relent.

"Milo, you can't . . ."

"Listen to me, Amory," Milo interrupted. "We're not going to get involved with this."

"We are involved with it," I said. "Whether you like it or not, Darien is your brother, and we can't just wash our hands of this whole thing."

"He has no claim on my time or my resources," Milo said.

I didn't know exactly how to reply. I was stunned. For some reason, Milo had already made up his mind about Darien.

I realized suddenly that something must have happened, something that had caused this bewilderingly sudden shift in his perspective, this iron resolve that I was apparently powerless against.

"What is it?" I asked at last. "Why have you turned against him?"

One dark brow rose. "The evidence isn't enough? The bloody boot, the money, and the missing necklace found in his possession?"

I shook my head. "It's too easy. I don't think he'd be so foolish as to leave evidence in his room."

He sighed. Turning, he walked to the sofa and sat down. I followed him.

"It was Ludlow's telephone call," he said. "He's discovered something about our Darien."

The pace of my heart increased at his words, and I realized in that moment how desperately I wanted Darien to be innocent. "What did he say?"

"Darien was involved in another situation like the one with Imogen. He was using his mother's surname then, Archer. There was a young woman—a married young woman. She had a much older husband who, after she began her affair with Darien, died by falling from his horse, leaving her with a good deal of money."

The comparison was clear enough. "You don't think he . . ."

"The accident aroused suspicion, but then the young woman in question threw herself in front of a train and brought an end to the matter."

I gasped. "How horrible."

"Yes. So you see, things don't look good for Darien. Even before Inspector Wilson arrived, I had my suspicions."

"But even that isn't proof that Darien was involved in that death," I said. "Perhaps the woman did it and then killed herself out of guilt."

His gaze was cynical. "You're much too smart to believe in such a staggering coincidence."

"But what if Darien is innocent?" I said at last. "He could hang for this, for something that he didn't do."

"That's what trials are for. You seem to think that sharing a bloodline automatically creates some sort of bond between us. His turning up on the doorstep unannounced does not constitute a relationship between us, and if he is guilty, he ought to hang for it."

I blanched at the callousness of this sentiment. "But, Milo . . ."

His eyes locked on mine. There was a flash of unguarded irritation in them—uncharacteristic of him to let me see it—and then he answered in a voice that had grown hard. "Amory, I'm done discussing this."

I blinked. He had seldom used that tone with me, and I was startled.

I clenched my teeth against the desire to retort, to plead with him that he could not let this happen without lifting a finger to prove his brother's innocence. I could tell from the way he had spoken to me, however, that it wasn't going to do any good to argue with him.

"Very well," I said, rising from my seat. Without another word, I turned and left the room.

I BLAMED MY pregnancy for the tears that sprang to my eyes as I hurried away from the drawing room. I was furious with Milo: furious for his refusal to at least consider the possibility that Darien was innocent, furious for the tone he had taken with me, and furious that he hadn't followed me when he knew I was hurt.

Swiping away the angry tears, I went into the morning room. Glancing at my knitting still sitting on the sofa, I knew that I was in no mood to sit still. Besides, on the off chance Milo did come in search of me, I didn't want to speak to him.

In this contrary frame of mind, I thought a walk might do me good. Since Winnelda always acted as though I'd suggested climbing a mountain or swimming the Channel when I attempted any sort of physical activity, I decided against going to my bedroom to collect a jacket. The light jumper I wore would have to suffice.

I ventured out through the French doors in the morning room. The early evening air was cool, and I breathed deeply in an attempt to calm myself.

It wouldn't do any good, I knew, to get overwrought. I just needed to calm down and think. I was certain that, in time, I would be able to talk some sense into Milo.

I set off down the little path that led from Thornecrest's kitchen garden, along the hedgerows to a little wooden gate and then across a field to a stone fence where there was a sturdy stile. The path on the other side of the fence led to the village, and I had taken it often. It was a safer path for an evening walk than the main road, as there would be no chance of encountering vehicles. I didn't move as fast as I once did, and I didn't want to walk along the curving road, in case of speeding automobiles.

It was a beautiful spring evening. The sun was shining through the clouds as it began to make its descent, tinting their edges with bright gold. The air was fresh and smelled of lavender, verbena, and wild roses. In the distance I could see the shadowy hillsides spotted with sheep.

A cool breeze blew, rustling my hair, and I pulled my jumper a bit more tightly around me as I looked across the landscape.

Thornecrest looked beautiful in the evening light. Looking at its serene stillness, its stones and spires bathed in golden light, one would never imagine the turmoil that had just occurred within its walls. That's the way it was with all houses, I supposed. They hid so much of what was happening within: years, even centuries, of joy and heartbreak. The fleeting foibles of its occupants insignificant in the scope of time.

Only they were not insignificant to us.

My anger fading slightly, I tried to see things from Milo's perspective. I could understand how Darien's arrival was difficult for Milo. Indeed, it was not exactly convenient for me. This was not something I had expected to deal with in the weeks leading up to the baby's birth. We had been prepared for a baby; we were not prepared for the arrival of a heretofore unknown male relation and the inherent problems that came with him.

The suspicion of murder aside, I didn't know what to make of Darien. There was something very reckless and selfish about him. I suspected he'd been indulged much of his life, the same way Milo had been. He hadn't been raised with Milo's money, but being extremely good-looking was a definite boon in life. It was already quite apparent that he charmed women with the same skill and ease Milo had always done. There was no telling what else he had done to benefit himself.

Nevertheless, I could detect in him something of the uncertain young man he had no doubt been only years ago. He was illegitimate, abandoned by his father, and had been raised in less-than-prosperous circumstances. He had enough confidence in himself, that was certain, but he lacked the confidence Milo had always had in his situation in life, the knowledge that there were always vast resources at his disposal.

Though Darien could be a most unlikable young man, I couldn't help but feel a bit sorry for him. And, after all, he was my husband's brother. I felt as though it was our duty to help him in some way. At the very least, we needed to be sure that he wasn't falsely convicted of a crime he hadn't committed.

I considered, objectively, the possibility that he might have killed Bertie Phipps. The threat I set aside as a hotheaded response to a physical altercation. And lovely as Marena Hodges was, I didn't see Darien as the type of young man to kill for love, or his version of it. No, those things were less concerning to me than the items that had been found in his room. But, as I had told Milo, surely Darien was too clever to leave the proof of his crime sitting about. It seemed more likely that someone had put the items there. I just didn't believe that he was guilty.

Beyond all that, there was a feeling I had, the instinct that had served me well in other such situations. It was the expression on his face when the inspector had come to arrest him, the mixture of disbelief and uncertainty, that had really convinced me. And perhaps it was my newly developing maternal instincts, but there was something in Milo's cold rejection of Darien that made me want to care for him.

My thoughts were interrupted by the rustling of footsteps on the grassy path, and I turned to see Imogen approaching. She caught sight of me a moment later and stopped, surprised.

"Oh! Mrs. Ames. What are you doing here?" she asked.

"Just taking a walk," I said, wondering the same thing about her.

"I was, too," she said. "It's lovely here, looking across the countryside."

"Yes."

We stood for a moment, looking out at the pleasant vista before us. I didn't believe, of course, that she had merely been taking the evening air. While it was true that this path led directly to the village, few people took it unless they were coming to Thornecrest. There were a great many country paths at a closer proximity to Mrs. Cotton's rooming house Imogen might have taken if she were merely seeking an evening constitutional.

As I had hoped, the weight of silence seemed to do the trick.

"I . . . I . . . in truth, I was coming to see you," she said at last. "Or, at least, I was working up the nerve to do so."

"Oh?"

"I . . . I need to confess something."

I waited. "Confess" was such a strong word. I wondered momentarily if she might have had something to do with Bertie's death. But the two of them had been strangers. Hadn't they? I realized that I knew very little of Imogen's background. She worked in London and had holidayed in Brighton, but that was the extent of my knowledge of her past.

In the time all of this passed through my mind, Imogen had summoned the courage to come out with her admission. "I told the police that I saw Darien leaving the scene of the murder."

I stilled. So Imogen had been the witness that Inspector Wilson had mentioned.

"I see," I said noncommittally. I had found, in the past, that it was better to say as little as possible. People with something on their mind generally filled the silence, and there was often useful information to be gleaned.

"You're going to think I did it to be spiteful," she went on. "But I didn't. It's the truth. I saw him walking across that field where . . . where they found the . . . body later."

"Did you speak to him?"

She shook her head. "He didn't see me, and I didn't want to talk to him. Not then. I was still so confused about everything. And then I heard that a body had been found and that it was murder. And I knew . . . I knew I had to tell the police what I had seen. I didn't mean to hurt Darien. But I had to tell the truth."

I studied her, trying to gauge her sincerity. It was one thing to say one loved a young man and quite another to implicate him in a murder. Telling the truth to the police had been the right thing to do, of course, but I didn't think she should be surprised by the results.

"You were angry with him," I pointed out, waiting to see what effect the words would have.

She flushed, looking very pretty in the gloaming. "Of course I was. Wouldn't you be if someone had done such a thing to you? But I didn't lie about it." Her eyes met mine and held. "I didn't."

I didn't know what to think. I had believed Darien when he proclaimed his innocence, but it seemed to me that Imogen was just as sincere. Which of them was lying? Or was there some way that they might both be telling the truth?

I supposed only time would tell.

Time, and some well-placed questions.

15

AFTER A BIT of crying on her part and a bit of ineffectual soothing on mine, Imogen and I parted ways. I had told her we would see what we could do for Darien, though by "we," I meant myself, as Milo clearly had no intention of getting involved.

It was nearly dark by the time I returned to Thornecrest. I entered the house the way I had left it, through the morning room doors. I walked quietly through the hallway and up the stairs to our bedroom. My anger had cooled, but I was still not much in the mood for Milo.

Winnelda found me instead. She had an uncanny knack for seeking me out at a moment's notice. Perhaps that was the mark of a good lady's maid.

"Where have you been, madam?" she asked worriedly, eyeing the bits of wet grass clinging to my discarded shoes.

"Out for a walk."

"By yourself?"

"Yes." I suppose there was an edge to my tone that discouraged further questions on that score, for she let the matter drop.

"Will you be dressing for dinner?" she asked.

"No, I think not. Perhaps you can just bring me up a tray with a bit of something?"

I knew that "a bit of something" would likely turn into a tray heaped with all manner of food, but I hadn't the energy to argue with her.

To my relief, she returned a short time later with a small bowl of soup, bread and butter, and a pot of tea. It was just the right thing after a long day, and I was touched at Winnelda's thoughtfulness. Though normally chattiness personified, she seemed to sense that I needed time alone and left me to eat my dinner in silence.

I had bathed, dressed in my nightclothes, was already in bed when Milo at last made his appearance in our bedroom.

I briefly considered feigning sleep, but I knew that was childish and might also prove a boring ruse to maintain should Milo stay awake for any length of time. So, instead, I waited to see what he would say. If, however, I expected contrition on his part, I was to be disappointed. He didn't even ask me where I had been for the past two hours. Instead, he went to the bathroom to wash up and then changed for bed himself.

There was a heavy silence in the room. I was reminded of the troubled times in our marriage, when we had been virtual strangers to each other's thoughts. At least it didn't appear that Milo intended to sleep in the adjoining bedroom as he had for the rockiest year of our union, for at last he came and got into bed beside me.

"I have to go back to London tomorrow," he said as he leaned back against his pillows.

"All right."

"I shall perhaps have to stay overnight."

"I'll be fine."

I could sense his eyes on me, but I didn't look at him. At last he leaned over and switched off the light.

There was silence, except for the rustle of bedclothes and the slightest creak of the springs as Milo settled himself beside me.

I resisted the urge to sigh loudly. I didn't like us being at odds. I wanted to discuss things with him, to be the team we had learned to be over the course of several other investigations. It seemed strange that this one, which ought to matter most to him, was the one he had set himself against.

The baby kicked hard, and I gasped in surprise and shifted uncomfortably in the bed, trying to find a better position.

"Are you all right?" Milo asked into the darkness.

"Yes. I just can't seem to get comfortable."

"I'll fetch you some extra pillows, shall I?"

He got up without waiting for my answer and moved with ease across the dark bedroom. I heard the door to the adjoining room open, and a moment later he returned with pillows.

"Thank you," I said as he helped to arrange them around me in a passably comfortable configuration. I hadn't anticipated all the little ways in which pregnancy would change my life, least of all the ways in which I walked and slept.

Milo slid back into bed, and we settled again into the quiet darkness.

"I meant it, Amory," he said at last.

"Meant what?" I asked, though I knew perfectly well what he was talking about. Pillows or no, he had not softened his stance.

"We're not going to get involved with Darien's case," he said, his tone lacking the edge it had held earlier, despite the words. "He'll be condemned or go free based on the evidence, not on whatever sort of information we can dredge up about alternate suspects."

I was not going to argue with him; it would be useless.

"If that's the way you feel," I said at last.

"It is."

There was silence for a moment.

"I know I can't keep you from going around asking questions, as you're bound to do while I'm gone, but I'm asking you not to muddy the waters. Let the police do their job."

I didn't know how to respond. I wouldn't make any promises I didn't intend to keep.

When I didn't reply, he let out the sigh I had been so valiantly holding in. "If you're determined to go about nosing into village business, I don't want to hear about it."

If that was the way he wanted it, that was the way it would be.

"You needn't worry," I said coolly. "I shan't breathe a word."

ONCE I WAS rid of Milo the next morning, after a strained breakfast in which neither of us went out of the way to be pleasant to the other, I went about plotting my next course of action.

As far as I could see, there were, besides Darien, six possible suspects: Mrs. Hodges, Marena, Lady Alma, Imogen, the vicar, and Mrs. Busby.

Mrs. Hodges was under consideration based on Lady Alma's suspicions. Granted, I had only Lady Alma's word to go on. It was common knowledge, however, that Mrs. Hodges had never approved of her daughter's young man. Perhaps there was some motive of which we had no knowledge. There was, too, the question of whether he might have learned something about her, some secret she wished to keep hidden.

Marena was a suspect for the obvious reason: a lover's quarrel of some sort. Though they had parted ways, she was still angry at him for having struck Darien. Might she have confronted him and hit him in a fit of passion? I thought it unlikely, given how distraught she was at his death. But, then again, guilt and grief had many of the same symptoms.

As for Lady Alma, it was possible Bertie knew something about her and she had killed him to hide it and then tried to lay the blame elsewhere, claiming Bertie had learned a secret about Mrs. Hodges. I didn't like to think such a thing of Lady Alma, but it was possible.

Imogen wasn't necessarily a good suspect. After all, she hadn't known Bertie. But she had implicated Darien in his murder. Was it possible she had committed the crime in order to frame the man who had scorned her? It was a bit far-fetched, but not impossible.

Then there was the vicar and Mrs. Busby. While I was reluctant to include them, I could not entirely discount them. After all, Bertie had allegedly broken into the vicar's desk drawer. Had he discovered something that one of them thought it necessary to kill to conceal?

I sighed. There were so many possibilities and none of them much better than the last.

I decided the best place to start would be with Mrs. Hodges, especially as it was apparently she who had some secret that Bertie had known.

I had Markham, our driver, drive me to the Hodges home. It was a small, tidy cottage set away from the village. Contrary to Mrs. Hodges's stern personality, the house had a cheery appearance. The shutters were painted a bright yellow and the fence was a spotless white. There was a profusion of flowers around the outside: hyacinth, daffodils, narcissus, and foxglove. All the better to attract the bees she loved.

I stepped from the car and noticed a bicycle resting against the gate just as Marena came out of the house.

She looked up when she saw me, froze for a moment, and then came quickly toward me. Her hair appeared windblown, though she had just come from inside, and her face was red.

"Oh, Mrs. Ames. Have they arrested Darien?" she asked. "Have they really?" She was gripping the gate so tightly her knuckles had turned almost as white as the wood.

Word certainly traveled fast in the village.

"Do try to calm down, dear . . ."

"But my mother just said someone had been arrested, that it was a relation of yours. I had to get out of the house before I screamed . . ."

"Listen to me, Marena," I said, gently but firmly. "You're not going to do Darien—or yourself—any good by going to pieces. You must calm down. Do you understand?"

My schoolmarm tone of voice seemed to do the trick, for she nodded. Drawing in a deep breath, she brushed the loose strands of hair from her face and seemed to collect herself.

I reached out to pat her hand, noticing her grip on the gate had lessened ever so slightly. "That's better, isn't it? The best way to face the news is calmly."

"Then they did arrest him?"

"Yes, but . . ."

As I was afraid would be the case, she burst into tears as soon as I confirmed the story. I felt sorry for her, especially as I was fairly certain Mrs. Hodges had not been at all sympathetic.

"Did you tell your mother about your relationship with Darien?" I asked.

She shook her head. "No. She merely told me that some relation of yours had been arrested. I had to try to hide my distress from her. When I saw you, I couldn't bear it any longer."

I looked back toward the door of her mother's house, wondering if I should take her inside. I was fairly sure Mrs. Hodges would only make the situation worse.

Marena sniffed loudly then and looked up at me, her eyes bright. "He didn't do it, Mrs. Ames. I know he didn't."

I studied her, her tawny eyes filled with tears. I didn't know what to say to her. She appeared as though she truly believed what she was saying. But how could she know? She had been acquainted with Darien for less than a fortnight.

"The police will investigate the matter thoroughly. I'm sure they'll come to the truth." I was a bit disgusted with myself for repeating Milo's platitudes when what I really wanted to do was tell her I was investigating the matter. I knew, however, that I couldn't afford to take anyone into my confidence.

"But . . . what will happen if . . ." she whispered.

I knew what she was asking. What would happen if Darien were convicted of the crime? I didn't feel as though Marena was in the best state of mind at the moment to dwell on the possible outcomes.

"We won't worry about that now," I said gently.

"That girl did it, didn't she?" she said suddenly, anger sparking in her eyes. "She told the police, mother said. I think she's the one who killed Bertie."

"What girl?" I asked, reluctant to share the information with which Imogen had entrusted me.

"Imogen. She probably killed Bertie and tried to frame Darien for it."

I had considered the same possibility, but hearing it aloud made it seem even more unlikely than it had in my head. "Wouldn't she have just killed Darien if she were so desperate for revenge?" I pointed out.

She shook her head stubbornly. "She has something to do with all of this, I'm sure of it."

"Well, if Darien is innocent . . ."

"Oh, but he is!" she cried. "He would never do something like that, never."

"I'm not disagreeing with you," I said, knowing that we wouldn't be able to resolve this situation here in front of Mrs. Hodges's gate. "We shall just wait and see what happens. I'm sure the true killer will be brought to justice in time."

"Yes. Yes, I'm sure you're right." She suddenly seemed to take note of our location as well, almost as though she had appeared at her mother's house without really realizing it.

"But . . . but what are you doing here, Mrs. Ames? How did you know I was here?"

"I didn't, in fact. Actually, I came to see your mother."

A frown flickered across her face. I thought she looked almost worried. It passed quickly, however. "Mother's not feeling very well, I don't think. She denies it, but she's not a well woman."

It crossed my mind, unkindly, that I would have thought, given Mrs. Hodges's iron disposition, that she would outlive us all.

"I'm sorry to hear she's unwell."

"We've never got on especially well, but I do worry about her." She smiled at me. "She's quite well enough to see you, however."

"I purchased some honey from her at the festival, but I didn't have a chance to pick it up . . ." I left the rest of that sentence unfinished, lest the reminder provoke Marena to further tears. "Perhaps now isn't the best of times, but you know how women in my condition often have their fancies."

It was a flimsy excuse. After all, I could very well have sent Winnelda to collect it without coming myself. It didn't seem, however, that Marena had noticed.

"You may have to go around to the kitchen door. She often pretends she's not here when visitors knock on the front door." I didn't miss the little look of contempt she gave as she glanced back at the house.

"I'll just go and speak with her then. Go back to the vicarage, dear, and do try not to worry so much. Everything's going to be fine."

"I hope you're right, Mrs. Ames," she said softly. She got on her bicycle and went off down the lane toward the village without a backward glance.

I looked back toward the house and was startled to see the face of Mrs. Hodges watching us through the curtains. Then the curtain dropped, and she was gone.

While I was standing, debating whether I should go to the front door and knock or go to the kitchen door as Marena had suggested, she opened the door.

"I thought I heard Marena causing a scene out here," she said flatly. I marveled at her lack of compassion for her daughter. Whatever one thought of Marena's romantic escapades, surely one must feel sorry that a young man she had once cared deeply for had died.

I fought down my irritation, however. As Mrs. Hodges would be, I was sure, the first to say, one caught more flies with honey than with vinegar.

"She's quite upset," I said. "She cared very much for Bertie Phipps."

She let out a short breath through her nose, either impatience or disagreement, I wasn't sure which. "She didn't care for that boy as much as she pretends to now that he's dead. What can I do for you, Mrs. Ames?"

"I was wondering if I might collect my jar of honey. I didn't have the chance at the festival."

Her eyes narrowed ever so slightly, and I could tell that my excuse was not entirely satisfactory. Nevertheless, she stepped outside and closed the door behind her.

"Come this way," she said. She led me around the side of the house, through a tidy kitchen garden. At the edge of the field of lavender and yarrow beyond the back gate I could see the stacks of her hives, waiting for their occupants to return. We went in through a door that led into a clean, sunny kitchen. I had imagined the interior of her house to be a bit grimmer than this, and I was a bit surprised at the homely warmth of it.

There were filmy white curtains on the windows, admitting the sunlight, and every surface had been scrubbed until it shone. The floors, too, practically gleamed. Beeswax, no doubt.

There was a teapot on the table with a milk pitcher and a small jar of honey.

It smelled pleasantly of herbs, and I looked up to see bunches of dried lavender, thyme, and rosemary and bundles of sage hanging from one of the ceiling's wooden beams.

She went to a cupboard against one wall and pulled it open. "You're in luck. I've only a few jars of the lavender left," she said. She nodded at the jar on the table. "And that's the last of the rosemary. Marena's favorite, though it's too strong a taste for most. I'll be glad when the bees return. I'm hoping to have a larger colony this year than last."

"I meant to collect it after the race," I said. "But with everything that happened, it slipped my mind. It was all so unfortunate . . ."

"That boy getting himself killed, you mean? Yes, I suppose it was."

There was something very unpleasant about Mrs. Hodges, but one couldn't help but feel that there was also something clever about her. I decided that she would, perhaps, appreciate the most direct approach.

"Who do you think might have done it?"

She turned her hard gaze on me. "It doesn't matter what I think."

Another thought occurred to me, and, before I could think better of it, I asked the question out loud. "Why were you in the field near the Priory during the races?"

I expected, perhaps, a look of surprise, but, if anything, her expression became more calmly guarded. "Who says I was?"

"Someone mentioned it to me," I said vaguely.

Her eyes narrowed ever so slightly even as the corner of her mouth turned up in a grim smile. I recalled suddenly the illustration of a woodland witch in a storybook I'd read as a child.

"You're a clever one, Mrs. Ames," she said. "But I'm not the one you need to be questioning."

"You were wearing a different dress after the races than before," I said. Now that it was all out in the open, I might as well be direct.

She shrugged, unfazed by this piece of evidence. "I broke a jar of honey and walked home to change my dress. No crime in that, is there?"

"No, of course not." Could the explanation really be so simple? I found it unsatisfactory somehow, though it made perfect sense. The property line between Bedford Priory and Thornecrest was nearly a direct route to this cottage.

"I wouldn't have gone out of my way to harm him to keep him from Marena, anyway, if that's what you're thinking."

I didn't bother to deny it, and she went on. "People must take the consequences of their actions. If Marena wanted him, I wasn't going to stand in the way."

"Lady Alma said Bertie mentioned he knew a secret about you."

I had said it bluntly, to see if I could catch her off guard, but the only thing that crossed her face was a confused frown. "It must have been secret indeed, for I've no idea what you mean."

"Are you sure?" Even as I asked the question, I felt somehow that she was telling the truth. She had been surprised, not afraid, at the suggestion. I had seen it clearly in her face.

"I've a better question for you," she said. "One that's been on my mind since that afternoon."

My skin prickled a little, as though I were about to learn something very important. "Oh?"

She leaned a bit closer, her sharp dark eyes meeting mine. "What was that Imogen girl doing that day talking to Bertie Phipps in the field where he died?"

"YOU SAW IMOGEN Prescott talking to Bertie Phipps?" I asked, surprised by this latest bit of information.

She nodded. "I didn't think much of it at the time. But after he turned up dead, I started to wonder what she was doing with him."

"How did you know who she was?"

"It's hard to keep things quiet in this village."

That was true enough. But what connection was there between Imogen and Bertie? Thus far no one had given any indication that the two of them had known each other, Imogen least of all.

My mind immediately began sorting through the possible reasons for this deception. What was Imogen hiding? I knew Bertie had often gone to London. I supposed they had met there, though the nature of their connection was a bit harder to discern. A romantic liaison was perhaps the most obvious choice, but I had been so sure that Bertie genuinely cared for Marena. Could there be some other relationship between Bertie and Imogen?

"Were they arguing?" I asked, curious about the tenor of their interaction.

"Not that I could tell. But they had the look of two people that knew each other. They were comfortable together, if you take my meaning."

"You didn't much care for Bertie Phipps, did you?" I asked.

Her brow furrowed. "I didn't care for Marena chasing after him. She's not a good girl, and I knew what kind of trouble could come of it."

If she had disapproved so heartily of wholesome Bertie, I shuddered to think what she would say when she realized Marena had taken up with Darien.

"Perhaps you're too hard on her," I suggested. "Marena's a lovely girl."

"She's her father's daughter," Mrs. Hodges said darkly. "When she started asking about him, I knew there would be trouble."

Mrs. Hodges's husband had died many years ago, long before I had married Milo and moved to Thornecrest. No one, it seemed, knew much about him, for he had died before Mrs. Hodges came to the village, but I couldn't help but think that Marena must have inherited her good looks and sunny disposition from him.

"Well, thank you, Mrs. Hodges," I said, taking up my jar of honey. "You've given me a good deal to think about."

"There's more to all of this than meets the eye," she told me as I reached the door. "I'd be wary of digging too deep."

"I shall bear that in mind."

I crossed back through the garden and exited the front gate. Sliding into the backseat of the car felt rather like making an escape.

I wondered if I should go to the village and confront Imogen about what Mrs. Hodges had told me. I realized, however, that a short time in the woman's company had drained the energy from me. Detective work was very tiring in my condition.

By the time I returned to Thornecrest, I was feeling weary indeed. So it was with no great enthusiasm I received the news that my mother had rang and left word she intended to arrive in a week.

"Maybe she'll be detained again," Winnelda said, in an attempt to cheer me.

"I very much doubt it," I answered with a sigh.

My mother had been visiting more often since I'd become pregnant, and I was very much afraid that this time she meant to stay with us until the baby was born. At least I still had a week before she came. It would give me time to brace myself.

I had completed the nursery, so I would not need to finish it while contending with her input. There was, however, still the matter of a name to be settled. Milo and I had different ideas of what we wanted to call the baby. I preferred traditional names like Mary and Alice or Thomas and Henry. Milo said that he thought we ought to choose something a bit more exotic.

I supposed that Amory and Milo weren't the most traditional of names, and it had never done us any harm.

My mother, who in every other matter adhered to the strictest conventions, had chosen an uncommon name for me on the basis of familial loyalty hedged by prudence. Her favorite great-aunt was named Delilah Amory, but she had balked at so scandalous a given name. "There was nothing Christian about Delilah, now, was there?" she had once noted.

And so she had compromised by bestowing her aunt's surname upon me. Though I might have been more glamorous had I been christened Delilah, I supposed that Amory was fairly well-suited to me.

My middle names were the more traditional Rosamund Frances, so I supposed we might use one of those if it was a girl. Milo's were Anthony Lucien, but he had said he didn't care for either of them enough to give them to a child. He was especially opposed to Anthony, which had been his father's name.

My mother, though she would never deign to say so directly, had made several comments that had informed me that she would not be displeased if the baby were to be named after her or my father. I had dutifully added Luella and Franklin to the list of possibilities.

I had no doubt my mother would be advocating for them for the remainder of my pregnancy.

"I found a trunk in the attic, madam, when I was looking for baby things," Winnelda said. "I didn't open it, but it was near the nursery furniture, so I had Nathan bring it to the nursery for you to look at later."

I had been so lost in thought that I had forgotten she was still in the room.

"Oh. Excellent. Thank you, Winnelda."

She looked at me closely. "Are you feeling all right, madam? You look a bit peaked, if you don't mind my saying so."

"I am a bit tired," I admitted.

"Why don't you lie down for a bit before tea?" she suggested. "It will do you good."

"Yes. I think I shall." Though I would never have admitted it, I was in dire need of a bit of rest.

I supposed that now, with the baby's arrival nearing and my mother's impending visit, was not the ideal time for a murder investigation. Perhaps Milo was right; perhaps it would be best to let the police handle things.

Unlike Milo, however, I could not just abandon Darien to his fate. He might be a thoroughly unprincipled young man, but I didn't think he was a killer. And, whatever Milo said, I felt it was our responsibility to help him.

I needed to speak to Imogen about what Mrs. Hodges had told me. I found it very suspicious she had left out the fact she knew Bertie Phipps. What was the relationship between them, and what had she been doing in that field shortly before he died?

She had told both the inspector and me that she had seen Darien there, but apparently no one had thought to question her about why she had been in that spot to see him.

There was still information to gather and avenues to be explored. But it could wait until I'd had my nap.

As I drifted off to sleep, I had a sudden thought: today had shown me that I could count my blessings. My mother might drive me to distraction, but at least she wasn't Mrs. Hodges.

AS LUCK WOULD have it, the next opportunity for investigating presented itself at my doorstep that afternoon.

"Inspector Wilson is here asking for Mr. Ames, madam," Grimes said as I took my tea in the small sitting room.

I didn't hesitate. "I'd like to speak with him. Show him in, please."

Grimes had no discernible change in expression, but I could sense that he was not exactly thrilled with this request. He knew, as everyone did, the sort of intrigues in which Milo and I had been involved over the past years. Though he would never comment upon such things and had, naturally, kept his feelings on the latest developments within the Ames family to himself, I was sure that even his well-honed sense of professionalism must be strained by this point. Grimes was of the old school, and we were all behaving in much too modern a fashion for his tastes.

He made no further comment, however, and left to show the inspector in as I considered how best I might be able to use this unexpected visit to my advantage.

To be honest, I was not entirely encouraged by the fact that Inspector Wilson was on the case. He had always seemed a pleasant enough gentleman in our brief encounters, and I had no reason to believe that he was anything other than genuinely devoted to the cause of justice. The fact remained, however, that he was not a man of great imagination. He was the sort of person to look at facts and assume the most straightforward interpretation. The evidence pointed to Darien, and so he assumed Darien was guilty.

That didn't mean that he was a poor investigator. It simply meant that he might need someone to open his eyes to alternate possibilities.

The first step would be to get him to relax his guard, even if just slightly.

"Inspector Wilson, madam," Grimes said as he returned to the room with the policeman in tow.

"Thank you, Grimes. Good afternoon, Inspector."

"Good afternoon, Mrs. Ames," he said. He still held his hat in his hand, apparently unwilling to relinquish it to Grimes's charge. That meant, it seemed, that he did not intend to stay long.

"I understand you've come to see my husband, but I thought perhaps I might do just as well," I said brightly.

He looked uncertain about this, as men often do when a woman suggests she might serve just as well as a man, but I wasn't about to let him get away without at least gleaning a bit of information from him.

"I thought you might give me an update on the case."

"I don't want to trouble you with this unpleasant business, Mrs. Ames."

If he expected me to be a delicate wife, I might as well play the part. I put a hand on my stomach to draw attention to my condition. "It would set my mind at ease to hear it directly from the authorities."

He cleared his throat. "Well, I'm happy to do what I can, ma'am."

I smiled. "Excellent. There's no need for us to be formal. Would you care for some tea, Inspector?" I thought for a moment that he would refuse, but I could see that he was tired—no doubt the investigation and Darien's arrest with its incumbent paperwork had kept him occupied for long hours over the past days—and knew the prospect of a hot, strong cup would likely be a worthy enticement.

"I would like that very much, Mrs. Ames."

I moved to the tea tray and poured him a cup.

"Milk or sugar?" I asked.

"Both, please."

I fixed his tea as he sat uncomfortably on the edge of the yellow velvet cushion of the Thomas Sheraton chair across from the sofa.

"Now," I said when we were settled with our cups and saucers. "This is better, isn't it? Much more civilized. What is it that you've come to see us about?"

He took a sip of tea. I noticed that, despite his apparent discomfort, his hands were steady and his movements assured. "I know your husband isn't best pleased that I've arrested his . . . ah . . . brother."

I had the sense from these words that there was some resistance on the part of the villagers to recognizing Darien as Milo's brother. It wasn't just the fact of his illegitimacy, though I was certain that played a part.

The other reason was that Milo's family had lived here for generations. A great many of the villagers had watched him grow up, had read of his wild ways in gossip columns for years, and had watched as he mellowed into his own rough-edged version of respectability.

Whatever there was wild in Milo's past, there had also been his bond with Thornecrest and the people of Allingcross. That a stranger should come here claiming to be an Ames and then be charged with murder was a lot more than many people wanted to accept.

"It's been a surprise to all of us, naturally," I said, holding out a tray of biscuits. He accepted one, crunching on it as I continued. "We had no idea about Darien's existence until a few days ago, but one doesn't like to imagine that one's relative might be a murderer. After all, there are any number of people who might have killed Bertie Phipps. Most of the village was at the festival that day."

"That's true," he said. "But most of the village hadn't threatened to kill the young man."

"People often say things rashly in the heat of the moment that they don't mean."

"That doesn't answer for the evidence, I'm afraid." He said this mildly, as though not to give offense, and I was careful not to give the impression that I was growing combative.

"Of course," I agreed. "But it seems strange, doesn't it, that he would have kept the stolen objects in his room? Darien might be a reckless young man, but he isn't stupid."

Inspector Wilson shrugged. "People do strange things at times. I've seen the brightest of criminals do something thoughtless and swing for it in the end."

He seemed to realize what he had said and flushed, taking a quick sip of tea to cover his embarrassment. I pretended as though I hadn't noticed the faux pas of referring to the possibility of my brother-in-law's execution.

"Yes, I suppose." I leaned forward to refill his teacup. "Just for the sake of argument, have you considered anyone else?"

"We like to consider everyone who might have done it, naturally." He wasn't affronted by the question; the tea had mellowed him. He reached for a second biscuit.

"Who else, for example?" I asked, taking a biscuit myself.

I was fairly certain that he would tell me he could not divulge this information, so I was surprised when he answered me. "There were strained relationships in his life, of course."

"Of course."

"I shouldn't say too much. Reputation is a delicate thing, after all."

I nodded sagely, my expression soft with understanding. "Yes, it certainly is." I stirred my tea. "I know, of course, that he was dating Marena Hodges and that things didn't end entirely well between them."

"She broke it off with him and took up with your . . . eh . . . brother-in-law."

"Yes."

He hesitated. "You didn't hear that from me."

"No, I heard it long ago. In fact, I was at the inn during the altercation between Darien and Bertie. Marena herself told me that she was quite angry with Bertie over it." I was not trying to implicate her in the crime; I merely meant to point out to Inspector Wilson that there were other possibilities.

He seemed to consider this, and I hoped that my words would be weighty enough to keep the matter in his mind after our tea was finished. "That may be," he said. "But that blow . . ."

"The doctor was of the opinion that either a man or a woman might have done it, I believe. My husband was at the inquest and told me all about it."

He looked at me, his gaze sharpening ever so slightly, and I realized that I would need to tread carefully.

"That's so," he admitted at last. "But physical violence is often done by a man. Poison is more a woman's weapon."

"Perhaps," I said. "Though, in the heat of passion, a woman might as soon pick up a rock to do harm with it as a man."

"I suppose you're right." I felt a little hint of triumph that was immediately dampened by his next words. "Of course, I'm certain we've the right man, so speculation is useless. After all, Darien Ames was seen walking across the field around the time Bertie Phipps must have been killed."

"It was my understanding that Mrs. Hodges was seen walking across the field around that time as well."

The more I thought about it, the more ridiculous it seemed that no one had witnessed Bertie's murder. With all the people in that field, they might as well have held the festival there.

He looked at me, his gaze narrowing ever so slightly as he began to realize what I was about.

"You've been talking to Lady Alma," he said at last.

So she had told him, had she? "She mentioned something to me about having seen Mrs. Hodges walking across the field. Surely that's just as compelling as Imogen Prescott having seen Darien doing the same thing."

"I don't think Mrs. Hodges had much of a motive."

"What about Imogen Prescott?" I asked casually. "Did you ask her what she was doing in the field when she witnessed Darien walking across it?"

He sighed, leaning forward to set his empty cup and saucer on the table. "Mrs. Ames, I'm not really at liberty to discuss the case with you. I've already said more than I ought."

I realized I had pressed him too far, but an idea occurred to me, and I thought I might well seize upon it while I had the chance.

"Inspector Wilson," I said. "I should like very much to visit Darien in prison."

17

"Mrs. Ames, I don't think this is the sort of place you should be visiting," Inspector Wilson said for what seemed like the hundredth time in the last quarter of an hour. "Especially as you . . . well, as you are . . ."

He broke off, finding himself unable to reference my condition. "It just isn't the place for you, madam."

He had been saying as much since I had convinced him to let me accompany him back to the police station. We had just walked through the front doors, and his unease seemed to be increasing by the moment. I only hoped he wouldn't change his mind after we'd come this far.

"I'm certain I have been in worse places, Inspector," I said soothingly.

He looked doubtful.

"I'd just like to speak to him for a few minutes."

Torn between his desire to be accommodating and what he felt was his duty to shield me from the rougher elements, he eventually relented, realizing, I supposed, that I would not be easily thwarted.

"If you'll come this way, I'll show you to our interview rooms. We'll have him brought to you there."

I thanked him and followed him down the corridor and into a dim, sparsely furnished room. There was a table that looked as though it had seen much better days, and two rickety wooden chairs. I sat carefully in one, testing it to be sure it wouldn't collapse beneath me before settling my full weight in it.

With one last doubtful look in my direction, Inspector Wilson left me alone.

I felt a little hint of triumph that I had succeeded thus far. I felt certain that if I could speak to Darien, I might be able to clear up a few points that were troubling me.

A few moments later, Darien was led into the room by a burly officer. Inspector Wilson came in behind them.

Darien still wore the expression of indifference, but he seemed a bit paler than when I had seen him last, and his clothes were rumpled. They had taken his necktie.

"Oh, it's you," he said when he saw me. I wondered who he had been expecting. I suspected he had hoped it would be Milo.

"Hello, Darien," I said. "How are you?"

"I'm all right."

The officer led him to his seat and pushed him down into it. He set his arms on the table between us, and I saw that they were shackled together. I felt sorry for him, though everything in his expression said he didn't want it.

"May I speak to him alone?" I asked Inspector Wilson. "Just for a few moments?"

"I'm sorry, but I don't think . . ."

"I'm sure with an officer right outside the door, no harm will come to me," I said in my most imperious of tones. He hesitated. I sensed he wasn't the sort of man to back down easily, but he was weighing whether or not it was worth it to argue with me. One had to pick one's battles.

At last he gave a shrug. "Five minutes, no more."

I nodded. I would take what I could get.

Inspector Wilson and the officer went out, and we were alone.

I turned back to Darien and smiled. "There. That's better, don't you think?"

"Do you have a cigarette?"

I didn't smoke, but I had known this would likely be his first question. I reached into my handbag and brought out one of the cigarettes I had taken from the box Milo kept in the sitting room.

He took it and put it between his lips, and I flicked on the lighter and leaned forward to light it.

He inhaled deeply and let out a relieved breath of smoke. "I've been waiting for a cigarette. It tastes almost as good as freedom."

"I'm afraid this is no laughing matter, Darien."

He looked up at me, a flicker of amusement in his eyes. "Do you think I don't realize that? I may enjoy a risk now and then, but I certainly don't fancy being hanged."

"You're not going to be hanged," I said. I hoped I was right. This was all much more serious than he seemed to realize.

"I didn't kill that fellow," he said.

I wanted to believe he was telling the truth, but, as with Milo, it was very difficult to tell. Looking into those blue eyes was like standing on a ship and looking for answers in the depths of the ocean.

Remembering what Milo had learned about Darien from Mr. Ludlow, I decided to change tactics. "What happened with the other woman, the one whose husband supposedly died in a fall from a horse?"

He looked surprised. "How did you hear about that?"

"You have to admit, it looks bad," I said, ignoring the question.

"That man's death was an accident. Pure chance, nothing more. There was a lot of nasty gossip about it because of my involvement with the wife."

"And then she killed herself." I was watching him closely as I said it, and I was certain a flicker of something like sadness crossed his features before he concealed it.

"In the end, it got to be too much for her, I suppose," he said, looking down at his cigarette.

"This information certainly doesn't help your case."

"I've done a lot of bad things," he said, his eyes coming up to meet mine. "But I haven't killed anyone."

I wanted very much to believe him.

"Who do you suppose did kill Bertie Phipps?" I asked.

He shook his head. "I haven't the foggiest idea. I hadn't seen him since our row at the inn. I certainly didn't go about looking for him to bash his head in."

I frowned. Whether or not he had killed him, he was very casual about all of it.

"What were you doing in that field?"

The hesitation was so slight it was almost unnoticeable. "Just walking. Having a look at Thornecrest. I'm curious about my origins."

I had the distinct impression he was lying, but I moved past it for the moment, going to my next question.

"How do you explain the blood on your boots and Bertie's money and chain in your room?"

"Those aren't my boots," he said. "I only have the pair I was wearing."

"Can you prove it?"

"Can you prove how many pairs of shoes you have?"

"What about the chain and the money?" I asked, determined not to let his impudence dull my determination to help him.

"I didn't take it. Why should I? If I killed him in a rage, why would I steal from him afterward?"

"Why not?" I asked. "Perhaps you needed a bit of extra money and decided to take it."

I said this to goad him, to see what his reaction would be. If it made him angry, I couldn't tell. He merely watched me with those pale blue eyes. "I could have. But I didn't."

I studied him, and he looked back at me steadily. I had had this feeling before when looking into Milo's eyes, the feeling of decisions being weighed behind that inscrutable gaze. I hoped that he would make the right one, but if he really was anything like Milo there was no guarantee.

"This won't, perhaps, make me any more trustworthy," he said at last, "but I wouldn't kill for a woman. Why would I waste my life for one when there are so many to be had?"

Though this was a distasteful sentiment, I had to admit that it made sense. I didn't know Darien well, but it seemed very apparent that he was the sort of young man who had a short attention span where women were involved.

"I don't much care for your principles," I said at last. "But you do have a point."

He smiled, though it was more a smile of relief than the usual one of calculated charm. "I knew you would see it that way."

"But what of the fact that you were seen in the field that day, Darien?" I asked. "The truth."

He gave a little sigh. "If you want the truth, I went to meet Marena."

I felt a little surge of hope at this admission, but I tried not to let it show. Like one of Milo's high-tempered horses, I had to be sure that he didn't become skittish and bolt.

"Why?"

"Why does a man ever meet a pretty young girl in a secluded spot?"

"That field isn't exactly secluded."

"It's secluded enough. There's a path from the village that goes that way that's easy to find. We were to meet on it, find a haystack or something of the sort."

I sighed. How tedious he was.

"Then why didn't you tell the police that you were with Marena at the time of the murder?" I demanded. "You might have saved yourself all this trouble."

"Because Marena never arrived."

"No?"

"No." He waved a hand, the shackles at his wrists clanging. "And there goes my chance at an alibi."

"Did Marena ever tell you where she was at the time?"

He shook his head. "I haven't seen her since."

I considered this. If Marena had missed their assignation, there must have been a reason for it. Was the reason that she had encountered Bertie Phipps in the field?

"Did you see Bertie? You can tell me if you did," I said in a calm, soothing manner.

His mouth tipped up at one corner, just as Milo's was wont to do. "And what if I did? Are you going to save the day sister Amory?" There was something just the slightest bit mocking in his tone that set me on edge.

"Would you rather hang?" I challenged.

His smile widened. "You've got spunk. I can see why my brother fancies you. Most women wouldn't have the nerve to come into a prison, let alone to champion the cause of a ne'er-do-well."

I hadn't come here to have a discussion about Darien's ridiculous opinions on the fairer sex. I wondered if he knew I was quickly losing patience with him and that my desire to help was steadily becoming more of a burden than a cause. He didn't seem to realize what hung in the balance. Or perhaps he did, and this show of insolent nonchalance was all an act. I wondered if beneath the bravado, he was more worried than he let on.

"I think you underestimate women as a whole," I said, unable to let the matter drop entirely.

He shrugged. "Perhaps. Marena is a strong woman. And Imogen certainly has spirit. Despite how she looks. Oh, I know she makes a pretty picture with those wide green eyes and rosy blushes, but there's more to her than that. She's a lot stronger than she appears."

I hadn't needed him to tell me as much. After all, she had come to Thornecrest alone looking for a missing husband. Though she had been a bit uneasy about it, that was an act that had required courage. I had seen that streak of strength there, beneath the vulnerable exterior.

In fact, I hadn't entirely dismissed her as a suspect. Though I should have thought that if Imogen had been inclined to murder anyone it would have been Darien.

Marena, however, was a different story. Was it possible that she had killed Bertie? I was beginning to wonder.

Another thought occurred to me, one that should have occurred to me long ago. "Marena works at the inn. Do you suppose she might have put those things in your room?"

He considered. "It's certainly possible, though I don't know why she should have."

"Yes," I mused. "That's the question, isn't it?"

"I never bothered locking the door to my room, though. I don't own anything worth stealing. Anyone might have gone upstairs and put those things there. That girl at the desk certainly isn't much of a guard."

Yes, I had seen Jenny's level of proficiency firsthand.

He finished his cigarette and dropped it on the floor, grinding it out with his shoe. "I wish I could get out of here," he said. "I don't much care for this place."

"You're not meant to care for prison."

"Guilty people aren't meant to care for it. Innocent people aren't supposed to be here. It's not at all comfortable."

As if comfort was the most important consideration. I fought down my annoyance with the young man. He was so incredibly selfish that I found it very difficult to feel sorry for him. Nevertheless, I reminded myself that his off-putting manner did not mean that he was guilty, nor that he should be wrongfully convicted of a crime he didn't commit. Besides, I still sensed that, beneath it all, there was a young man whose audacity masked his insecurities.

"Well, we'll just have to hope that something will occur to prove your innocence," I said.

One must be careful what one wishes for.

WITH INSPECTOR WILSON not doing much to hide his relief to see me gone, I left the police station.

I thought I might next go to see Imogen. I was curious about Mrs. Hodges's assertion that Imogen and Bertie had been seen speaking to each other. I still couldn't fathom how the two of them might be connected.

When I stopped at Mrs. Cotton's rooming house, however, I was told she was out. I didn't know whether to be disappointed I couldn't speak with her or relieved that I might soon be back at Thornecrest and able to put my feet up. They were aching considerably.

"Back to Thornecrest, madam?" Markham asked as he opened the car door for me. I thought he looked a bit concerned. Perhaps I hadn't hidden my slight limp from too-tight shoes as well as I thought. I wondered if Milo had told him to keep me from overexerting myself.

Despite the temptation to head for home, I shook my head. "Just one more stop, if you please. Take me to the vicarage."

I wanted to see Marena, to ask her where she had been when she was supposed to have been meeting Darien.

We pulled up before the vicarage and I alighted from the car to see the vicar standing near the fence, working on his flower bed.

"Mrs. Ames," he said. "How are you?"

"Hello, vicar. I'm well. And you?"

"Right as rain," he said. "Just working on the flower beds a bit before I go in to tea."

"I thought I might come and check on Marena."

He nodded. "That's very kind of you, my dear. She's in the parlor having tea with Lady Alma and Mrs. Busby. I believe Mrs. Hodges brought over a basket of sweets earlier. I'm sure they'd love for you to join them."

That certainly wasn't ideal company for questioning Marena as to her whereabouts. I would have to do it another time. As for tea, I would much rather take a cup while sitting shoeless in my own home.

"I shan't disturb them," I said.

"I'm sure they'd love to see you."

"I really should be getting back to Thornecrest. I'll come back tomorrow, perhaps."

"As you wish, my dear."

I was about to turn back toward my car, but I realized this was an excellent opportunity and felt I should take advantage of it.

"I wonder . . . Might I have a word with you, vicar?" I asked.

He looked up. "Of course, Mrs. Ames. What is it?" He fixed me in that sincere, caring gaze of his, his flowers immediately dismissed, and I felt a bit guilty at what I was about to do.

Of course, it was all for a good cause. I was quite sure God would take that into account.

"I'm afraid I'm a bit at loose ends after all that has happened. It's just so shocking, what happened to Bertie. I was going to check on Marena, but, to be honest, I'm still disturbed about it myself." It wasn't a lie, after all.

He nodded sympathetically.

"I just find that I have so many questions."

"It's natural in the case of sudden death for one to question the nature of life." It was a lovely theological sentiment but not quite what I was getting at.

"I'm not at all convinced that the police have the right man," I said. "What do you think?"

It seemed to me that his expression grew slightly less transcendent than it had been a moment before. "As to that, I couldn't say. My realm is the spiritual; the law is that of the police." He smiled. "'Render unto Caesar' and all that."

"Yes, of course. But the search for truth is the duty of us all, is it not?"

"Yes, yes. You're quite right, my dear."

"I have heard that Bertie seemed to have broken into your desk."

If he was surprised by this sudden change of subject, he gave no sign of it.

"I'm afraid that's true."

"What do you suppose he wanted?"

"I assume he was looking for trinkets to sell. There were a few other items missing from the office that weren't recovered, small silver items of negligible value."

"Did you ask him why he did it?" I was genuinely curious.

"That's the sad thing. He denied it all. I told him that all was forgiven. That he had only to come to me, and I would have been glad to help him." He shook his head. "But he wouldn't admit it."

I decided to pose my next question, though there was the chance I was revealing too much of what I knew. "I noticed at the festival that you gave him an envelope."

He frowned. "I . . . gave him . . . I don't recall . . . ?"

I pushed on, despite his show of ignorance. "There was no envelope found on him when he died, but there was one found with his necklace in Darien's room at the inn. I don't suppose you gave Bertie money?"

He smiled kindly, shaking his head. "No. Though I would have, if he had asked for it. It is a lesson we could all learn, how to ask for help."

He was being purposefully obtuse now, though I couldn't be certain why.

"I couldn't agree more, vicar," I said sweetly. "That's another reason I'd like to speak to Marena. You see, I've heard that Bertie had a secret, one that he felt burdened to tell. I thought that perhaps it might hold a clue as to his death."

"Is that so?" It occurred to me suddenly that what I'd always taken to be an expression of perpetual serenity on his countenance might also be an exceptional poker face.

"I don't suppose he confided in you?"

"As a clergyman, I would be unable to share it if he did, of course." He said this in a gentle, almost apologetic tone.

"Oh, yes, of course. Well, perhaps he said something to Marena."

"Perhaps he did."

I could see I wasn't likely to learn anything more. It was time to take my leave.

"Well, good evening, vicar," I said. "I'll come back to speak to Marena tomorrow."

"Very good. I'm sure she'll be happy to see you."

I got back into the car and Markham started toward Thornecrest.

I looked once out the back window and saw the vicar was watching me drive away.

I RETURNED TO the house and, despite the strands of the mystery weaving themselves through my brain, I fell asleep early and slept well and late.

I was surprised when I turned in bed the next morning and saw the clock. It was much later than Winnelda usually let me sleep. I supposed, however, that she had thought I needed rest.

She had been right, apparently. I felt like a new person after a good night's sleep. Even my sore feet felt better. Traitorously, I thought how nice it had been to have the bed all to myself in Milo's absence.

I rang for Winnelda then went to the bathroom to wash. As I cleaned my teeth, I considered what needed to be done today.

My first order of business would be to go back to the vicarage. I wanted to have another conversation with the vicar. There had been something strange in his demeanor the previous evening, and I thought perhaps another conversation might reveal more. If not, perhaps Mrs. Busby would be able to tell me something.

I wanted to check in on Marena, too, of course. And perhaps, as I had mentioned to the vicar, I might ask her if she knew anything about Bertie's secret.

I had just come out of the bathroom when Winnelda burst into the bedroom. I was accustomed to her high level of energy, but I was still a bit taken aback by her entrance.

"Oh, madam!" she said. "I've been wanting to wake you up, but you were resting so peacefully! Something dreadful has happened."

"What is it, Winnelda?" I asked, my mind automatically turning to Milo. But no. Surely she would have awakened me in that case.

Her face was flushed, and her voice, when she spoke, was hushed with reverent horror.

"It's Marena Hodges. She's dead."

"MARENA'S DEAD?" I repeated, not quite knowing what to make of the words.

The first thought to cross my mind was that she might have, in her distress, done harm to herself. But no. She was a strong woman, full of life. She wouldn't have done that. I had seen her only yesterday, and, though upset about Darien's arrest, she had given no indication that she was in a dangerous frame of mind.

All these thoughts passed through my head in the space of an instant, even as I stepped toward Winnelda. "What on earth happened?"

"Poison, they say."

Poison? I felt a cold rush of shock run through my veins. It seemed incredible, impossible.

"But . . . are you certain that it wasn't some sort of accident? Or an issue with her health? Perhaps her heart was weak . . . after Bertie's death?" I knew I was grasping at straws. Marena had been young and healthy. A sudden death wasn't likely to be anything but murder.

"No, madam, I heard all about it," Winnelda said. "Tilly heard it from May, who was at the vicarage when it happened. They were having tea last night, the vicar and his wife and Lady Alma and Miss Marena. Miss Marena took a sip of her tea, and May heard her make a strangled cry. She said, 'This tea tastes strange!' and then she started grasping her throat. She was trying to say something, but no one could make it out."

I felt the color drain from my face at the grim description, at the awfulness of it all. Poor Marena.

Winnelda continued, oblivious to my distress. "There was blood and foam on her lips, May said. Isn't that awful, madam?"

"Awful indeed," I said faintly. I pressed down the growing ill feeling in my stomach. It wasn't just the description of Marena's death; it was the fact that such a lovely girl was gone.

I couldn't seem to make sense of it. My mind was in a fog of disbelief.

Someone had killed her just as they had killed Bertie Phipps. But who?

I DRESSED QUICKLY and hurried downstairs. I would have a quick breakfast and then go to see Lady Alma. It was too early to visit the vicar and Mrs. Busby, but I would go later in the day to pay them my condolences. In the meantime, perhaps Lady Alma could tell me what exactly had occurred since she had been there at the time.

I had reached the bottom of the stairs when Grimes approached from the direction of the drawing room.

"Mr. Darien is here to see you, madam," he said.

I stopped short. "Oh. Is he? I . . . Thank you, Grimes."

Darien was here? Had he escaped? I certainly hoped not. What was I meant to do if he had? Tackle him to the ground if he tried to leave? It wasn't as though I could move very quickly in my current condition.

I felt quite at a loss. I had slept for a few hours, and now the world was very much askew.

Mustering up an outward serenity that I did not feel, I went into the drawing room. Darien turned from where he stood near the window to smile at me. "Hello, Amory."

"How did you get out of prison?" I asked, forgoing the pleasantries.

"Good morning to you, too," he said with a little laugh. "Inspector Wilson let me go this morning. You've heard what happened?"

"Yes," I said. "I'm sorry, Darien. Marena's death is a great shock."

He nodded. "We hadn't known each other long, but I cared for her, in my way."

It was a lackluster declaration, and I decided it would be best if neither of us went on pretending he was grieving.

"He let you go because he believes the murders are connected, and you couldn't have murdered Marena when you were in prison," I said, putting the facts together.

"Yes, though I'm not entirely cleared of suspicion, it seems. I've orders not to leave the village. I told him you would look after me."

"You did, did you?"

"Yes." He stepped forward. "I wanted to thank you for coming to see me yesterday."

There was something earnest in his expression, and I immediately distrusted it. He was Milo's brother, after all. I knew he was perfectly aware of his charms and how to use them. One didn't grow up to be that good-looking without realizing the advantages it afforded one.

"What do you want, Darien?" I asked bluntly.

"What makes you think I want something?"

"I can tell. But you should know, I am immune to flattery and to that particular sort of smile. I've seen it often enough from Milo."

He laughed. "You're sharp as a thorn, Amory."

I waited.

"I didn't suppose I would have much in common with him, other than our looks. I suppose I ought to have known that one can't escape heredity."

"No," I said. "It's a very difficult thing to do."

"I came to ask if I might stay at Thornecrest," he said. "Just until the matter is cleared up, of course."

The matter. As though two violent deaths were a mere inconvenience to be swiftly resolved.

"I'm afraid I gave Inspector Wilson the impression that I would be welcome here," he said when I didn't answer.

I hesitated. I knew what Milo would have to say about it. But things were different now, weren't they? Darien was no longer the prime suspect. Surely Milo couldn't object.

I knew the answer to this well enough, but I decided to deal with the consequences later. After all, if he wanted to be rid of Darien, he was going to have to do it himself.

"Milo's in London," I said. "We'll discuss it when he gets back. I've got somewhere to be, but you're welcome to have breakfast here."

"It's good of you," he said. "Thank you."

It was an unexpected moment of sincerity, and I was momentarily thrown off my guard. I suspected that might have been his intention, but I felt a little of my goodwill return.

"You'll behave yourself, I trust?" I asked.

He put his hand to his heart. "I shall be a perfect angel."

"Let's not get carried away," I replied. "Perhaps you might start with being a decent human being."

"Touché," he said with a grin.

EVEN WITH DARIEN'S unexpected visit, I knew it would still be too soon for me to go to the vicarage. The police would likely be there, and no doubt the Busbys were still in shock over what had happened.

Poor Mr. and Mrs. Busby. They were so very fond of Marena, had looked upon her almost as their own child. I could only imagine the blow this would be for them.

So my first stop would be Bedford Priory. Neighbors often shared their concerns, after all. And Lady Alma had been present at the time of the incident. Perhaps she would be able to shed some light on this latest tragedy.

Leaving Darien in Grimes's capable hands, I asked Markham to drive me to the Priory. It was still almost unbelievable to me that Marena had died. Who would have done it? How had she been poisoned? It was all so horrible.

I reached the Priory and was shown into Lady Alma's comfortable drawing room. It was decorated in shades of gold, red, and dark brown, and, as one might expect, there were numerous paintings of horses on the walls, including a Stubbs and a Landseer.

I had only just taken a seat in an oversized leather chair when Lady Alma came striding into the room. "Hello, Mrs. Ames."

"Lady Alma," I said, beginning to rise from my seat.

"No, no. Don't get up," she said. "I know you must be uncomfortable. I've dealt with enough pregnant horses to realize that."

I fancy I managed to hide my surprise at this comparison. I certainly hoped I didn't look like a pregnant horse.

"Can I offer you some tea or coffee?"

Given the nature of my visit, I supposed it would be polite to refuse. But I had neglected breakfast due to Darien's unexpected arrival, and I was already feeling its absence.

"Coffee would be lovely," I admitted.

Lady Alma issued brusque orders to a maid and then came and settled heavily into a chair across from me. She looked tired, as though she hadn't slept, and her normally tanned skin had taken on an unhealthy color, highlighted by the darkness beneath her eyes.

"I suppose you've heard what happened," she said.

"Yes. It's awful."

"Awful doesn't begin to describe it. That poor girl . . ." Her voice trailed off. Lady Alma had never been a woman of strong emotions, but I could see that she was clearly upset.

"I . . . I heard it was poison," I said. There was no sense, I supposed, in beating about the bush.

She nodded. "It couldn't have been anything else, not the way it happened."

"Do you want to talk about it?" I asked. I have to admit that I was rather hoping she would say yes. Not from any sense of morbid curiosity, but rather because I felt it was important to get firsthand information about what had happened.

"It was all so unexpected. I'd stopped by to talk to Mrs. Busby about the festival. Marena came down to have tea with us. The maid brought it in. Nothing out of the usual. Then that girl came to the door."

I frowned. "What girl?"

"Prescott, I think she said her name was. Mrs. Busby let her in, though it was late for a social call of that nature. She was looking for Marena."

Imogen had been there? I felt a sudden cold chill. Why hadn't Winnelda mentioned this aspect when she'd related the story she'd heard from May? Perhaps, since Mrs. Busby had let her in, the maid didn't know about it.

"What did she want?" I asked.

"It was something to do with a young man." She looked at me searchingly as she said this, wondering, I supposed, just how much I knew about that particular triangle.

"Darien," I said. "My husband's brother."

She nodded. "It seems both fillies had taken a liking to him. They exchanged some terse words with each other."

"What did they say?"

"I have to admit, I wasn't paying much attention. Such matters have never been of much interest to me. I wandered to the other end of the parlor and was looking at Mrs. Busby's collection of sheet music. Never knew there were so many hymns."

This was incomprehensible to me, as I would have found it impossible not to at least listen unobtrusively to the conversation between the two young women. How could one be uninterested in such a thing?

"What about Mrs. Busby?" I asked. "Was she uncomfortable?"

"You know how she is, always soft-spoken. She got a bit flustered, I think, but then the vicar came in and set everything to rights. The two young women managed to be civil, and then the girl went away. The tea had just about gone cold by the time she left, but we decided to drink it anyway. More's the pity.

"Marena took a drink of hers and said, 'This tastes strange,' or something of that nature. I thought nothing of it at first. Cold tea isn't good, after all. But then she made a strange strangled sort of sound and grabbed her throat. A moment later she was on the floor."

I couldn't imagine the horror of it.

"I didn't know what was happening at first. Mrs. Busby seemed to think she'd fainted or some such thing. She cried out for the vicar, and he came back in and tried to revive the poor girl. I rang for Dr. Jordan. But it was no good. She was already dead."

Lady Alma had recited this in a fairly calm manner, but her hand was a bit unsteady as she lifted her coffee cup to her lips. She set the cup back down again and pulled the familiar flask from her jacket pocket. Instead of adding it to her coffee, however, she took a long drink directly from the flask.

"What did the doctor say?" I asked.

"He seemed to realize it was poison right away. Said none of us should touch anything and rang for the police."

"I imagine Mr. and Mrs. Busby were in quite a state."

"Mrs. Busby was crying a great deal. She was very close to Marena. Almost like a daughter to her. The vicar was calm, as he usually is, but I could tell he was much affected by it. He was very fond of Marena, too."

I nodded. Marena had been almost like a second daughter to them after they had lost Sara. And now Marena was gone, too. It seemed almost unfair that they should have to deal with so much grief.

Belatedly, my thoughts turned to Marena's own mother.

"I suppose the police told Mrs. Hodges."

"The vicar went to see her," Lady Alma said. "He thought it his duty to do so."

"I suppose she was quite distraught."

She looked up at me, her gaze suddenly hard. "I suppose that's the question, isn't it? Was she really?"

"What do you mean?"

"Who killed Bertie and who killed Marena? No doubt the killer is one and the same. And you know who I suspected of killing Bertie."

I remembered her accusation against Mrs. Hodges. "But surely she wouldn't . . . not her own daughter," I said.

"There has never been a natural mother-daughter relationship between those two," she said. "Everyone in the village could see that Jane Hodges cared very little for her daughter."

"But why? What possible reason could there be?"

She shrugged. "That woman has always been strange. Who knows what notions she's taken into her head?"

Somehow this explanation didn't sit well with me. Mrs. Hodges was an unusual woman, yes, but I couldn't see her killing two people, including her own daughter, on a whim.

"If . . . if it wasn't Mrs. Hodges, who else might it have been?" I asked.

Her eyes narrowed. "I don't see who else it could have been. Unless you believe the vicar or Mrs. Busby might be capable of such a thing." There was something in her tone that didn't entirely rule out the possibility.

"One doesn't like to think that any of one's acquaintances are capable of such a thing," I said vaguely.

"No, one doesn't," Lady Alma replied. "But someone killed Marena Hodges. Someone that we know."

There wasn't much else to be said. I left a few moments later, my mind a whirl.

Of course, I had to include Lady Alma on my list of suspects. I wasn't sure why she might have wanted to kill both Bertie and Marena, but the fact remained that she had had the opportunity to do so in both cases. As had Mr. and Mrs. Busby. As had Imogen.

Any of the suspects in Bertie's death might also have been responsible for Marena's untimely demise, I realized. The field had not been narrowed at all.

That meant I would have to narrow down the suspects myself.

SINCE I WAS already out, I had Markham drive me to the village. While I supposed it was still too early to pay a visit to the vicarage, I thought I would go and speak to Imogen next.

So she had decided to confront Marena Hodges, had she? I supposed it was inevitable that it would happen eventually. Truth be told, however, I hadn't pictured Imogen as the sort of person who would meet the issue head-on, at least not with an audience. Of course, she likely hadn't known that Lady Alma would be there having tea with the Busbys and Marena.

This also meant, of course, that she might have had the opportunity to poison Marena's tea. The cup had been sitting there in the open. It would have been a risk, but not impossible. After all, someone had accomplished it.

Markham pulled up before Mrs. Cotton's boardinghouse, and I went through the gate in the little white fence and up the flagstone walkway.

I knocked on the door and was greeted by the maid, who informed me that Miss Prescott had gone out. She certainly was a difficult person to contact.

What was keeping her in Allingcross? I wondered suddenly. Things were clearly not going well with Darien. To my knowledge, she had not even seen him since she had been here. It seemed perfectly plain that he had neither the desire nor the intention to continue their brief romance.

In her position, I would have returned to London and tried to get on with my life. Of course, it was easy to speculate what one might do in another person's position. Imogen might have her own reasons for wanting to linger in the village.

Some little part of me wondered if she had stayed just to seek her revenge.

I was just approaching the car when I spotted Imogen coming back up the street. She smiled and waved when she saw me.

"Hello, Amory," she said when she reached the gate.

"Hello, Imogen." I searched her face for any sign of guilt in the wake of what had occurred last night in the vicarage, but I saw none. She merely looked pleasantly surprised to see me.

"Were you coming to visit me?"

"Yes. I wanted to speak to you for a few moments . . . if you have the time?"

"Of course." She hesitated. "But do you mind if we walk? Mrs. Cotton's parlor is so small. And I have the impression that she listens at keyholes." She said this with a little laugh, but it was an astute assessment. Mrs. Cotton was our resident busybody. If there was gossip to be had in the village, she was the one who would know it.

It occurred to me then that I might have a conversation with Mrs. Cotton at another time. Who knew what she might be able to tell me?

"I won't be long, Markham," I said, turning to my driver. "If you'll just wait for me here?"

"Certainly, madam."

"I'm sorry," Imogen said suddenly with a glance at my stomach. "I didn't think . . . if you don't feel up to walking . . ."

"I'd very much like to walk," I assured her. "I spend much too much time stationary these days."

"All right."

We began walking, passing the apothecary shop and the post office before Imogen spoke. We saw only two or three villagers, but I noticed a few curious glances our way. News of the circumstances surrounding Marena's murder had spread by now, I was sure. And Imogen, as an outsider, was no doubt viewed as the likely suspect.

"I suppose you wanted to talk to me about Marena Hodges's death," she said, her thoughts moving in the same direction as mine.

"You've heard what happened then."

"Yes. The police came to see me late last night." She sounded very calm about it. It was almost a bit strange. In a similar situation, I might have been alarmed to have the police question me about the death of a girl with whom I'd had an argument moments before she died.

"I understand you quarreled with her."

"Something like that," she admitted quietly.

"Why did you go to see her last night?"

She sighed. "I started thinking, about everything. I thought that perhaps we ought to discuss the matter, face-to-face. I know she's heard things about me. I saw her once, across the street, and the look she gave me was hateful."

"It wasn't her fault that Darien . . . is the way he is."

"I know," she said. "I thought about that, too, that she didn't understand what sort of person he is. I thought if we talked about it, we might be able to clear things up."

"But she wasn't interested in doing that."

She shook her head. "I think she's under Darien's spell. She . . . she said some rather cruel things to me."

"Did she accuse you of killing Bertie Phipps?"

Her face went white and then crimson. "I . . . I . . . yes, she did. It's so silly because . . . I didn't even . . ."

She was fumbling for excuses, and I decided not to give her time to formulate them. "I was told you were seen talking to Bertie Phipps the day of the festival."

I watched her carefully to see what her reaction would be.

To my surprise she nodded, her eyes downcast. "I was."

"Did you know him?"

"Yes."

I tried not to appear too encouraged by this admission. After all, I didn't know what it meant. I only knew that there was another tie to Bertie Phipps, another line of inquiry that might keep Darien out of prison.

"How?"

She didn't answer at first. When she did, her answer didn't entirely make sense. "I . . . I'm not a typist," she said.

I waited.

She let out a little breath and then spoke the words quickly. "I'm a barmaid at a tavern not far from Alexandra Park Racecourse. Bertie used to come in there after he'd gone to the races. We became friends."

They'd become friends, had they? What sort of friends? I wondered.

As if I'd asked the question aloud, Imogen said quickly. "Just friends. That's all. I swear. Bertie loved Marena."

"Then why didn't you tell anyone that you knew him?"

She shrugged. "At first it was because I didn't want anyone to know how we'd met. I didn't want anyone to know I was a barmaid instead of a more respectable occupation. I was afraid it would get back to Darien."

"Do you honestly believe that sort of thing would make a difference to Darien?"

"Not now. But when we met, I did. He was so handsome and elegant. And so I lied to him about my job. It all seems so silly now."

Could it be true, I wondered, that something so trivial was the reason behind Imogen's secrecy? I supposed it might be the case. After all, if she had thought Darien came from a wealthy family, they weren't likely to have welcomed a barmaid into their bosom. A typist, on the other hand, was a position that spoke of industry and respectability.

There was just enough plausibility to her story to make me believe that she might be telling the truth.

I recalled how Mabel, the fortune-teller at the festival, had said Imogen had hurried from her tent, upset at the mention of the past impacting her future.

"What were you doing talking to Bertie in the field?"

"I saw him walking away from the festival, and I caught up with him. I just wanted to make sure that he hadn't told anyone. It was a friendly conversation. We talked for just a moment or two, and then I left."

"So you didn't see anyone else, aside from Darien?"

She shook her head. "I spotted Darien walking across the field just as I neared the festival again."

"And you weren't there when Marena died," I said, though I'd already had Lady Alma's account of it.

"No. I understand it happened shortly after I left. What a dreadful thing."

"She was a lovely girl," I said, watching her face closely.

Imogen stopped walking and turned to me. "I'm very sorry that she's dead. I would never have wished for anything like that to happen to her."

She sounded sincere. I was beginning to wonder, however, if she was a better actress than I had given her credit for being. Darien certainly seemed to believe that she wasn't as innocent as she appeared. Of course, I hesitated to take Darien's word on anything where women were concerned.

"Who do you think might have done it?" I asked.

She shook her head. "I don't know. I don't know anything anymore."

"Did you know that Darien has been released from prison?"

Her eyes widened. "No. He . . . he has?"

"The police believe, given Marena's death, that he is not the murderer of Bertie Phipps."

I expected her to look happy at the news, but it seemed that her expression clouded before she did her best to appear cheerful. "Well, I suppose I'm happy for him. I never did believe he killed Bertie."

"The question still remains," I replied. "Who did?"

IMOGEN WENT BACK into Mrs. Cotton's house, and I turned toward the car. But then a thought occurred to me.

"Just one more moment, Markham," I called to him before turning back toward the apothecary shop next door to the boardinghouse.

I stepped inside. The interior was dim and cool compared to the sunny warmth of the morning outside. I had always liked the shop, with its mahogany shelves stacked with neat rows of jars and colorful bottles, the scent of herbs and tinctures in the air.

The apothecary, Mr. Peters, was standing behind the counter, reading over some notes in front of him, his glasses perched on the end of his nose. He looked up when I entered and offered me a welcoming smile.

"Ah, Mrs. Ames. Good morning."

"Good morning, Mr. Peters."

"How are you feeling?" Mr. Peters had supplied me with several remedies over the years. He was a kind, cheerful fellow, and clever as well. Which meant I was going to have to be very careful.

"I'm feeling quite well, thank you," I said with a smile. "The doctor says all is as it should be."

"I'm glad to hear it. What can I do for you today?"

"I wonder, do you have any raspberry leaf tea?"

The apothecary nodded. "Yes, of course. It's wonderful for women in your condition. Especially as the time may be approaching. Let me see . . ."

As I had hoped, he stepped away from the counter, moving toward the corner of the room, his back to me.

"And a jar of witch hazel," I added. I knew where it was kept, and it would give me an additional moment or two to do what I had come to do.

Quickly, I stepped behind the counter and pulled out the poison register.

I knew where it was, for I had been here once on the occasion that someone was purchasing some toxic material. They had been required to write both their name and the poison in the book, a useful measure when one was granted possession of a deadly substance.

I looked up. Mr. Peters was still focused on the tea, scooping it out of its jar into a little tin for me to take with me.

I opened the book, flipping to the most recent page, and quickly scanned the list of names. Many of them were familiar to me, local farmers who could use the stuff to keep rodents away from their orchards and hops.

I stopped when I caught sight of a listing from three weeks ago.

Cyanide salts.

I looked at the name beside it. The signature was written in an elegant, tidy hand.

Elaine Busby.

I PUT THE register back and composed myself as Mr. Peters brought back my tea and witch hazel, though my mind was very much preoccupied for the rest of the transaction.

I supposed there were any number of reasons why Elaine Busby might have bought cyanide salts. But none of them seemed as relevant at the moment as the possibility she had used them to poison Marena's tea.

Of course, she was bound to know that the police would check the poison register. Surely she wouldn't be so naïve?

What was more, I found it difficult to believe she could have come here alone. After all, it was not easy for her to get around in her chair.

Nothing seemed to make sense, and the more I investigated, the more complex things seemed to have become. It was very frustrating.

I was tired when I returned to the house. I intended to have some tea and sit near a fire in the drawing room while I finished sewing the hem on a blanket for the baby and thought over all that had happened.

I would need to see Inspector Wilson at some point, of course. Though I was certain the poison register would be the first place he would look after a death of this kind, I wanted to be sure that he had seen Mrs. Busby's name there.

I had just settled myself into the chair and picked up my sewing when Milo came into the room. I didn't know he was back from London, so I was a bit surprised to see him standing in the doorway.

"What is Darien doing in this house?" he asked.

So that was it. He was wearing riding clothes, though the spotless nature of his boots told me he hadn't been out yet. He must have been waiting for me.

"Hello, Milo," I said pointedly. "How was your trip to London?"

He didn't reply, waiting, I supposed, for an answer to his question.

"I don't know if you've heard, but there's been another murder," I said.

If this surprised him, he didn't show it. Indeed, he seemed very uninterested in this latest bit of village news.

"That doesn't explain what he's doing here."

I could see he was not in a pleasant mood, but I was tired and on edge myself. If he wanted a fight, I was prepared to give him one. I set my sewing aside. "Inspector Wilson has released him into our charge."

"Why the devil should he do that?"

"He couldn't have committed the second murder, so Inspector Wilson has begun to believe he didn't kill Bertie, as it seems likely one killer committed both murders. Aren't you interested, by the way, in who else has died?"

"I know who else has died," he replied. I ought to have known he had already heard the news; there was little that happened in the vicinity of Thornecrest that Milo didn't know about almost immediately.

"I should think you'd be glad to learn your brother is no longer the primary suspect."

"Just because he didn't kill Marena doesn't mean he didn't kill Bertie."

I sighed. "Milo, do try to be reasonable."

"I think it's perfectly reasonable not to want an accused killer in my house."

My brows rose. "Your house, is it?"

We were perilously close to a blazing row. My energy was low, but I could feel my ire rising.

"You know very well what I mean," he answered evenly.

"It's not for long," I said, matching my tone to his. "Besides, I told him we'd discuss it when you got back from London. If you hadn't come charging in here so rudely, I might have had a chance to mention that."

"I'm back from London," he said. "So let's discuss it."

I studied him. "Do you know something about Darien that you haven't told me?"

"No."

"Then why have you set your mind against him?"

"I find it difficult to believe he hasn't given you reason enough to distrust him in the time you've known him."

I was growing exasperated with his whole attitude.

"Milo, I don't see why you're so angry."

"Don't you?" he replied. Despite his calm tone, his eyes were that bright shade of blue I recognized from the one or two occasions when he had allowed me to see how furious he was. "You're putting our child in danger."

"I'm doing no such thing!" I resented the implication. Nothing was more important to me than the safety of our child, and the accusation made me angry.

"What do you call it? Inviting a murder suspect into our house. And what's more, going around asking questions when someone has been killed."

I hadn't expected him to change topics this way, to shift some sort of blame onto me, and I wasn't prepared for it.

For just a moment I considered the accusation. It was true that our investigations had placed me in danger before, but this time was different. I was being careful. I wasn't acting recklessly or going anywhere alone with potential suspects. I was only doing what would be natural for me to do under the circumstances: talking to those involved, offering my sympathies as a friend.

It wasn't fair of him to characterize it as a risk.

I was about to make an angry retort when I thought better of it. I was suddenly too tired to go on arguing. If he wanted Darien out of the house, he would have to get rid of him himself.

"I can look after myself and the baby," I said. "As for Darien, do what you like. It's your house, after all."

We looked at each other for a moment.

"I'm going for a ride," Milo said.

"Very well."

He turned and left then without a backward glance. And good riddance to him.

Xerxes must have been saddled and waiting, for a moment later I saw through the window as they galloped off across the lawn. Xerxes was already prancing and pulling on the bit. Perhaps the exertion required to handle him would do something to improve Milo's temper.

I drew in a deep breath, calming myself. It would do no good for me to get upset. We would just have to discuss the matter again when both of us were in a better frame of mind.

There was a chattering as Emile, our pet monkey, made his appearance in the drawing room. I had grown very much attached to him since he had come to us and often talked to him as I would a child, though I had to do it in French, as it was his native language, so to speak. He answered me, too, with little chirps and enthusiastic clapping of his paws.

"Hello, Emile," I said. I was glad to see him; I could do with a bit of cheering.

He came over to my chair and picked something up off the ground. "What have you in your hand, dearest?"

He climbed up to the arm of my chair and held out a thimble I had dropped when I had set my sewing aside.

"How clever you are, Emile. Thank you."

He chattered happily, pleased with himself. He had a habit of returning lost items to their owners, which had proven useful on more than one occasion.

For the most part now, however, he lived a life of luxury and ease. Most of the time he was at his leisure to roam about, though Winnelda was tasked with keeping an eye on him and making sure that he didn't get into too much trouble. All of the more valuable fragile items in the house had been moved behind closed doors.

Milo and I had discussed what would happen once the baby was born. I was a bit nervous as to how Emile would react to an infant. There was no question of our giving him away, not when he had become so dear to us, but I thought that a period of separation would be the best thing. Thornecrest was certainly large enough to keep them apart from each other, or, if need be, he could be moved to our flat in London until the baby was no longer an infant.

"A sprawling country house, a beautiful wife, exotic pets, what more could one ask for? My brother is a lucky man."

I looked up as Darien came into the drawing room. I couldn't tell, either from his tone or his expression, how I was meant to interpret this observation. I wondered, too, if he had overheard any part of my conversation with Milo.

I decided to proceed as if nothing had happened. I reached over to a little cup of nuts I kept for Emile and held one out for Darien. "You can feed him if you like. He'll be your friend forever afterward."

Darien paused and then came forward and took the peanut, holding it out in Emile's direction.

"Here you are, little fellow."

Emile tipped his head to one side and studied Darien.

"Come on then," he said.

"We got Emile in Paris," I told him. "He doesn't speak English."

An expression I couldn't quite read flickered across Darien's face.

"A pity, then, for I don't speak French." He popped the peanut into his mouth.

I realized again that gap that existed between the two men. Darien might be Milo's brother by blood, but there was a world of difference between them. Milo's life had been a series of advantages afforded by money, a family name, and an abundance of good fortune.

Things had obviously not been so easy for Darien, and a part of me understood why he was resentful of his brother. Then again, it had not been Milo's fault that their father had abandoned Darien and his mother. There was only so much he could do to remedy it.

I held another peanut out to Emile, and he scampered over to collect it, looking meaningfully at Darien as he ate it.

"Where is my brother this fine morning?" he asked, settling himself into a chair.

"He just went out riding."

"A pleasant pastime."

"Yes, he just returned from doing business in London. He enjoys riding to clear his thoughts, I believe."

"Ah, yes. Always busy, isn't he?"

There it was again, that tone that indicated there was something more beneath the words. I was in no mood to play games with him. If there was something on his mind, he had better come out with it.

"Is there something I can do for you, Darien?" I asked.

He looked at me. "It's an interesting question."

I waited for him to say more.

"I had hoped to have an ally in you, but it seems Milo isn't the sort to be easily persuaded."

So he had overheard our conversation after all.

"He wants to protect the things that matter to him," I replied. I was angry with Milo, but that didn't mean I wouldn't come to his defense.

"Yes, I can see that. I suppose I've gone about things the wrong way," he said lightly, though I could sense a bit of uncertainty beneath the question. Was he asking me for advice?

"If you were hoping to win your newfound brother's approval, seducing a young woman under false pretenses and getting yourself caught up in a murder investigation wasn't precisely the way to go about it."

"I hadn't thought about approval initially," he admitted. "I've always done just exactly as I please."

Though it was a ridiculous remark, I couldn't hold back a smile. "You're very much alike in that respect."

"I don't imagine it's easy for either of us to make concessions."

"No," I agreed. I didn't want to discourage Darien, but I found it difficult to imagine that Milo was going to make any concessions at all.

"I always wanted a brother," he said. "When I was growing up, I mean. I asked my mother often if I might have a sibling—before I knew where siblings came from, of course. When I learned the particulars, I began to understand why she always looked so sad when I asked her. She never found anyone else after my father left."

"What was your mother like?" I asked, suddenly curious.

"She was lovely," he said. "The kindest woman you'd ever meet. I'm afraid I was something of a disappointment to her." He said this with a self-mocking smile, but it was there again, that flicker of vulnerability that made its way through the cracks in his countenance. His veneer was not yet quite as hardened as Milo's.

"I'm sure she saw your potential and knew you'd one day live up to it," I said.

He looked at me. I thought for a moment that he was going to make one of his sarcastic quips, avoiding the emotion that lay beneath the topic. But then he nodded.

"I suppose. We were fairly happy, all told," he said. "She did what she could to make life easy for me."

I imagined she had tried very hard. Darien seemed as though he was the sort of young man who had been given a great deal of latitude. Too much.

"What was his mother like?" Darien asked, shifting the subject back to Milo.

"He never knew her. She died when he was born."

"I didn't know that," he said.

I wondered if Mr. Ames had ever spoken to Darien's mother about his wife. Somehow, I doubted it. It seemed that her death had been something he had bottled up and hidden away.

Milo's father, Anthony Ames, had been a man who seemed to have lost his way in life along with his wife. I sometimes wished I had been able to meet him so that I might have had a better understanding of Milo.

There were few people I'd met who had known him, aside from Milo, and his side of the story was not exactly impartial.

"His life hasn't been all comfort and ease," I said. "It sounds like you had the advantage of him in one respect: a mother who loved you."

"Yes, I suppose you're right."

We sat in silence for a moment.

"Milo is much as I expected," Darien said at last. "But you're not how I thought you'd be."

I looked up at him. "Oh?"

"I'd seen pictures of you in the society columns, of course. Beautiful and glamorous and dressed to the nines. I thought you'd be a thorough snob. But you care about people. I can tell."

I didn't quite know how to respond to this assessment, the compliments mingled with insults.

"I suppose none of us are exactly what we might appear to be to outside observers," I said pointedly.

He took my meaning and smiled. "I'm afraid I'm as much of a cad as I seem to be."

"Are you?" I challenged him.

He studied me for just a moment. "What do you think?"

"I think you're a spoiled young man who would do better to use his considerable talents for good rather than going about getting into trouble."

He laughed. "You're a marvel, Amory. I wish I had met you before Milo did."

"Nonsense. I'm much too old for you." Even as I said it, I realized we were probably very close to the same age, Milo being five years older than me.

"I've always liked older women," he said. Good heavens, he was flirting with me. I knew it was an act of charity, given my condition, but it was naughty nonetheless.

"That will be enough of that," I replied. "You'd better go. I'm very busy."

He rose from the chair, a grin on his face. "If you ever decide to leave him, you could marry me. You wouldn't even have to change your surname."

The young man was thoroughly incorrigible.

I pointed at the door. "Out."

I heard him laughing as he exited the drawing room.

21

THOUGH HE HAD proved an amusing diversion, I had other things than Darien's outrageous behavior to worry about at the moment. Or even Milo and his off-putting surliness, for that matter.

There had been two deaths in the village, and the killer needed to be stopped before he killed again.

I went back to my sewing as I thought, my mind attempting to stitch together a row of facts as neat as the hem of the blanket.

It was just so strange. Bertie's manner of death spoke of passion, not of planning. But there was premeditated malice behind what had happened to Marena. Which individual might be responsible for both?

Imogen was the most likely suspect, I supposed. Despite what she had told me about her innocent meeting with Bertie, there was the possibility that their relationship had been more involved than she let on. Perhaps she had killed him, worried he would stand in the way of her winning Darien back. And then she might have killed Marena to clear the rest of the path. It seemed outlandish, but the reasons for murder were seldom logical.

The vicar and Mrs. Busby had both been displeased with Bertie and close to Marena. Was it possible that Bertie had discovered a secret about one of them and shared it with Marena, and either Mr. or Mrs. Busby had decided that they both had to be silenced?

I found it difficult to believe that either of them would have killed Marena in such a cruel way, especially after the death of their own daughter. But the fact remained that Mrs. Busby had purchased poison only three weeks ago. What had been her intention?

Lady Alma had also been there at the time of Marena's death. I wasn't sure why she would have wanted to kill Marena, except perhaps if she thought Bertie had shared something with her and she, too, needed to be silenced.

I just couldn't seem to wrap my head around what might have happened. What I needed was someone to talk things through with. Milo was clearly out of the question at the moment, which was disappointing. He was usually so useful at times like these.

An idea occurred to me. I might ring up my friend Detective Inspector Jones of Scotland Yard. If anyone could help me sort out these matters, it was him. Though we had met under less-than-ideal circumstances, we had formed a friendship that was, I thought, based on mutual respect. He didn't always approve of my interference into criminal matters, but he always took me seriously and offered excellent advice.

I went to the telephone, and, after a series of switchboard operators and secretaries, I was at last greeted by a familiar voice.

"D.I. Jones."

"Inspector Jones. It's Amory Ames," I said.

"Ah, Mrs. Ames! How are you?" There was geniality in his tone, but also a certain wariness. I could not blame him for this, as my contact with him usually meant there had been a murder. This time was no different.

"We've had a death here in our village," I said. "Two, actually."

"Have you indeed?" There wasn't the faintest hint of surprise in his tone. More like resignation.

I quickly explained the circumstances surrounding the murders, leaving out the bit about Darien's involvement for the moment. He listened quietly.

"It does sound like an interesting problem," he said noncommittally when I had finished.

"It's all so very strange. I don't know what to make of any of it. I feel as though I should have enough information before me to give me the answer, but the solution keeps evading me. I thought, perhaps, you might have some insight."

"Who's the inspector on the case?"

"His name is Wilson," I said. "He's perfectly competent, but he doesn't seem at all keen on sharing information or letting me involve myself in any way."

"Imagine that," Inspector Jones said dryly.

I ignored this bit of irony in his tone. As Milo did, Inspector Jones had frequently reminded me that the business of solving crimes was not really my concern. I had proven to him on more than one occasion, however, that sometimes an invested bystander could be instrumental in bringing a case to a close.

"I'm very much afraid the murderer might strike again before he's caught," I told him pointedly.

"Yes, we don't want that," Inspector Jones agreed. There was a slight pause. "You are taking care of yourself, Mrs. Ames? Not getting yourself into danger, are you?" The real question was there beneath the surface: Are you sticking your nose into places where it doesn't belong?

"Certainly not," I assured him. "I just thought . . . perhaps if I could discuss the case with you, something might come to light. Then perhaps you could mention it to Inspector Wilson. He would take it seriously coming from you."

Again, there was a pause as he seemed to consider the matter. I hoped he might have a few salient questions or offer an insightful remark that might give me a new avenue for thought. What he said, however, was even better than that.

"You're in Kent, aren't you?"

"Yes, Allingcross."

"It just so happens that I'm following up a lead in Maidstone this afternoon. If you'd like, I could stop in on my way back in this evening, and we could discuss things in more detail."

That was a bit of luck indeed. A chance to sit and talk the matter over with him face-to-face was more than I had hoped for. I felt, somehow, as if a weight had been lifted from my shoulders.

"Inspector Jones," I said, "nothing would delight me more."

AFTER A HEARTY lunch and a short nap, I decided I would return to the village. I needed a bit more information before Detective Inspector Jones arrived.

The time had come to visit the vicarage.

Truth be told, I was dreading the visit. Paying grief calls was never a pleasant pastime, and now that I was constantly tired and emotional, it was even less appealing. I knew, however, that it had to be done.

There were several cars outside when I arrived, as well as a stunning black mare tied to the gate. It seemed Mr. and Mrs. Busby had several visitors during their time of sorrow, Lady Alma among them. I realized now would not be the time for questions, but paying my respects was the least I could do.

I knocked at the door, which was opened by May, the maid. Her face was red as though she had been crying, and she sniffled repeatedly as she led me into the parlor.

Mrs. Busby looked up at me as I entered. She wore a black dress and looked as though she had aged years in the space of a day. "Amory, dear, it's so good of you to come."

"I'm so sorry, Mrs. Busby," I said, leaning down to embrace her.

"Thank you. It's been . . . rather like a nightmare. I feel as though I should awaken at any moment and find it isn't true."

"Hello, Mrs. Ames," the vicar said as he, too, approached me. His face, usually shining with good humor, was solemn and drawn.

"I'm so sorry for your loss, vicar," I said as he took my hand in his cool, damp ones. "I know Marena was very special to you."

"Yes, she was a wonderful girl," Mrs. Busby said. Her eyes filled with fresh tears, and she pressed a crumpled handkerchief to her face. The vicar patted her gently on the back. He was composed—force of habit from a long career dealing with loss, I supposed—but I could tell it was an effort.

"It has been very hard on us, I'm afraid," he said. "We looked on Marena almost as a daughter."

They both looked shattered. After their daughter Sara's death, they had weathered the storms of their grief with the help of their faith and the support of their parishioners. I hoped they could do the same with Marena's death.

"I'm so sorry," I said again. There was little else to be said in times like these, for I knew that no words of mine would be able to give them comfort. Not now. The grief was still too fresh and raw.

"There'll be no . . . arrangements made until after the inquest, of course," Mrs. Busby said. "But we will send word to Thornecrest."

"Thank you."

Another visitor had come in behind me, and they excused themselves and moved to greet her, the vicar maneuvering his wife's chair as though they were two parts of the same whole.

I nodded at the other visitors seated around the parlor, most of whom I knew. I was glad Mr. and Mrs. Busby had company. We could not ease their sorrow, perhaps, but I thought it helped to know they had the love and support of the village behind them.

I noticed there was a pot of tea on the table, but no one was drinking any of it. I couldn't say that I blamed them.

Glancing around at the faces of those gathered there, I saw that Marena's mother was not among the mourners. Had she decided to bear her grief alone? Or was there some other reason she hadn't come?

Lady Alma sat in a corner, staring into the middle distance, her mind clearly occupied. There was an empty chair next to her, and I moved toward it. She didn't notice me until I was nearly upon her.

"Oh. Hello, Mrs. Ames," she said, looking up at me.

"Lady Alma."

I sank carefully into the chair, glad for a moment of rest. I was uncommonly tired these past few days. "I see you rode here," I told her. "Is that Medusa tied up outside?"

She shook her head. "I wouldn't trust Medusa alone tied to a fence post. Besides, her leg is still on the mend. That was a nasty scratch."

"I hope she's all right?"

"Yes, she's coming along fine."

"I'm glad to hear it."

"I've been thinking," she said in a low voice.

I turned to look at her. "Oh?"

She glanced around the room. Everyone appeared to be in subdued conversation. There was little chance of our being overheard in this corner of the room, but she leaned closer and lowered her voice a bit more before she spoke.

"I got to wondering what Bertie might have discovered when he broke into the vicar's desk."

Lady Alma knew about that, did she? I wondered who else might have known that Bertie could potentially be in possession of village secrets.

"I suppose there's no way to know," I answered.

"There you're wrong," Lady Alma said. "I went in and had a look."

My brows rose. "When?"

"A few minutes ago. Excused myself and slipped in. You'd have thought he'd be more careful after finding Bertie in there, but it was still unlocked. I knew they were preoccupied and I'd have a chance to take a look."

I was shocked and a bit jealous that I hadn't had the idea myself.

"He still hadn't fixed the lock on the drawer?" I asked.

She shook her head. "You know he can be absentminded at times."

"What was in it?" I asked.

"Didn't seem to be much at first. Parish records. Births, marriages, deaths. That sort of thing."

I waited. The "at first" told me she was saving the best for last.

Her eyes met mine. "And the vicar's journal."

I looked sharply at her as she said this. Surely she hadn't read it. The proper society lady in me could think of few things more scandalous than reading a vicar's private journal without permission.

"I flipped through it," she said in a low voice. "Too much to read it all at once, of course. Besides, his handwriting is abominable. But when I was looking, a sheet of paper fell out. It was a banking notice."

"Oh?" I was thoroughly invested in her story now.

"His account balance is . . . quite high. It seems he's made several large deposits as of late." She raised her eyebrows meaningfully.

"What are you saying?" I asked in a whisper.

She shrugged. "Nothing in particular. Only that that money must be coming from somewhere. One can't help but wonder where."

AFTER WHAT I felt was an appropriate length of time, I left the house, trying to shake some of the heaviness of grief off me. Grief and suspicion. It was all so very sad and upsetting.

Surely there were any number of reasons why the vicar might recently have added a good deal of money to his bank account. I could think of very few, however. Unless he was embezzling from the church.

I didn't like to believe such a thing of Mr. Busby. In fact, I found it almost impossible to believe. But it did lead to more questions.

If, for example, he had been taking money from the church, was it possible Bertie had found out? If so, perhaps the envelope he had given Bertie was meant as a blackmail payment. Was that how Bertie had been able to afford his new horse?

And what of Mrs. Busby? Had she known about it? Would she have been willing to kill to protect her husband?

I felt the heaviness of sadness and suspicion weighing on me. I desperately needed someone to talk to. I would be glad when Inspector Jones arrived.

It occurred to me then there might be another untapped source of information nearby: the proprietress of the rooming house where Imogen was staying, Mrs. Ursula Cotton.

She was what could most kindly be described as the village gossip. There was nothing the woman did not know. I had always wondered how it was that she managed to maintain a comprehensive catalog of all the indiscretions committed within a five-village radius of her comfortable cottage. I supposed having a rooming house helped. There were always people happy to chat about what was happening in their own lives.

In the past, I had tried to avoid Mrs. Cotton, mainly because my own life had been fodder for gossip among the villagers for years. Milo had never been at all concerned with appearances, and his behavior over the years had provided more than enough speculation for even the most gluttonous of county scandalmongers.

I debated, as I made my way to her rooming house, what might be the best means of approaching her on the subject of the murders. The more I considered it, however, the more I came to realize that she would no doubt be immediately suspicious upon my arrival. She would have heard of Bertie's death, of Darien's arrival and his connection to our family, and of Marena's murder.

Moreover, she was no doubt familiar with my forays into the world of detection. My appearance at the scenes of several different murder investigations had been the stuff of much speculation among residents of the village. Not that I could help it that people happened to be murdered in my vicinity. As Milo had pointed out, murders happened all the time. In the course of our extensive travels, we were bound to encounter some of them.

Of course, this murder had not happened on our travels. It had happened on our doorstep. And Milo's brother had been a suspected culprit.

All of this led me to believe that the best way to approach Mrs. Cotton would be directly. She would know I had come to learn something, and somehow I doubted she would oblige me freely. As with my old friend Yvonne Roland, notorious telltale and perpetual widow, I would be most successful if I came with an offering of information.

I would need to give gossip in order to receive it.

While I debated what I could tell her without giving away too much of my private family affairs, I hoped that she would be more in the mood for talking than listening.

The door was opened by the maid, who led me to a comfortable parlor. The furniture was all hung with colorful knitted throws. There was a cheerful fire crackling in the grate, chasing away the afternoon coolness, and a bouquet of bright flowers sat on a table near the window.

I took a seat in one of a pair of emerald-green chairs, and a moment later Mrs. Cotton made her appearance.

There was something very fitting about her name, I had always thought. She was small and pale with a halo of fluffy white hair that reminded one of a ball of cotton. Her cheeks were pink, however, and her brown eyes were warm and cheerful. If one looked closely enough, one could also see the sparkle of mischief in them.

"Well, Mrs. Ames. Welcome," she said as she came into the room. "I must say, I'm not entirely surprised to see you here."

"Yes, I've been stopping by frequently as of late. I'm acquainted with Imogen Prescott."

"That's not what I mean, my dear."

So I had been correct in my assumption that she knew I would be asking for information. I was glad that my own instincts had been correct. And perhaps it was better this way. After all, we understood each other.

"Would you like some tea, dear?" she asked as she took the seat across from me. A white cat, who had apparently been lurking beneath the chair, jumped immediately onto her lap, and she began to stroke it gently.

"That would be very nice, thank you."

"I thought you might think so. I've told Sarah to put the kettle on."

She seemed to be in the habit of anticipating my wishes, and so I knew I would have to tread carefully. Despite her rather innocuous appearance, I knew there was a sharp brain behind those kind smiles.

"I suppose you've come to talk about the murders," she said, not bothering with any of the normal social pleasantries.

I smiled. "I did think perhaps you might have heard something about it."

"I've heard your husband's brother is suspected of Bertie's death."

One could not accuse Mrs. Cotton of being indirect. I suspected this was one of her means of gathering information. People often gave away more than they meant to when they were caught off guard. Fortunately, I had been in such situations too often to easily lose my poise.

"It's all a misunderstanding," I said. "The police have let him go now. He'll be proven innocent in no time, I'm sure."

She offered a skeptical yet sympathetic smile. "Perhaps. One never knows, though, does one? After all, you know very little of the boy's upbringing. Your husband had every advantage and turned out rather wild. One wonders what his brother might be capable of."

There was nothing malicious in the comment. She wasn't saying anything that people hadn't said for years. Indeed, it wasn't anything that wasn't true. Milo had always had the best of everything, and he had still run riot for much of his life. Perhaps it was the advantages that had been part of the problem.

However, I had not come here to discuss my husband's past escapades. I really wanted to know what Mrs. Cotton knew about other potential suspects. If anyone knew of hidden motives and secret agendas, it was sure to be she.

"Darien was in prison when Marena was killed, and it stands to reason that both murders were committed by the same person. If it wasn't Darien, then who do you think it might have been?"

"The weather's been lovely for this time of year, don't you think?" she asked abruptly.

This change of subject surprised me momentarily, but then Sarah, the maid, came in with the tea tray, and I understood that Mrs. Cotton had heard her approaching. It seemed the lady did not like to share her gossip with the domestic staff.

"Yes, I agree. I've been pleasantly surprised."

"Have you chosen a name for the baby?" she asked, changing the subject again when we had settled down with our tea. The china was floral-printed Wedgwood.

It did cross my mind momentarily that the tea might not be safe to drink, but Mrs. Cotton had had no involvement with the murders. What was more, she drank heartily from her cup and suffered no ill effects. I supposed it was safe to drink from mine, which had been poured directly from the same pot.

I took a sip. "Not yet, no. We've several ideas but haven't settled on anything."

"Flower names are always lovely for girls."

"Yes. There are a great many nice ones."

"I myself have always been fond of the name Octavius for a boy. It's a very strong name."

"It is indeed."

The maid left and closed the door, and Mrs. Cotton set her cup in its saucer with a delicate clink.

"Lady Alma had a temper in her younger days," she said without preamble. "It comes from being raised with all those brothers, I suppose, but she wasn't above coming to blows with those she disagreed with."

I wasn't entirely surprised by this revelation. Lady Alma had something of a domineering personality, and I could picture her reinforcing it with fisticuffs in her youth.

"Yes," Mrs. Cotton went on, "she once beat a stable boy for causing harm to one of her horses. Went at him with her crop, I believe. In the end, she had to pay for doctor's bills and a bit extra to hush things up. You can't really keep things quiet, of course. The story followed her here. But she's been the model of propriety ever since she came to Allingcross. Breeding her horses and founding the Springtide Festival. It seems one can outgrow such violent behaviors in time. Don't you think?" She looked at me over her teacup.

I knew what she was insinuating, that Lady Alma's temper might have got the better of her again with Bertie. She had been so fond of

Bertie, though. Was there anything that might have induced her rage to that extent?

A scenario occurred to me. Perhaps Bertie had been working with Medusa, and perhaps he, and not the killer, had been responsible for the cut on her leg. Lady Alma might have discovered it and flown into a rage and then been forced to try to cover what she had done.

I supposed it was possible. Anything was possible, really.

"I know she's very fond of her new horse, Medusa. If Bertie had injured her in some way . . ." I said, thinking aloud.

"Ah, yes. Her horse. I heard she's been boasting it was sired by a famous racehorse."

I nodded.

"It makes one wonder why she keeps everyone so far from the horse."

"What do you mean?" I asked, suddenly alert.

She adjusted her shawl. "I've just heard talk that she's the only one allowed to work with it. Almost as though she doesn't want anyone to get a good look at it?"

"Why wouldn't she?"

"I don't know. That's the question, I suppose."

"Even supposing she did kill Bertie for some reason, it wouldn't account for Marena's murder."

Mrs. Cotton nodded thoughtfully. "Yes, that is a bit tricky."

I had never seen any particular interactions between Lady Alma and Marena. They had been casual friends at best. I could think of no reason why she would have resorted to murder. Unless perhaps Marena had had suspicions about Bertie's death.

She had, after all, been nearby around the time of his murder. Perhaps she had seen something and had confronted Lady Alma. It was a stretch, but it was something to consider.

"What about Marena's mother?" I asked.

Mrs. Cotton's face darkened. "Jane Hodges has always been a dour, unpleasant woman. Even before her husband was sent away."

I stared at her. "What do you mean?"

"He died in prison, you know. He killed a man in a pub brawl. Well, rather, he got in an altercation and waited for the man outside. Beat him to death."

"No," I said. "I didn't know."

"Few people do, I suppose. It happened in London, and when Jane Hodges returned to Allingcross, she never mentioned it again. She changed her name back to her maiden name, and Marena's with it, but no one asked any questions. Assumed he had run off with a nicer girl, perhaps. I heard of it in a roundabout way some years after, but I kept it to myself, for Marena's sake."

"Marena didn't know either?"

She shook her head. "She was a wee thing at the time. I used to call her Jane's dumbledor, a little bumblebee always buzzing about. She looked just like her father, though. He was a handsome man."

So that explained Mrs. Hodges's bitterness toward her daughter. She had always reminded her of the poor choices she, a woman so unforgiving of others, had made. And perhaps Marena had also reminded her of what she had lost. Just the way Milo's father had been reminded of his wife whenever he looked at his son.

"I always wondered about the accident," Mrs. Cotton said, drawing me back to the present.

I frowned, confused. "What accident?"

"The accident that killed Sara Busby."

I was even more confused now. "What has that to do with Lady Alma?"

"Nothing. My mind just wandered, I suppose." She shook her head, tutting gently. "That accident was a very bad business. Tragic."

I wondered if Mrs. Cotton was, perhaps, losing a bit of her edge. One didn't like to judge an elderly lady by her appearance—indeed, it was often fatal to do so—but her mind did seem to wander.

"Yes, very sad," I agreed. "I didn't know the Busbys at the time, of course, but I imagine it was heartbreaking for them."

"They both adored Sara," she said. "Their pride and joy, she was. I worried for a while that they would never overcome it. The vicar, perhaps. He's always been strong of faith. But Mrs. Busby loved that girl, and I've always thought . . ." She paused.

"Yes?" I felt suddenly as though I was going to learn something important and found myself leaning forward slightly in my chair. The baby registered its disapproval of my change of position with a sharp kick beneath my ribs, and I sat back.

"I shouldn't say such things, I suppose . . ." Mrs. Cotton said.

I had found that, with village gossips, these half-hearted protests were usually used to preface interesting but totally unfounded speculations. This case was no different.

"There was something more to that accident than met the eye."

"What do you mean?" I asked.

"I don't know. In fact, I know almost nothing about what happened. That's what was curious," she said. "There was so little said about it. Usually there is talk, but there was nothing. Mrs. Busby was driving and went off the road. Sara was killed and Mrs. Busby paralyzed. And that was it."

"Perhaps there was nothing more to be said. It might have been as straightforward as that."

"Perhaps," she said, but the word was heavy with skepticism.

I understood what she was telling me. "You think something else happened, something that only Mrs. Busby and Marena lived to tell about."

"I don't know. I just find it curious." She took a sip of her tea.

I considered the possibility. What sort of secret might have been worth keeping? Sara Busby was dead; was there anything greater than that they might have had to hide? It just didn't seem to make sense.

"Have you been to the vicarage?" I asked, taking up her strategy of shifting the topic to see what might come of it.

She pulled her shawl a little more tightly around her. "No, not yet. I don't get around as easily as I used to."

"I'm very sorry for the Busbys. Marena had been almost like a second daughter to them, and I know this loss has hit them very hard."

"Some people, it seems, attract tragedy to them."

I looked at her. "What do you mean?"

She shrugged. "Some people have a great many sad things happen to them, unexplained things. Some may think it fate, some the will of God, and some may think that there's no smoke without a fire."

I took my leave not much later. As I left the little cottage, I recanted my uncharitable thoughts about Mrs. Cotton's age; she was sharper than I had given her credit for being. Sharper, perhaps, than I was.

I RETURNED HOME. Tired but too on edge to rest, I went into the nursery. I had found myself coming to this room more and more often now that the baby was soon to arrive. I liked to stand in the warm, sunny space and think about what it would be like when its tiny resident had made his appearance.

The room had been Milo's nursery as a child. It was a large room with windows that looked out over the eastern side of the property where a small lake in the distance glinted in the afternoon sunlight. Milo had sailed his toy boats on that lake as a child.

The room had been decorated in white, with accents in shades of yellow and pale blue. I'd had someone in to paper and paint, and the cradle, curtains, and most linens were new. I liked the idea of our child having a fresh start in life. There were several items, however, that remained from Milo's tenure here: the rocking horse in one corner, a shelf of well-read books of adventure stories, a stack of colorful blocks.

Milo's mother had chosen those things for him. She had died shortly after giving birth, and it was sad to think that she had never had the chance to hold her child in her arms here. I had often wondered how Milo's life—his very personality—might have been different had he not been deprived of a mother. Of course, the what-ifs would do no good. Milo would not have been the same person if his family history had been altered. Nevertheless, I wished he could have known her, that I could have known her. I wished she could have met our child.

I didn't hear him come in, but somehow I knew when he was standing at the doorway. I didn't turn from where I was folding a blanket to place in the linen cupboard.

"That was a long ride," I said.

"Yes, I suppose it was."

Silence fell between us as he came into the room. I put the blanket into the cupboard and turned to face him.

Milo was looking around the room. "I haven't been here in more than twenty years."

"There are a lot of memories, I suppose."

He nodded. "Madame Nanette used to read to me on that window seat," he said, indicating the cushion set into the window. "I always liked it best in winter, with a fire crackling in the grate. When it was cold, I would draw little shapes in the frost on the glass to match the stories she was reading."

I smiled. It was such a whimsical recollection. It was hard for me to imagine sometimes, that Milo had once been a cheerful, boisterous boy. He was always so very poised, so completely in command of himself. I had never seen any hint of vulnerability in him, any trace that anything that happened made much difference to him one way or the other.

Oh, he was happy we had a baby on the way. He was excited that he was going to be a father. Yet, even in that, there was something very restrained.

"You have good memories of Madame Nanette."

"Yes. It wasn't a bad childhood, all told."

We were both silent for a moment, each of us lost in our own thoughts. I was glad that we could be civil toward each other, glad that he had sought me out rather than avoiding me.

It was then I noticed the trunk tucked away in the corner, the one

Winnelda had brought down from the attic. It was dotted with cobwebs, though she had made a good show of trying to clean it off.

"Do you know what's in this trunk?" I asked Milo as I made my way toward it.

He glanced at it. "I haven't any idea. Where did you find it?"

"It was in the attic near some of the old nursery furniture."

He shrugged. "I haven't been up there in years."

My curiosity increased.

I moved to the trunk and unfastened the clasps. Raising the lid, I found several items wrapped in cloth. I removed the first. It was a photograph in a silver frame. The subject was a beautiful woman. Her shiny dark hair was piled high on her head in the Edwardian style, and she was wearing a high-necked lace collar with a cameo attached. She had blue eyes, a fact that was clear even in the faded sepia coloring of the photograph. There was something elegant about her, and I knew at once that this must be Milo's mother.

I had never seen her photograph before now. There was a very good painting of her in the family portrait gallery, but Milo had mentioned to me once that his father had put away almost every reminder of the wife he had lost.

I had seen photographs of Milo's father, for the elder Mr. Ames had often been in the society columns, though not for the same scandalous reasons as Milo. He had been a striking man with handsome, symmetrical features he had passed on to both his sons. And he'd had a dimple in one cheek, like Darien. I had always assumed that Milo took after his father, but seeing a picture of his mother made me realize how much he looked like her as well.

It occurred to me that Milo may never have seen a photograph of his mother either.

"I . . . I think this is your mother," I said, handing it to him.

He took the photograph and examined it. I watched his face, but whatever he was feeling he didn't reveal.

"I never understood my father," he said at last. "We never saw eye to eye about anything. But now, with you facing what killed my mother, I understand him a bit better. I thought about it as I rode today: they were in the same position in which we are now, anticipating a child and their future happiness. It must have been a great shock to him when she died."

"Yes," I agreed softly.

His eyes came up to meet mine. "And it occurred to me that I could lose you as he lost her."

My heart clenched at these words. Though his tone was perfectly composed, some unguarded emotion had flashed momentarily across his eyes, and I felt a surge of love for him. He didn't often express himself in sentimental terms, but there were moments like these when I knew with absolute certainty how much he cared for me.

"Nothing's going to happen," I assured him quickly. "The doctor says everything is going very well. And medicine has advanced a good deal in the last thirty-three years."

"I know," he said. "I'm quite confident that everything will be fine. It just . . . occurred to me."

I reached out and caught his hand and squeezed it, and he brought my hand to his lips for a brief kiss.

"What else is in the trunk?" he asked then, the brief moment he had let his guard down passed.

I turned back and carefully lowered myself to the floor so I could reach farther into the trunk. How difficult it was to move freely with a large round object attached to one.

I removed the next item. It was a stack of letters, the envelopes yellowed from their time in the trunk. I looked at the writing on the outside. "Letters from your father to your mother. Love letters, I suppose."

There were a great many of them. Knowing what I did about Milo's father, I found it difficult to imagine him penning effusive words of love, but I suspected he had been a different sort of person before the loss of his wife.

Milo didn't reach out to take the letters from me, so I set them on the floor beside the trunk, pulling out the next wrapped item. It was a stack of five leather books, the covers embossed with the initials D.A. Dora Ames.

I flipped one open to find an elegant hand across the pages. A few lines told me what they were. "These are her journals," I said softly.

I closed it, not wanting to read them before Milo had the chance. He deserved to be the first to learn something about his mother. I was glad that we had found them, that he would get to hear something of her voice after all.

There was one more item in the bottom of the trunk, fabric of some sort beneath the wrapping.

I pushed the wrapping aside and saw a sea of white. I knew immediately what it must be.

"Her wedding gown," I breathed.

I carefully lifted it out of the trunk. It was a stunning creation of satin and lace, with puffed sleeves and an off-the-shoulder bodice. I could imagine how beautiful she must have looked in it, but I didn't have to. As I pulled the skirts of the gown, yards and yards of gleaming fabric, from the trunk, a second photograph fluttered to the floor.

Milo reached to pick it up and handed it to me. It was a photo of their wedding day. I studied it. Milo's parents stood side by side, dressed in their finest. They both looked so young, and, despite the stiffness of their poses, I saw the unmistakable brightness of happiness in their eyes.

I felt a fresh pang of sadness that her joy had been short-lived, and I wished again that she was here to meet our child. A thought occurred to me. "What would you think if we took a bit of the train and made a christening gown for the baby? I think it could easily be done without destroying the gown."

"I think it's an excellent idea, my love."

I carefully folded the wedding gown and put it back in the trunk with the other items. I would see about making the christening gown soon, once things were a bit more settled.

"That was rather like discovering a treasure chest," I said as Milo helped me to my feet and I brushed the dust off of my hands.

"I'm surprised my father kept these things," Milo said. "I thought he'd disposed of everything that belonged to her."

"It seems he couldn't bring himself to part with her most cherished items."

Something else occurred to me. "I suppose that was the reason your father left Darien's mother before she gave birth to him. He wanted to sever the connection on his own terms, before he could lose another woman he cared for."

"But she didn't die. They might have been happy together. It was a selfish and cowardly thing to do."

"Yes," I agreed. "He ought to have married her. Or at least provided for her."

"I always wanted a brother when I was a child," Milo said, unconsciously repeating what Darien had told me. "I suppose it was an ally I really wanted."

I felt a little pang of sadness for the loneliness of his childhood. I was lucky enough to have had my cousin Laurel as a friend and confidante growing up. Milo had not had any such luxury. It was no wonder he was often so vexingly aloof.

"Perhaps your wish has come true," I suggested.

"I'm an adult now, darling," he said. "Wishes are nonsense, and I no longer have need of an ally."

"That doesn't change the facts, Milo. Darien is still your brother," I said gently. "And he *is* in need of an ally."

Milo sighed. "It would've been better for everyone concerned if he'd never come here," he said.

"But aren't you glad that you've had the chance to meet your brother?"

"A brother who may be a murderer?" he asked. "I think, given the option, I'd just as soon have never known."

"I don't think he did it," I said. "I truly don't."

He studied me. "I suppose you have someone else in mind."

I hesitated. I knew he wouldn't like it if I told him I had been investigating. I supposed, however, that he already suspected as much.

At last I gave a sigh of defeat. "I have a few suspects, but there are so many loose ends. I haven't the faintest idea who they all lead back to."

"But you're confident it isn't Darien." There was skepticism in his voice.

"I just don't think he had sufficient reason."

"My beautiful darling, always the optimist."

"Why don't you give him a chance, Milo? You may find out that you have more in common with him than you think."

"Then you're still bound and determined to find out who did it and prove his innocence."

I knew he wasn't going to be at all pleased at what I had to say next, but there was nothing to be done about it. "You may as well know. Inspector Jones is coming here this evening to talk things over with me."

"Delightful. I'll be glad to see the old boy again." He didn't mean a word of it, of course, and he knew that I knew it.

"He's got business in Maidstone. It's just a social call."

He waved aside my explanations, something like resignation in his tone. "You needn't make excuses to me, darling. Since when have I ever had any power to stop you?"

"Would you stop me if you could?" I asked, curious.

A smile tugged at the corner of his mouth. "It's a tempting prospect, to be sure. But you wouldn't be my Amory if you were compliant and incurious."

I stepped closer to him and slid my arms over his shoulders, looking up at him. "And you wouldn't be my Milo if you didn't say the sweetest things to disarm me when I feel as though I ought to be cross with you."

His arms went around me. "It seems we shall both just have to make the best of it."

"I suppose you're right."

He leaned to kiss me, and I felt a sense of immense relief.

With Milo on my side rather than serving as a distraction, we could find out who had killed Bertie Phipps and Marena Hodges.

24

We assembled in the drawing room after a subdued dinner. Darien had been on his best behavior. We all had, I supposed, none of us wanting to say too much in front of the servants.

Brushing aside Milo's offer to collect my knitting for me, I went to the morning room. My back was aching from sitting too long in the uncomfortable dining room chairs, and I was glad for a chance to stretch my legs.

I returned to the drawing room and stopped outside the door, curious to see how Milo and Darien might interact without my presence as a cushion between their rougher edges. I was glad to hear them conversing very civilly. There had been a sharpness in both of their voices in most of their earlier conversations. Even at dinner they had been polite, nothing more. So I was glad to hear that there was an easiness to the tenor of their conversation.

I stepped into the drawing room. They were sitting at a table, cards spread out before them, both of them smoking cigarettes, drinks on the table.

They were too absorbed with their card game to notice me, and I stood in the doorway for a moment watching them.

Milo was relaxed at the moment, comfortable in his role of host. He was sitting back easily in his chair.

Darien seemed to be enjoying himself, too. There was an expression of genuine amusement on his face as Milo made a wry remark, and he swore good-naturedly as Milo put down a winning card.

I was glad they had found a moment when they weren't at each other's throats.

Milo, in that way he had of sensing when I was nearby, looked up.

"There you are, darling," he said.

The two of them started to rise from their chairs, but I waved them back. "Don't get up, please."

"Would you care to play a hand?" Darien asked. "Milo's just trounced me."

I smiled. "I don't think so, but thank you."

I moved to a chair near the fire and picked up my knitting.

"We're discussing the murders," Darien said.

I stilled, forcing myself not to glance at Milo. I might have known that there were ulterior motives behind this friendly game of cards with his brother.

"Oh?" I asked.

"Yes, we've theories on who might have done it."

I couldn't help but notice the "we." Though Darien might believe they were now on steady ground, I knew better. Milo, despite his show of sentiment in the nursery today, was not ready to accept his brother with open arms. I only hoped Darien realized it before he became too invested in forming some sort of relationship.

"And who have you decided upon?" I asked lightly.

"My money's on the vicar," Darien said. "Perhaps he was secretly in love with Marena. He killed Phipps to get him out of the way and then killed Marena when she wouldn't give in to his advances."

I tried to picture Mr. Busby as the lecherous bounder, in love with the girl who had been almost a daughter to him, and failed. It just didn't fit. The whole idea made me feel vaguely sick to my stomach.

"Inspector Jones has arrived," Grimes said, interrupting these unpleasant thoughts.

"Oh, yes. Show him in, Grimes," I said.

Darien's brows rose. "The police have come again, eh?"

"Inspector Jones is a friend of mine," I told him.

"Police friends. How very bourgeois of you."

A moment later the inspector came into the room. He looked exactly the same as the last time I had seen him. There was something cheering in the fact that he always looked just as one expected him to.

I rose from my seat to greet him, stretching out a hand as he came forward. "Hello, Inspector."

"Mrs. Ames," he said as he took my hand in his. "How lovely to see you. You're looking well."

My free hand went to my stomach. "I suppose one needn't be a detective to notice that I'm going to have a baby."

"Allow me to offer you my heartiest congratulations," he said. "Children are one of life's greatest rewards."

I smiled. "I'm very much looking forward to motherhood. How are your wife and daughters?"

"Very well, thank you. My eldest is soon to be wed."

"How wonderful."

"Her mother seems to regard it as a tragedy," he said with a smile. He turned then to Milo, who had risen from his seat but not made any effort to come and greet the inspector.

"Mr. Ames," he said. "It's nice to see you again."

"And you, Inspector," Milo replied. "Welcome to Thornecrest."

Milo and Inspector Jones had never regarded each other very warmly. Indeed, there had been a time when Inspector Jones had suspected Milo of a murder. Their relationship had thawed a bit since that point, however, and they both pretended to be friendly when the occasion called for it.

The inspector's eyes moved then to Darien. He was always adept at concealing his thoughts, but I saw the interest in his expression as he noticed Darien's resemblance to Milo.

"And this is my husband's brother, Darien Ames," I said. "We've only just recently met him. Darien, this is Detective Inspector Jones of Scotland Yard."

"Scotland Yard!" Darien gave a low whistle. "Brought in the real professionals, have you, Amory?"

Inspector Jones gave him a mild smile. "This is just a social call."

"Ah. Well, then I'll just give you all the chance to catch up, shall I?" It was clear that Darien had no intention of spending the evening chatting with the police, friend or no. "Nice to have met you, Inspector."

"And you, Mr. Ames."

Darien walked unhurriedly from the room.

"If you'll excuse me for just a moment," Milo said. "I need to have a word with my brother."

He followed him out, and Inspector Jones and I were alone.

The inspector turned back to me, his brows raised ever so slightly. "Another one, eh?"

"I'm afraid so," I said with a laughing sigh. Inspector Jones had a way with words. I realized that *another one* was precisely the way I had felt about having a second Milo dropped on my doorstep.

"Milo's father had a . . . dalliance that resulted in Darien. Darien only just discovered he had a half brother and came looking for Milo."

"I see."

I decided I might as well come out with the truth of it now. "What I didn't mention on the phone is that Darien was arrested for the crime."

"Ah." He said this with perfect equanimity, as though he had been waiting for some revelation from me and was glad to have it at last. As for myself, I felt again the sense of calm that always resulted when I knew Inspector Jones was on the case. He was so very competent, so thoughtful and slow to judgment.

"It's all been rather trying, especially at this particular time, with the baby soon to arrive."

"Yes, I can well imagine."

"Please sit down, won't you?" I said, realizing I had been remiss in my duties as hostess. "Would you care for some coffee?"

"That would be very nice. Thank you."

I turned to the tray of coffee things Grimes had brought into the drawing room after dinner. "Did you have a successful trip to Maidstone?"

"I'm one step closer to catching a ring of counterfeiters, so I believe it was successful, yes."

"I'm glad to hear it." I poured him a cup of coffee from the silver pot. "You prefer yours black, if I remember right?"

"Yes. Thank you. You have a lovely home," he said, looking around. "A bit roomier than your London flat."

I laughed at this bit of understatement. "Yes, Thornecrest has been in Milo's family for ages. His father made many updates in his time. We've been here the last few months, preparing for the baby. Milo thought to keep me away from trouble here."

Inspector Jones smiled. "And yet it found you."

"I'm afraid so, much to Milo's chagrin. You see, he's not particularly keen on my involvement . . . given my condition."

"A natural concern on his part," Inspector Jones said neutrally.

"Yes, of course. But Darien is his brother. I couldn't stand idly by and do nothing."

"The local police aren't performing to your satisfaction?"

"Inspector Wilson is a good enough sort of fellow, but he lacks imagination."

"Which Amory, of course, possesses in spades," Milo said, coming back into the room just in time to make this irritating observation.

I frowned at him and continued speaking to the inspector. "There's something about all of this that doesn't fit, something that doesn't make sense. I feel that if I could only put my finger on it then everything would fall into place."

Inspector Jones took a sip of his coffee. "Why don't you give me the details."

I had given him a brief summation on the telephone, but now I explained the deaths in more detail, outlining the theories I had surrounding each of the suspects.

"The vicar and his wife were at odds with Bertie Phipps," I said. "He had been seen going through the vicar's private correspondence, and it has come to my attention that the vicar had been receiving and then withdrawing large amounts of money from his accounts."

"How do you know that?" Milo cut in.

"I didn't go snooping through his desk drawers, if that's what you're insinuating," I said archly.

"I'm not insinuating it. I'm assuming it."

"Well, you assume incorrectly," I said. "Lady Alma was the one who had a look at the drawer with the broken lock. It hadn't even occurred to me."

"I'm astonished you didn't think of it first."

Inspector Jones cleared his throat gently, setting us back on course in the way a schoolmaster might correct bickering students.

"Mrs. Busby couldn't have killed Bertie," I said. "At least, I don't see any way it would have been possible with her wheelchair. She can wheel herself, of course, but to kill Bertie in the middle of the field and return to the festival without being missed or seen by anyone seems impossible. But she did buy poison at the apothecary shop."

Milo's brows rose at this revelation, but I didn't dignify this reaction with a response. Mostly because I had indeed been snooping in that particular case.

"Do you suppose they might have committed the murders together?" I suggested. "Perhaps the vicar killed Bertie because of something that he knew, something he might have shared with Marena. Perhaps it was necessary that Marena be killed, too."

I recalled suddenly that I had mentioned to the vicar the possibility Marena might know something, shortly before Marena had been killed. Was it possible my comment had been the impetus for murder? The thought made me ill.

"When was the poison purchased?" Inspector Jones asked.

"A few weeks ago," I said, realizing with relief it could not have been bought for the express purpose of silencing Marena before I could ask her questions. "And anyway, wouldn't it have been easier for the vicar to be the one to purchase it? Nothing is easy for Mrs. Busby in her chair."

"What of this Lady Alma you mentioned?" Inspector Jones asked.

I told him of Lady Alma and the provenance of Bedford Priory.

"And she is on your list of suspects."

"She has a temper and cares for nothing but her horses. Medusa, the pride of her stables, was injured, and I did wonder if Bertie might have had a hand in it. She may have killed him in anger."

"And why might she have wanted to kill Miss Hodges?"

"Marena was in the field the day that Bertie died. She might have seen something."

"Wouldn't she have gone directly to the police?"

I considered this. Marena had cared for Bertie a great deal, but I knew there had always been a bit of the mercenary in her. Was it possible she might have tried to blackmail Lady Alma?

"I . . . don't know," I said at last. "I would think so, but there is always the possibility that she might have been uncertain or only suspected it. Perhaps she even mentioned as much to Lady Alma, hoping to be proven wrong. And then Lady Alma felt that she had to be disposed of."

It felt wrong, somehow, discussing all these people I had known and liked for years as potential suspects. It was one thing to involve myself in murders where the majority of the suspects were strangers or distant acquaintances; it was quite another to have to suspect the people who I greeted in the streets and sat next to in a pew at church. I didn't want to believe that any of them was capable of something like this.

And so I seized upon the one person who I would not mind terribly being the culprit. "There's Marena's mother, of course."

Inspector Jones looked vaguely intrigued. "You think she might have killed her daughter?"

"There was something . . . off in their relationship," I said. "I could never quite put my finger on why it was they didn't care for each other, but they certainly didn't. Not in the way mothers and daughters usually do."

"But why might she have killed Bertie Phipps?" he asked.

"Bertie apparently told Lady Alma that he knew something about Mrs. Hodges, a secret he seemed troubled about. She might have killed him to silence him."

"What sort of secret?"

I sighed. "As to that, I don't know."

"And does that conclude your list of suspects?"

"There's also Imogen Prescott," I said. "She's in love with Darien, so that would account for her killing Marena, her rival. But she also knew Bertie from London and wanted to hide the fact that her past wasn't exactly what she claimed it was."

Milo didn't know this bit either, so I related my conversation with Imogen to him. It would have been so much easier if he had been my partner in all of this from the beginning, rather than stubbornly clinging to the possibility that Darien was the culprit.

It seemed that even now he had not completely dismissed the idea, however, for he added, "And there's always the possibility that Darien might have done it." He had been so nice and quiet for most of the conversation; I wished he would have stayed that way.

Inspector Jones turned to him. "You don't discount the possibility that he might be involved?"

"Not at all," Milo said. "In fact, I haven't trusted him from the beginning."

"He isn't exactly trustworthy, perhaps," I said. "But that doesn't mean that he's a killer."

"No," Inspector Jones agreed. "After all, a great many men of bad reputation have been cleared of murder in our time."

Milo's eyes glinted at the reminder, but he surprised me by saying nothing.

"What, then, is your conclusion, Inspector?" I asked. "Has anything

I've told you struck a chord? I feel that perhaps I'm too close to things, that perhaps I'm not seeing the big picture as I ought to."

He took a moment to consider. "It seems important to discover how the poison was administered and what type of poison it was," he said at last. "If it was the cyanide salts you discovered Mrs. Busby purchased, you may have an added reason for suspicion. And it occurs to me that you may want to speak to the mother."

"Mrs. Hodges?"

"Yes. I think she may know more than she lets on about who might have wanted to kill her daughter."

"What if she did it?" I asked.

He gave me the barest hint of a smile. "Then that is likely to reveal itself as well. If she did kill Marena, why would she have killed Bertie Phipps? Start at the end and work back to the beginning. It may give you fresh ideas."

He glanced then at his wristwatch. "This has all been very interesting, but I'm afraid I must catch my train."

"Of course," I said, rising from my seat. He and Milo followed suit.

"Do feel free to ring me again if you need to discuss anything else. And I should like very much to hear how things turn out."

I nodded. "Of course."

"It's been very nice to see you," he said. "I wish you both much happiness on the arrival of the baby."

"Thank you," Milo and I said.

Inspector Jones had just reached the door when one more thought occurred to me. "Inspector?"

He turned.

"Milo and I are having difficulties selecting potential names for the baby. It seems strange to me that I've never asked. What's your given name?"

"Sebastian," he said.

I never would have guessed it. I would have pictured him as more of a John or a William, something as straightforward and unobtrusive as he was. Now that he said it, however, I could see that the more ostentatious name suited him.

"It's a very nice name," I said.

He gave a wry smile. "My mother was quite a fan of Shakespeare. But I got the best of it. My brothers are called Romeo and Othello."

I BREAKFASTED ALONE the next morning, as Milo and Darien were both still abed. I was glad, for I didn't particularly want to deal with either of them this morning, let alone the two in combination.

I wasn't feeling particularly well. I had been uncomfortable for most of the night and slept fitfully. My back ached, and I felt vaguely nauseated, a sensation that did not entirely diminish even after I forced myself to eat and drink some tea.

Despite my discomfort, I hadn't given up on working to solve the murders. Inspector Jones had given me an idea. I needed to speak to Mrs. Hodges. I felt certain that she would be able to provide insight into Marena's death. Perhaps if I looked at it from that perspective, I might be able to find out why she and Bertie had died.

It would not be unusual for me to call and pay my respects. After all, Milo and I were well known in the community. Under any other circumstances, I certainly would have paid the grieving mother a call. Of course, I might have waited until a bit later to do such a thing, were a murderer not on the loose. As things stood, it would be better to visit now, when there might be some useful bit of information to be gleaned.

I chose a gown of dark navy and put a flowing scarf over it. I looked in the mirror and thought that my stomach was reasonably concealed.

Mrs. Hodges was one of that class of women who was likely to think I should be sequestered in my house until the baby was born, so I wanted to offend as little as possible. I wouldn't further violate her sense of propriety by walking there, so I asked Markham to bring the car around.

Luckily, Milo still hadn't stirred, and Winnelda was off on some errand, so I was left to my own devices. If my departure was observed, it was too late for anyone to object. Not that it would have mattered. I was on a mission now, and I didn't intend to be foiled.

Though a death in the village would often bring out a flurry of activity from the local women, both sympathetic and morbidly curious, the Hodges house appeared quiet when Markham pulled up in front of the white fence. There was no group of mourners as there had been at the vicarage.

I felt a little pang of pity for the woman. Though she was unpleasant, it didn't seem right that she should have to grieve alone.

Markham came around to open the door for me, and I went to the front door of the cottage.

The maid opened it. She was a young, dour-faced girl, and I forced away the uncharitable thought that she must be what Mrs. Hodges had looked like in her youth. I was led to a dim, sparse parlor and took a seat in a chair by the fire, which had burned down to embers. In contrast to the cheerful kitchen I had visited two days before, this room was dark and chill, and I thought how little comfort was to be derived from it. I hoped that Mrs. Hodges's own room was more pleasant. I hoped, at least, it was warm.

I sat for a few moments, the only sound the ticking of a great grandfather clock at one end of the room. Then I heard the sound of heavy footsteps, and a moment later Mrs. Hodges came into the room. She was dressed in unrelieved black, her mourning clothes indicative of Edwardian style, with long skirts and a high-necked blouse. I was almost a bit surprised that she didn't have a veil.

I rose from my seat. "Hello, Mrs. Hodges," I said. "I've come to offer my condolences."

She nodded. "Thank you." Her tone was flat, just as it had always been, and there was not a hint of any emotion in her expression as she spoke. I wondered if she was dazed with the grief of losing Marena. Or perhaps she wasn't feeling much at all.

She took the seat across from me, and I sat again. There was a quiet moment as she arranged the folds of her black shawl across her shoulders. I studied her face. It was drawn and pale, and it seemed as though she had aged a bit since I had seen her last. If her grief was deep, however, she was keeping it hidden. Her eyes were dry, and her thin lips were pressed together in an expression of grim stoicism.

"Marena was such a lovely girl," I said. "I can't believe she's gone."

She said nothing.

"I do hope you'll let us know if there's anything we can do."

She looked up at me, and I saw that her eyes were a golden brown, a warmer color than I had expected them to be in the dim light of the parlor, almost like the honey she was so fond of. They were very like Marena's eyes had been, and I felt a moment of sadness as I realized how difficult it must be to lose her only child.

Almost unconsciously, my hand went to my stomach. I had not even seen this child yet, and I loved it fiercely. I could not imagine what it must be like to lose a child you had lived with and cared for for more than twenty years. The very thought made me feel a bit ill, and I forced my mind away from that aspect of things.

The maid came in with tea, and we were quiet as she settled things between us. Then Mrs. Hodges poured.

"How do you take your tea, Mrs. Ames?"

"No tea for me, thank you," I said. "I've just had breakfast."

To be honest, I wasn't certain I trusted her to serve me tea, not when the matter of Marena's poisoning was still unsolved. What was more, I still didn't feel well and didn't particularly relish the thought of another cup of tea at the moment.

She poured herself a cup, but it halted on the way to her lips for a moment, as though she was considering something. Some cynical part of me wondered if she was trying to formulate what story she wanted to tell about Marena, how much she could speak of her loss without revealing anything too incriminating.

Did I really think that she might be responsible for the murder of her own daughter? It seemed to me to be very unlikely. However much she might have disapproved of Marena, I didn't think her strident sense of morality would allow her to commit a murder to remedy it. Indeed, I didn't see why she would want to.

Though she had never seemed a warm woman, I had always thought she must be fond of her daughter in her own way. Marena had stayed at the vicarage on and off over the past several years to help Mrs. Busby, but she and her mother had still spent a good deal of time together. As far as I could tell, there had never seemed to be more than the usual amount of animosity between them, despite the oddness of their relationship.

I was no stranger to difficult mother-daughter relationships, after all. My own bond with my mother was very often strained, and there were few subjects on which we saw eye to eye.

"I am still adjusting myself to the idea that she's gone," she said at last. "I keep thinking she might come knocking at my door."

I nodded. "I can understand that."

"There are a great many things to think about, things one never considers before something like this happens. I have quite a bit of savings. It was all to have gone to Marena, but now . . ." She shrugged. "I don't suppose it will do much good. I'll give it to a charity. I've no doubt that they'll make better use of it than she might have."

There was a certain bitterness to her words, but there was sorrow in them, too. Despite the disagreements she had had with her daughter, she was still mourning her loss. I realized, however, this didn't entirely preclude the possibility that she might be responsible for Marena's death.

"I don't suppose the police have told you if they suspect anyone?" I asked.

She shook her head. "They're all closemouthed. I think they view me as a doddering old woman, a woman too wrapped up in grief to be of any use to them. Well, I do grieve her, but my grief is tempered by the fact that I lost her long ago."

"What do you mean?" I asked.

She shrugged. "The older she got, the more Marena grew apart from me. I was not the sort of woman she wished for in a mother."

"Many young women have difficulties with their mothers," I said. At least I could offer that comfort honestly.

"Perhaps," she said vaguely. "But it was different with Marena. She had ambitions, and she intended to achieve them. She meant to leave me and Allingcross behind."

Poor Marena. She would never accomplish that goal now; she would never achieve all the dreams she had had. I had to fight back the tears that sprang to my eyes. It would do no good to cry in front of Mrs. Hodges. She was not the sort of woman who believed that tears were of any help.

I cleared my throat, changing the subject to something a bit less sentimental.

"Did they ask you if Marena had been seeing anyone? A man, I mean?" I knew, of course, there had been her relationship with Darien, but I wondered if Mrs. Hodges knew of it.

She snorted. "There were always young men," she said in a cold voice. "Too many of them for her own good."

"I knew about Bertie, of course," I said, hoping it would prod her on.

She nodded, her expression grim. "Bertie Phipps was a young man with ambition, too. Marena appreciated that in him, hoped she'd be able to mold them both, I suppose, but I knew better. Bertie Phipps was always going to be a village boy. Try though she might to change him, he was never going anywhere there weren't horses."

I was surprised at this bit of insight from Mrs. Hodges. She'd never approved of Marena's relationship with Bertie from what I'd heard, but it sounded as though she'd understood Bertie well. Perhaps it was that she, too, was not the sort of person who would ever leave the village where she had been born.

"Before him, it was that Langford boy," she went on. "The Crooks boy before that. She was always looking for someone who might sweep her off her feet, give her the kind of glamorous life she wanted."

It made sense that she had fallen under Darien's spell. He was definitely the sort of young man who might dazzle a woman into believing he could introduce her to a more lavish and exciting life.

"I don't suppose that any of those young men might have wished to harm her?"

She looked at me for just a moment, shrewdly, I thought, and then she shrugged. "I don't know. I suppose one of them might. She was always throwing one over for the other. The latest of them was that handsome young fellow, your husband's brother, isn't he?"

So she knew about Darien after all. Perhaps I had underestimated her.

"Darien is my husband's half brother."

She nodded. "I understand she had taken a fancy to him. He's the sort that's usually up to no good, but Marena wouldn't have minded that. I daresay it would have appealed to her."

She said these things with apparently no fear of offending me, though I certainly wasn't offended. I barely knew Darien, but what I did know of him led me to believe that she was quite right. He wasn't a young man to be trusted where matters of the heart were concerned. He had proved that already in his conduct toward Imogen.

Why was it, though, that she had the impression Marena might have enjoyed a liaison with a disreputable man? Marena had always seemed very proper to me. Why the unfair prejudice on her mother's part?

I decided, for the moment, to change tactics. "Do you think the same person killed her that killed Bertie Phipps?"

"It seems likely, doesn't it?"

"But who might it have been?"

She took a sip of her tea. I thought for a moment that she wasn't going to answer me, but at last she said, "I've been thinking it over. There are people who might have wanted Bertie dead and people who might have wished to kill Marena. But who wanted to harm them both? That is a more difficult question."

Though I hated to admit it, I agreed with her. It seemed that every motive for Marena's death led back to the fact that she might have known something Bertie had told her or seen something the day he was killed. But what? It was still so maddeningly unclear what it was Bertie had known that might have been worth killing for.

I thought suddenly of my conversation with Mrs. Cotton.

"Mrs. Hodges, what do you know about the death of Sara Busby?"

She looked up at me, her gaze suddenly sharp. "Why do you want to know about that?"

I had never really been directly challenged on one of my questions before, not in so harsh a manner, at least. I was momentarily taken aback, but then I realized that Mrs. Hodges was already grieving, and I had no doubt brought up something that must be very painful for her. After all, she had nearly lost Marena in that crash.

But no. It was not grief in her expression; it was something sharp and perceptive, something that told me my answer to her question was important.

"I don't know exactly," I admitted. "It just occurred to me."

"It's interesting that you should bring it up when discussing motives for Marena's death," she said.

My skin prickled suddenly, as though I was on the precipice of an important revelation. I leaned forward as much as the baby would allow. "Why do you say that?" I asked softly.

She looked up at me. "Because it was Marena who was driving when that car went off the road and killed Sara Busby."

26

"MARENA WAS DRIVING the car when the accident occurred?" I repeated.

Mrs. Hodges nodded. "It was she who drove them off the road, she who was responsible for the accident."

I sat still, trying to absorb this information and its implications. "Why did Mrs. Busby say she had been driving?" I asked at last.

"To spare Marena, I assume. The girl wasn't old enough to drive, but Elaine was often spoiling them, giving in to their pleas. I suppose Marena might have got in a good deal of trouble if the truth was known."

And so Mrs. Busby took the blame for the accident that paralyzed her and killed her daughter. It was an act of supreme sacrifice, and I marveled that she had been able to do it. "And she's never told anyone."

"Not to my knowledge. Elaine has always been a bit too saintly for her own good."

"And Marena has carried the guilt with her all these years," I mused aloud. "Even going so far as to live in the vicarage to help Mrs. Busby."

Mrs. Hodges gave me a grim smile. "If you want to believe that. I think the truth of it was that she was afraid Mrs. Busby would reveal the truth one day, and she would be forced to answer for it."

"Surely not," I said. "She always seemed very fond of the Busbys."

"My daughter was fond of whomever she thought might be able to benefit her in some way."

She must have seen the flicker of disgust in my expression, for she waved a hand. "Not a nice thing to say about one's dead daughter. I understand that. But I've never been a woman to sugarcoat the truth."

"It was only an accident," I said. "She was very young."

Her stern gaze met mine. "She was responsible for that child's death, nonetheless."

I wondered if Mrs. Hodges had expressed these sentiments to Marena. Somehow I thought she likely had—if not in words, then in her attitude. It certainly wouldn't have eased Marena's conscience at all to know that her mother viewed her as responsible for the tragic outcome of a terrible mistake.

It made even more sense now that the Busbys had taken her under their wing. No doubt they had realized that Mrs. Hodges was not the sort of person who would empathize with her daughter after what had happened.

"She was never a good girl," her mother said. "Too much like her father."

I tried not to show my shock at the dreadful thing this woman was saying about her only child, a child that had just died.

"A youthful accident did not define her goodness." I felt it my duty to say that much on Marena's behalf.

"That's not what I meant," Mrs. Hodges said.

I did not find out what she did mean, however, for the maid appeared suddenly in the parlor door, a concerned expression on her face.

"Inspector Wilson is here, ma'am. He wants to see you."

"Tell him I have a guest."

"I did, but . . ."

"But I wouldn't be put off," Inspector Wilson said good-naturedly, coming into the room.

"Have you found out who killed my daughter?" Mrs. Hodges asked by way of greeting.

"I've come to speak to you about a rather private matter," Inspector Wilson said, his gaze flickering to me.

I began to rise from my chair, but Mrs. Hodges held up a hand. "You may say what you like in front of Mrs. Ames."

Inspector Wilson looked at me, one brow raising ever so slightly. I knew he felt that I was interfering again. Perhaps I was. But we were so close to the solution that I simply could not give up the chase.

He cleared his throat. "We've had some results from our chemist."

"Yes?" She sounded neither concerned nor very interested, only impatient.

"It seems that your daughter was poisoned with cyanide salts."

My stomach clenched. So it had been the same poison that Mrs. Busby had purchased at the apothecary shop.

I thought I should mention it to Inspector Wilson, though I was sure he probably already knew as much. Nevertheless, this newest revelation about Marena's driving the car that killed Sara Busby had put things in a new light. Was it possible that Mrs. Busby had carried a grudge for all these years, that she had finally decided to enact her revenge? I found it difficult to believe, but that didn't mean it was impossible.

Inspector Wilson, oblivious to my inner turmoil, went on. "The poison wasn't in the tea. It was in the jar of honey. Honey you brought to the vicarage, I understand."

If he meant this revelation to startle Mrs. Hodges into a confession, I could only imagine he was greatly disappointed by her response.

"Nonsense," she harrumphed.

"The chemist is quite sure," Inspector Wilson said.

"There was nothing in that honey. I ate from that jar myself the very morning she died, shortly before she visited. I brought the remainder of it to her that afternoon with a few other dainties. It was the rosemary honey. Only she and I liked it."

"Inspector," I said abruptly. "Will you indulge me?"

He looked suddenly weary, but his patina of politeness remained intact. "In what way, Mrs. Ames?"

I knew what I was about to suggest was highly unusual, but I had an instinct that it might just be the answer to bringing the case to a close. "Might we all go to the vicarage? I think that, perhaps, if we get everyone together, we might be able to make some sense of this."

I awaited his answer with bated breath. I felt that we were so near the solution. It was almost as though it were hanging there, above us, just waiting to be snatched, if we could only reach up and grab it.

"I don't know . . ." Inspector Wilson began. "It's rather unusual."

"Nothing official," I said. "Just a conversation. I really do feel that it could be useful."

I put my hand on my stomach and tried to look in need of sympathy. It seemed my body was inclined to aid me in the performance, for there was a sudden gripping tightness in my abdomen that caused me to draw in a sharp breath.

"Are you all right, Mrs. Ames?" Inspector Wilson asked warily.

"Certainly," I replied, the pain letting up almost immediately. "But I do think it would be beneficial if we could speak to the Busbys about a few things."

He seemed to be considering it, but it was Mrs. Hodges, surprisingly, who settled the matter.

"If she thinks it'll do good, why not go to the vicarage. It can't harm anything, after all."

She was the last person I would have expected to be my ally, but at this moment I would take what I could get.

Inspector Wilson hesitated for just a moment and then sighed. "Very well. Shall we go?"

WE REACHED THE vicarage, and our odd little party was shown into the drawing room by the maid, May, who was clearly curious about the disparate group of characters that had gathered at the door.

"Mrs. Ames, Inspector Wilson, and Mrs. Hodges, ma'am," she said as we followed her into the room.

I was surprised to see Imogen sitting on the sofa. Mrs. Busby's chair was drawn up beside her. The vicar was sitting in a chair near the fireplace, but he and Imogen rose when we entered.

"Welcome, all," the vicar said brightly.

"Vicar," Inspector Wilson said with a nod. "And Mrs. Busby. Miss Prescott."

"Hello, Imogen," I said. "I didn't expect to see you here."

"No, I suppose not. I . . . I just wanted to talk a few things over with the vicar and Mrs. Busby."

"We're sorry to intrude," I said.

"We have a few questions, if you don't mind," Inspector Wilson said, using the officialness of his position to take charge of the situation.

"Shall I go?" Imogen asked.

Inspector Wilson glanced at me then. It had been, after all, my idea that we come here. Should she leave? She was as involved in this as any of us, I supposed. And she was still on my list of suspects. Perhaps it was a lucky thing that she had shown up here.

"No," I said. "Why don't you stay?"

"Have a seat, will you?" the vicar asked. He had been standing quietly to one side of the room, but now he ushered us toward chairs like a gentle shepherd.

We sat. I felt another pang in my stomach and back as I eased myself into the seat. It gripped me for just a moment before I shifted slightly and it let go.

"Now," said the vicar pleasantly. "What is it we can do for you?"

"We've discovered the source of Miss Hodges's poisoning," Inspector Wilson said without preamble. "It was in the rosemary honey that she had with her tea."

There was a hushed silence in the room. "Did she prepare her tea herself?" Inspector Wilson asked.

Mrs. Busby looked stricken. "I . . . I fixed her tea."

"And you put the rosemary honey in it?" There was no hint of accusation in Inspector Wilson's tone. I knew that he and Mrs. Busby had always been on good terms, and I didn't think he truly suspected her capable of the murder. But I inwardly applauded him for asking the question that had to be asked.

"Yes," she said. "Yes, I did. But I didn't . . . I didn't wish to harm her."

"Of course not, dear," the vicar said gently.

"Mrs. Busby, there is . . . the question of the poison's origin," I said.

Inspector Wilson looked sharply at me, but I pretended not to notice.

"I was purchasing something at the apothecary shop and happened to notice your name in the poison register."

"My . . . my name . . ." Her face clouded and then cleared. "Oh, yes, of course. I did buy some poison a few weeks ago. To kill rats. Marena told me there were a great many of them in the garden shed and asked if I might purchase it. I don't like to kill the creatures, of course, but I couldn't have them running about. They might spread disease."

"Why didn't Miss Hodges buy the poison herself?" Inspector Wilson asked.

"Oh, I don't know," Mrs. Busby said. "I believe I was on my way to the shop and asked if there was anything she needed."

"You went alone?" he asked, glancing at her chair.

"I often help her get to a place and then leave her to manage," the vicar put in with a fond smile. "She prefers to do things on her own."

Mrs. Busby nodded. "I like to do things for myself. It makes me feel . . . less helpless."

"I see," Inspector Wilson said. "So you purchased the poison and did what with it?"

"I gave it to the gardener. It went into the shed, I suppose. I haven't seen it since."

"I wonder," Inspector Wilson said mildly, "how it was that cyanide salts came to be in the honey?"

All the color drained from Mrs. Busby's face. "You . . . you don't mean that's what killed her."

"It's exactly what I mean," Inspector Wilson replied.

"But . . . but I didn't . . . Who would . . . I would never do such a thing. Why would I?" She burst into tears.

In the midst of this rather dramatic scene, May came back to the door, her face anxious. "You've more company, ma'am," she said to the still-crying Mrs. Busby. "Lady Alma and Mr. Ames and . . . Mr. Ames."

I wasn't sure what Milo and Darien were doing here with Lady Alma, but I supposed they might as well round out our little group of the players involved in this drama.

"Show them in," the vicar said. He sounded as though he was pleased to see more people traipsing into the strange tableau.

One person not pleased, however, was Imogen. Her face had gone white, and I realized that she had not seen Darien since arriving in Allingcross. I supposed we were about to have another scene.

A moment later Lady Alma, Milo, and Darien came into the room.

"We were out for a ride and saw your car and the inspector's, Mrs. Ames," said Lady Alma. "Thought we'd drop in and . . . I say, what's the matter, Elaine?"

"We've been discussing the murders," I said, feeling that things were suddenly getting out of hand.

"Chin up," Lady Alma said, going to Mrs. Busby's side. "It's all been rather hard, but there are brighter days ahead. Isn't that so, vicar?"

"Yes, it's very true, Lady Alma. There is always hope for tomorrow."

I looked over at Milo, a question in my gaze.

"Darien and I were out riding and came upon Lady Alma. Is everything all right?"

I nodded. In defiance of this answer, my abdomen clenched again. I did my best to ignore it.

I glanced at Darien. He had clearly noticed Imogen, but if he was surprised to see her there, he did a good job of concealing it. He smiled slightly, as though finding the woman he had wed under false pretenses sitting in the parlor was a pleasant surprise.

"Darien, don't you suppose you ought to at least say hello to Imogen?" I asked.

Darien frowned, glancing around the room. "Imogen? Is she here?"

I thought for a moment he was playing some sort of cruel joke, ignoring the woman as though he didn't know her. But then I saw Imogen's face. It wasn't sadness or embarrassment or even indignation that was written there; it was fear.

And then she turned and darted toward the door of the parlor.

27

IT WAS INSPECTOR Wilson who stepped in front of her and caught her. "Just a moment there, miss. Where are you going in such a hurry?"

"I . . . I need to get some air," she said. She tried to push past him, but his grip on her arm tightened.

"Wait just a minute."

She hesitated with the poised air of a bird about to take flight, and I thought she might make another run for the door. Then her shoulders slumped, and she moved back to the sofa.

I looked at Darien. He was watching her with interest, but no recognition.

"This isn't Imogen, I take it?" I asked him.

"I've never seen her before in my life." He didn't sound angry or even surprised, just a bit curious.

I turned back to look at the young woman who had been calling herself Imogen Prescott. Indeed, it seemed that all eyes in the room went to her. The thoughts swarmed through my head. If she wasn't really the woman who Darien had met in Brighton, who was she? What was her connection with Bertie? If not a lover, perhaps she was a relation who had arrived for some unknown reason and had an altercation with him.

Perhaps she was the killer after all, and I was still on the wrong track. But I had been so sure . . .

The room was silent as we all waited for some explanation.

She said nothing for a long moment, and then at last she began to speak, her voice low and a bit breathless. "Imogen Prescott is my sister."

"I don't understand," I said. So she wasn't a relation of Bertie's, but of the woman Darien had deceived. Why, then, had she come to Allingcross?

There was another pause, and then she drew in a deep breath, as though deciding it was time to unburden herself. "We both work at the pub near the racecourse," she said. "That's where we met Bertie. We were friendly, the three of us. Bertie was nice. Polite. I half hoped he would catch Imogen's eye, for she always fancied the wrong blokes. But Bertie only had eyes for Marena. Then Imogen went on holiday in Brighton, and she fell for the wrong sort of fellow again. She told me, when she got home, how she met Darien and that he was to meet her in London. I knew right away he wasn't telling the truth. When he didn't ever arrive, she was heartbroken."

"Where is she now?" I asked, afraid for a moment that something dire might have occurred.

"She's still in London. She was just going to let him get away with it." She didn't look at Darien as she spoke, and he made no attempt to interject.

"And you decided to come to Thornecrest and confront him for her?" I asked.

She nodded.

So it had all been an act from the beginning. I was surprised. She had seemed so genuine.

"I felt very sorry for you," I said, letting a note of disapproval into my tone. After all, she had deceived Milo and me in her quest for . . . for what?

"Why didn't you tell me the truth?" I asked. "We could have helped you and your sister."

"At first, I didn't know Darien wasn't really Milo. It caught me by surprise, when I arrived at Thornecrest and found you married to him and expecting a baby," she said. "That's why I cried when I found out. I felt so bad for poor Imogen."

It made sense now, how she had identified the photo of Milo as Darien. She had seen only her sister's photograph of him. In our wedding photo, taken several years ago, Milo had looked very much like Darien did now. I thought of the hesitant, searching expression she had had when meeting Milo. No doubt it was only upon seeing him, in the flesh and a bit older, that she realized he was not the same man her sister had met in Brighton.

"What is your name, miss?" Inspector Wilson asked her.

"Eloise," she said. "Eloise Prescott."

"But why did you go on pretending to be Imogen?" I asked, still not entirely understanding the ploy. It would have been one thing to arrive and confront Darien. It was quite another to go about impersonating her sister.

She flushed. "I don't know. Once I realized Imogen had been duped, and that it wasn't likely I was going to encounter Darien after all, I . . . I thought . . ." Her words trailed off.

"You thought we might be in a position to help you and, by extension, your sister."

She nodded.

"When I saw Bertie at the festival, I was afraid that he was going to mention to someone that I was Eloise and not Imogen. Of course, I had to avoid Darien as well. That wasn't hard, as he, cad that he is, had no interest in doing the honorable thing and meeting with me . . . Imogen. I knew from the moment she mentioned him that he was a rotter."

She said these things about Darien without being the least bit self-conscious that he was in the room. When I glanced at him, he seemed as unmoved as she did.

"Why didn't Imogen come herself?" he asked at last.

Her eyes flashed. "She was too proud. She'd never run after you . . . no matter how much you hurt her."

"It was only a lark," Darien said. "She knew that."

"You . . . compromised her for your own amusement." She said the words in a flat, hard tone that was somehow much more piercing than a loud voice might have been.

"It wasn't like that."

"What was it like?" she asked. "You seduced her, had your fun, and abandoned her. If I hadn't come looking for you, she never would have heard anything about you again. Do you deny it?"

Darien was unmoved by this attempt to make him feel guilty. Indeed, it seemed to have the opposite effect, for I saw his face harden ever so slightly. "It's nice you care for your sister, but she knew what it was all about."

She glared at him and then averted her gaze.

"Is that why you told the police you saw him in the field?" I asked, curious.

"No! I really did see him there," she said. "I didn't do it to be cruel, but if he had killed someone, he deserved to be caught. Anyway, I didn't kill Bertie, and I certainly didn't kill Miss Hodges. I had no reason to kill her."

"Neither did I," Darien said. "I didn't care a thing about Bertie, but I liked Marena a great deal."

None of us said anything at this lukewarm praise of the woman he had lost.

"If you weren't truly vying for Darien's affections," I asked Eloise, "why was it that you came to see Marena here at the vicarage?"

"I . . . I was going to try to tell her the truth about Darien."

"But you didn't tell her that you weren't really her rival?" Inspector Wilson put in. "It was a good time to make the truth known, I'd say."

"She didn't give me much chance. Our conversation grew heated. She was accusatory. So I left quickly."

It didn't entirely rule her out. If vengeance was in her heart, she might have killed Bertie to keep him quiet and Marena to clear the path for her sister. It was a weak motive, however. Eloise Prescott, despite her deception, did not strike me as the kind of woman who would be that obsessed.

"You weren't at the boardinghouse that evening when I came to see you," I said. "But when I stopped by the vicarage, you weren't here either. The vicar told me only Lady Alma was visiting."

"I took a walk before I came here," she said. "Sorting out what I wanted to say to Miss Hodges."

"She arrived shortly after you drove away, Mrs. Ames," the vicar said.

"Then I must have just missed her when I spoke to you at the gate."

"Yes," he agreed, then added thoughtfully: "You told me that you wanted to discuss the possibility that Marena knew what Bertie had been hiding."

"Interesting, then, that she died shortly afterward," Inspector Wilson said mildly, echoing what I was thinking but too well-mannered to say.

If the vicar was alarmed by this, he didn't show it. "That's true," he said. "The timing might be considered strange. It seems a very long time ago. To think, a few days ago my biggest worry was my missing garden boots, and now . . ."

I stopped suddenly, a strange shock of something like revelation coursing through me. "Your boots?" I asked.

"Yes. My old leather garden boots, you understand. I had them in the shed, but they'd gone missing. I asked Mrs. Busby, Marena, and May, but they knew nothing about it . . . Oh, what does that matter!"

He said something else, but I had stopped listening. With this one tiny bit of information, everything began to fall into place. My mind whirled as the various strands of clues began to work themselves into a complete picture.

Start from the end and work your way back, Inspector Jones had said. Not who had wanted to kill Bertie, but who might have killed Marena. If one looked at it like that, it all began to make sense.

"Inspector," I said suddenly. "I . . . think I might have an idea."

He didn't seem overly enthusiastic, but he was too polite to dismiss me out of hand. "What is it, Mrs. Ames?"

Another spasm went through my midsection just then, and I paused for just a moment to let it pass. The baby was apparently growing as excited as I was. I forced myself to calm down.

"It was clear from the beginning that Bertie knew a secret," I said. "After all, he said as much to Mr. Ames and me shortly before he died. I knew that whatever it was must weigh against his conscience, his sense of duty."

"But you didn't know whose secret it might be?" Inspector Wilson asked.

I shook my head. "Not at first. My first thought was Mr. Busby." I looked at the vicar. "I'm sorry. One doesn't, naturally, think that a vicar is capable of such a thing. But the truth of the matter is that one never knows what is in anyone's heart, and Bertie asked me that question shortly after I'd seen an exchange of money between the two of you."

"You're right to not think anyone above suspicion, Mrs. Ames. 'All have sinned and fall short of the glory of God,'" he quoted with a small smile. "I know I cannot be immune to questioning. My position makes me no more infallible than any other man, perhaps even less so."

"Why did you give Bertie that money?" I asked.

A small frown flickered across the vicar's forehead, and then he sighed. "Confession is good for the soul, they say."

He glanced at his wife. She was watching him with a serene expression, as though there was nothing in the world he could do to shake her faith in him.

I looked over at Milo. He stood near the door, his handsome, impassive face taking in the scene. His gaze caught mine as I looked at him, and his mouth turned up ever so slightly at the corner. It might have been almost imperceptible to anyone else, but I recognized it as a gesture of both affection and encouragement.

"I'm sorry, my dear," the vicar said. Then he turned to me. "I told you the truth when I said I didn't give Bertie any money."

I was momentarily caught off guard. I hadn't expected him to continue denying it.

"Perhaps you'd better explain, vicar," Inspector Wilson said. "There was, after all, an envelope of money found in Mr. Ames's—Mr. Darien Ames, that is—room with Bertie's things."

Mr. Busby nodded. "Yes, I suppose that's true, but, you see, I didn't give it to him. He was trying to give it to me."

"Trying to . . . give you money?" Inspector Wilson said, the faintest hint of disbelief in his tone.

The vicar glanced at his wife again. "He took it from his pocket, but I refused it, and he put it back. I didn't want to be seen taking it at the festival, though I can see how you might have assumed the opposite, Mrs. Ames."

"But why was Bertie giving you money, dear?" Mrs. Busby asked. "Was he trying to pay you back for the things he took from your desk?"

"I wish that were the case," the vicar said. He drew in a breath and let it out. "You see, I'd been giving money to Bertie to place bets for me at Alexandra Park Racecourse. I'm afraid once I'd won a time or two, it became rather a habit. I've been making a good deal of money."

I stared at him. This was his secret sin? Behind me, I heard what seemed to be a snicker from Darien.

"Gambling is not, I suppose, a noble hobby for a vicar. Indeed, there are many better ways in which I might have spent my money . . . should I have lost it, that is. But I should like to say that a great deal of my winnings were given to good causes."

It accounted for the frequent deposits and also the withdrawals.

It was a bit unsatisfactory that the vicar's secret was that he was donating his gambling winnings to charities. Granted, I had sincerely hoped he would not be the killer, but this was almost disappointingly tame.

I looked at Inspector Wilson. He looked as nonplussed as I felt.

Clearing my throat, I continued. "Then I thought perhaps the secret had to do with Lady Alma." I turned to her. "That he had perhaps discovered something working for you that you didn't want anyone to know."

Lady Alma, uncharacteristically, flushed. "Like what, for example?"

"Like the fact that Medusa wasn't really sired by Damocles." This came from Milo. I looked over at him, surprised.

Lady Alma was surprised, too, and I thought she might deny it. Instead, however, she charged ahead. "How did you know?"

"I'm afraid I guessed," Milo said. "When I went to London, I stopped by my club and saw an old friend in the racing game and asked him about Damocles's foal. He said he'd heard something about it from a friend but couldn't remember what."

I shot Milo a look that said how much I appreciated his keeping this information from me. Granted, it wasn't much, but I would have liked to have known that he cared enough to look into things.

"He telephoned me this morning," he went on. "He informed me that the foal had been sold a year ago and then broke her leg in a fall. She had to be put down."

She sighed. "I'd wanted that foal for a long time. It was going to be excellent breeding stock. When I came across this horse, I thought I might be able to pass her off as a breeder. Not just for the money, mind. She's a beauty of a horse. Why should such fine blood be passed over just because she hadn't a pedigree? So I paid Medusa's owner for her papers."

It was astounding to me how many imposters had been masquerading about in Allingcross. Darien, Imogen, Medusa. Who might be next?

"How did Bertie find out?" Milo asked.

"He knew from the beginning. It was he who told me the original Medusa had died. He met one of the grooms from the stable of her owner. I gave him a bit of money for helping me with the transaction. It's how he bought Molly."

"You paid him off," Inspector Wilson said.

She met his gaze with a slightly imperious one of her own. She was an earl's daughter, after all. "Call it what you will. Nothing came of it, so I've done nothing wrong."

"Not where the horse is concerned, perhaps," he said. "But what about Bertie?"

"He was a good boy, a fine young man. I didn't kill him, but I think perhaps I know who did."

She looked directly at Mrs. Hodges.

Mrs. Hodges returned her gaze, her stern face unchanging.

"Lady Alma," I said. "You told me that Bertie mentioned to you that he had a secret, one that concerned Mrs. Hodges."

This brought a response from Mrs. Hodges. "I told you, I haven't any secrets."

"I'm not entirely sure that's true," I told her carefully.

She stared at me, as though challenging me to come up with one.

"There was the matter of your husband dying in prison after killing a man," I said. I didn't want to embarrass her, but it was important that the truth came out. Hopefully she would realize it.

There was not much reaction to my announcement, at least not from Mrs. Hodges. The others, however, turned to look at her.

"It wasn't a secret, not really," she said. "It just wasn't something I cared to talk about."

"But you hid it from Marena all these years. And from the other villagers."

"There was no need for anyone to know. Least of all Marena."

"But she started wondering, didn't she?"

Her expression darkened. "She did. She'd begun asking questions about her father. I think she thought he was living the high life in London somewhere and hoped she could go off and meet him there. She was never satisfied with life in the village."

"There's also the matter of you bringing her the honey that was used to poison her," Inspector Jones said.

"I told you. I had some of that honey myself that very morning.

There was nothing wrong with it. Someone must have put it in the jar once it arrived at the vicarage."

"But why would they do that?" he asked. "How could they be sure that no one else would eat it?"

"I can only suppose it was because it was the rosemary honey. No one else much cared for it but Marena and me."

"And everyone here at the vicarage knew that," I said.

She nodded. "I've brought a jar of it here before. Marena said the Busbys wouldn't touch the stuff."

"Too strong for my taste," the vicar said, then added, so as to avoid giving offense, "though it has a very pleasant aroma."

"Then that's another reason to rule out strangers. No one else could have known that Marena specifically would be killed by the poisoned honey."

"That's right," Inspector Wilson said. "That narrows it down to Mrs. Hodges and Mr. and Mrs. Busby, doesn't it?"

"I also wondered about you, Mrs. Busby," I admitted.

She looked up at me from her chair, a slight flushing coming to her cheeks. "You thought I might be a murderer? Goodness me."

"Yes, you see, I recently discovered that it was not you who was driving the car that killed your daughter. It was Marena."

Mrs. Busby's face went white, and her eyes again filled with tears.

"Elaine, I've told Mrs. Ames all about the accident," said Mrs. Hodges, apparently both unmoved by the woman's distress and willing to connect the poisoning to a possible motive.

Mrs. Busby opened her mouth to speak, but no words came out. She swallowed and tried again. "Yes, it's true that she was driving when the accident happened. She wanted to drive, and I didn't see any harm in it. But then she and Sara started quarreling about some silly childhood matter. What it was I don't even remember now. And then suddenly the car was going off the road. It's the last thing I remember . . ." Her voice broke off with a stifled sob, and the vicar went to her side, placing a hand on her shoulder.

"But I didn't blame her," she said at last. "I blamed myself. She was just a child, and I shouldn't have let her drive the car."

"There, there, dear," Mr. Busby said soothingly. "You mustn't blame yourself."

"Mrs. Busby, I didn't think it would be possible for you to kill Bertie, not with your wheelchair. But when Marena died, and the poison was purchased in your name, things looked bad. It made me begin to fear you might be involved. But then an old friend told me I should consider things from a different angle."

I looked again at Milo, and he gave me a nod of encouragement.

I took a deep breath, preparing to plunge ahead. I wasn't sure Inspector Wilson would believe me, but I had to try.

"Just now the vicar mentioned his missing boots. They had been in the shed, where the poison was kept." I turned to Inspector Wilson. "And that's what made me realize there isn't a murderer to be arrested here after all."

He looked at me as though I had lost my senses. "What do you mean, Mrs. Ames?"

My stomach clenched again; the excitement was becoming too much for me. I gritted my teeth and let out a breath through my nose.

"Because . . ." I said. "Because Marena wasn't murdered. She killed herself."

28

EVERYONE STARED AT me, dumbfounded by this announcement. I suppose I would have been skeptical myself had someone proposed the idea to me a few hours ago. Now, however, I was very certain.

Mrs. Hodges was the first to break the silence. "Nonsense," she said. "Marena would not have done such a thing."

"No, no," Mrs. Busby agreed, her voice still thick with grief. "Something like that wasn't in her nature."

Inspector Wilson paid little attention to either of them.

"Killed herself?" He stared at me, his gaze sharp. "You think she gave herself the poison."

I nodded. "I'm afraid so. Only she didn't mean to do it. It was all an unfortunate accident."

Inspector Wilson frowned. "You mean to say there was no crime committed here? Begging your pardon, madam, but that's preposterous. After all, the poison was in her tea."

"Yes," I agreed. "And she put it there. Though she didn't know she did."

He was looking at me strangely, so I knew I needed to start from the beginning. It was still coming together in my head, though I was as certain of the solution as I had ever been of anything. I tried to think of how best I could explain.

The next part was the most difficult, but I had to come out with it. "You see, the entire time, Marena had been hoping to poison her mother."

This was met with a stunned silence. I knew that it was going to be difficult to believe, perhaps even more difficult to prove. But it made sense, if one looked closely at the facts.

"Marena and her mother had never seen eye to eye." Everyone knew that Mrs. Hodges was not at all liked by many of the people in the village. Marena had been clever and beautiful and ambitious, and she had wanted to use those qualities to her advantage, not hide them as her mother had hoped she might.

"Always thought herself destined for something more," Mrs. Hodges said, following up on my train of thought. I noticed that she had not come to her daughter's defense. She didn't even look shocked at my revelation.

It was Mrs. Busby who rallied to defend Marena, just as she had always done. "But I really don't think . . ."

"Let her continue, if you please, Mrs. Busby," Inspector Wilson said.

"As you told me, Mrs. Hodges," I said. "Marena was often dating boys from the village, looking for someone who might sweep her off her feet and give her the sort of life for which she longed. I think that's also why she began asking questions about her father."

Mrs. Hodges nodded. "She wanted to know who her father was. There was no good that could come of it. I told her again and again."

"Sometimes one wants to know where one comes from." This was the first I had heard Darien speak up, and something in the words touched me.

Now, however, was not the time for sentiment. I needed to lead the others along the path of clues I had followed.

"That's what induced her to break into your office, vicar," I went on.

He looked at me, his eyes wide. "You think Marena did that?"

I nodded. The next bit was difficult to explain, as it involved Lady

Alma's foray into the vicar's office and her examination of the documents in the desk drawer. She had called my attention to the financial documents, but there had been something else there, something that had seemed insignificant when she first mentioned it. But now I recalled something else.

"When I came to visit Marena after Bertie's death, there were documents on her desk that she quickly cleared away. I believe they were parish records."

"She wanted information about her father," the vicar said.

I nodded. "I believe she was looking for him but trying to keep things quiet. I think it might also have been she who stole your things, though it would be hard to prove whether she did it or put Bertie up to it."

"Bertie was quite mad for her," Mrs. Busby said sadly.

"Not so mad that he would have stolen anything." Lady Alma's tone brooked no argument.

"Whatever the case," I said, "she had taken up with Bertie, believing that it might be the way to a better life. Unfortunately, he was no more interested in a life outside his horses than her mother was with a life outside her bees. But then the idea came to her. If she killed her mother, she would have an inheritance. And then she would be free to live the life she wanted with whoever she chose."

Mrs. Hodges's perpetually grim expression grew a bit grimmer.

"I just can't believe it," Mrs. Busby whispered.

"I think she first mentioned the idea to Bertie, hoping he would go along with it. Perhaps he did break into your office, vicar, and she thought he would help her with another, larger crime. Whatever the case, I think things grew more complicated after the altercation with Darien at the inn.

"Bertie realized Marena had thrown him over for good and that she had her sights set on another young man. I think the idea that she was going to kill her mother weighed on his conscience. That's why he mentioned a secret about Mrs. Hodges to you, Lady Alma, and why he also said something about it to Milo and me. Perhaps he thought she didn't really mean it. Or perhaps he thought he could talk her out of it. When he learned that her affections had shifted, he knew he had to do something."

"And things came to a head at the festival." Inspector Wilson said. He seemed to realize the unintentionally macabre pun of his words and cleared his throat. "That is, she confronted Bertie about it."

I nodded. "Marena was to meet Darien in that field, but somehow she encountered Bertie instead. Perhaps he followed her there to speak with her. He must have told Marena that he couldn't allow her to go through with it, that he was planning to spoil her scheme by revealing the truth to her mother. They quarreled. She picked up a rock and hit him over the head with it."

Mrs. Busby gasped.

"She then came back to the festival and pretended to be distraught when his body was discovered." I considered it for a moment. "Perhaps she was, in a way. I think she cared about Bertie as much as she could care about anyone."

"Where did I come into all of this?" Darien asked.

"Perhaps she thought you would come into money, being an unknown Ames relation returned to Thornecrest," I said. "But then Imogen arrived in Allingcross, and Marena likely began to realize that your intentions were not necessarily of the long-term variety. Perhaps she had thought it would be best to go ahead with her original plan to kill her mother. That was why Bertie needed to be silenced."

Another thought occurred to me. "Did you tell Marena about the woman you knew whose husband died in a riding accident?"

Darien nodded. "Marena seemed to enjoy hearing about the scandals from my past."

"That must have given her the idea," I said. "After she killed Bertie, she realized that your quarrel with him had presented her with the perfect opportunity. She could frame you for the murder."

"She said she loved me," Darien said in an injured tone. He had, I thought, some nerve to sound affronted after the way he had been treating women. Then again, the fact that he hadn't plotted to murder any of them was a definite point in his favor.

"She acted quickly," I continued. "She was always clever. After killing Bertie, she went and let Medusa out of her stall, spooking her in the process, and then put the saddle near Bertie's body. I think it was her intention to make it look like a poor attempt to cover up a murder."

"Then she must have put those things in my room," Darien said. "But what about the blood on the boots?"

"Those were the vicar's boots," I said. "I think she put them on when she came to meet you in the field. She was wearing pale-colored shoes that day, and I assume she wanted to keep them clean. When she killed Bertie, she must have gotten blood on the boots."

"She'd sometimes wear my garden boots when out walking," the vicar said quietly. "To keep mud or damp grass from her own shoes."

I remembered now that she'd been wearing them that day the festival committee had met for the final time at the vicarage. She'd come in windblown with muddy leather boots.

"She couldn't very well return them to the shed with blood on them," I said. "So I suppose she thought she might as well use them. She took the necklace and money Bertie had on him, and, when she returned to work at the inn, she put all of the items in Darien's room. After that, she had only to wait for the right opportunity to introduce the likelihood of his guilt."

"Only I did that," Eloise said softly.

"It wasn't your fault," Darien said graciously. He was doing his best to charm her. I glanced at Eloise to see how this performance was affecting her, but she was not at all starry-eyed. Whatever her sister had seen in Darien, Eloise was seeing something much less appealing.

"You deserve to be punished for what you did to my sister, but not to hang," she told him.

The corner of his mouth tipped up. "Decent of you to say so."

"But how . . . how did Marena end up being poisoned?" Mrs. Busby asked, bringing us back to the matter at hand. Her voice shook with the question, the weight of her part in placing the honey in Marena's tea visible in the slope of her shoulders, and the vicar moved closer, reached out to take her hand.

"With Bertie gone and Darien accused of the crime, she decided to go ahead with her plans to kill her mother. After all, she already had the poison she had convinced Mrs. Busby to buy."

"She did it the day you came to see me," Mrs. Hodges said suddenly. "The day we were in the kitchen together. She asked me about rosemary honey, and I said I had only the one jar left. I offered it to her, but she declined. She must have slipped the poison in when I wasn't looking, knowing I would eat it in due course."

I nodded. "When she saw me, she made sure to say that you were ill. I think she wanted to introduce the idea so it wouldn't be a surprise when you died. But then you gave her the rest of the rosemary honey," I said.

She nodded. "I brought it round in a basket here to the vicarage. I . . . I thought she would like it."

It was horribly ironic that a small kindness on Mrs. Hodges's part was what had killed her daughter. Marena hadn't counted on this consideration from her mother, and it had ultimately cost her her life.

"Lady Alma told me that she sipped the tea and suddenly her expression was stricken. She said 'this tea tastes strange,' or words to that effect, before she collapsed. But I wonder if what she was really going to say was 'this tea tastes like rosemary.' I think she realized, in that instant, what had happened."

To some extent, I felt pity for her. It must have been dreadful to know that she was dying by her own hand. But, in a way, I suppose it had been justice. I was only glad no one else enjoyed Mrs. Hodges's rosemary honey.

"I . . . I just can't believe it. Marena . . . my dear Marena . . ." Mrs. Busby's face crumbled then, and she began to cry again, great sobs that shook her shoulders.

"There, there, dear," the vicar said softly, patting her back. "It's going to be all right."

I felt sorry for her. I knew that Marena had been a replacement of sorts for the daughter she had lost. A part of me also wondered, given that Marena and Sara had been quarreling at the time of the accident, if Marena had driven the car off the road on purpose. I suppose there would never be any way to know.

I looked then at Mrs. Hodges. She was watching me, and her honey-colored eyes caught mine and held. There was no anger in them, no condemnation in the fact that I had revealed her daughter was a killer.

"I was afraid she was like her father," she said, and there was very little sadness in her voice. The hardness that was usually there had gone, too. I found it surprising that it was only now, when she knew her daughter had wanted her dead, that there was some softness in her tone toward her. "From the time she was young, there was something about her that worried me. I tried to do right by her, but I suppose there was nothing I could have done to change her, not really."

A bit of kindness might have helped, I thought to myself. But, then, Mrs. Hodges could not be held responsible for the decisions Marena had made of her own free will.

The vicar turned to Inspector Wilson then. "If it's all right, Inspector, I'd like to take my wife to her room. She needs to rest."

Inspector Wilson nodded. "All right, vicar."

The vicar began to push Mrs. Busby's wheelchair toward the door, but he stopped as he reached me. His usually tranquil expression had slipped ever so slightly, and he suddenly looked tired. However, his words were as selfless as ever, as soothing as they had always been to those in pain or in need of comfort. "You've done a good thing, my dear. A difficult and brave thing. Bless you for your courage."

"Thank you, vicar," I said softly.

Then he wheeled Mrs. Busby from the room.

"Well." Inspector Wilson looked at me. "I'll have to look into a few things, Mrs. Ames, but it seems you may have got it right. I'll be in touch soon."

He tipped his hat to us and left.

"I'll be going now, too," Mrs. Hodges said, rising from her chair. She would no doubt need some time alone to think things through.

She left the room, and I let out a breath. It was finally over. At least, in theory. I knew the reverberations of all of this would be felt in the village for a long time to come.

"I suppose I'll go back to London now," Eloise Prescott said. "Imogen was right. I should have just let things be. Coming to Allingcross was more trouble than it was worth. Much more trouble."

She shot a meaningful look at Darien, who at least had the good grace to look slightly repentant.

"For what it's worth," he said. "Tell Imogen I'm sorry."

"It's not worth much," she retorted. Then her expression softened slightly. "But it's worth something."

When she was gone, Darien turned to me. "You're a marvel, Amory."

"Thank you, Darien."

"If it wasn't for you, it might have meant my neck."

"I only did what was right."

"Perhaps I ought to try that sometime," he replied. And then he winked at me, audacious boy.

"I feel I need some air," Lady Alma said suddenly. I didn't know what she felt about all of this, but I knew she wasn't going to share it with us. It wasn't in her nature. What was, however, was her love for her horses, and she was ready to turn to them for comfort.

"Ames," she said to Milo, "if you and your brother would like to come to the Priory and see Medusa for yourself, I think you'll still agree to let me breed her with your Xerxes."

Milo looked over at me. "I think I'd better go back to Thornecrest."

"Nonsense," I said. "Go ahead. You and Darien will enjoy it."

"Are you sure?"

"Yes. I could use with a bit of air myself. Send Markham back to Thornecrest, will you? I'm going to walk." I had another cramp in my side, and my back was aching. A walk would do me good.

"Are you all right, darling?" Milo asked as we all left the vicarage, Lady Alma and Darien a bit ahead of us discussing Medusa and Xerxes. Milo's eyes were searching mine. I wondered if he could see the discomfort in them.

"Perfectly fine," I reassured him, even as I pressed a hand to my throbbing side. "I'm just a bit tense from all the excitement, I think."

"I'm going to take you home and ring for Dr. Jordan."

"No, no. You go riding with Darien. It will be good for you."

He glanced at his brother, who was doing his best to charm Lady Alma. He had a difficult task ahead of him; she was no one's fool.

"Give him a chance, Milo," I said softly. "Whatever the past, he's your brother, and you can't escape that."

He sighed but gave me a smile. "I suppose I can see how things play out."

"That's all any of us can do."

He dropped a kiss on my cheek, then sent Markham on his way and went to meet his brother and Lady Alma. They mounted their horses and rode away as I turned toward the little path that led to Thornecrest, lost in thought.

It was hard to believe that all of this had happened in our little village, hard to believe that Marena Hodges had been responsible for Bertie's death and her own. I supposed one never could tell what lay behind closed doors or veiled eyes. Our village might be a quiet one, but deceit is universal.

I was halfway home when another sharp pang in my stomach stopped me cold. This was different from the annoying cramps that had come before. It was so intense it took my breath away. I clenched my teeth and tried to shift my posture, hoping it would ease the pain. This was most inconvenient when I still had a good distance back to Thornecrest.

And then suddenly I felt the water leave me, and I realized the truth of just how inconvenient the matter was.

I was having the baby.

I TRIED TO remain calm, fighting the pain that was coursing through me. I forced myself to draw in deep breaths through my nose and let them out through my teeth.

Things were progressing very swiftly, of that much I was certain. When at last the pain subsided, I began walking as quickly as I could along the path toward Thornecrest.

It was rough going, the pain intensifying between short periods of blessed relief.

At last I reached the grounds and walked toward the entryway, trying to keep my composure should I encounter someone. I rather hoped I would. Anyone. I needed someone to ring for the doctor.

But, as luck would have it, not even Grimes appeared as I made it through the front door and started toward the telephone. I thought about calling for Winnelda, but I wanted to make sure the doctor was on his way before Winnelda flew into a fit of hysterics.

Alas, it was not to be. I was halfway across the foyer when I was seized by another paroxysm of pain. Fighting back a groan, I reached out to grip the banister at the bottom of the stairs just as Winnelda was making her way down them. She looked at me, her eyes taking in my face, the clenched hand on the rail. I wanted to try to tell her not to panic, but I was near to panicking myself.

"Madam, are you . . ."

I knew I had to keep calm. It wouldn't do for both of us to go to pieces. "Yes," I said. "I believe . . ." The words were cut off by the intensity of the pain, and I gritted my teeth as I waited for the inevitable squeals and wringing of hands that usually accompanied any sort of excitement that occurred in Winnelda's presence.

But then something quite unexpected happened. The general look of flustered discomposure that usually appeared on her face at any hint of chaos gave way to one of understanding and immediate action. In a moment she was at my side.

"You're having the baby, madam."

Though it wasn't a question, I nodded. I couldn't speak just then, for I was grinding my teeth.

"Let's get you into the bed. We'll tend to things from there."

"But . . . I . . . Mr. Ames . . . He's at . . . the Priory."

"I'll fetch him presently," she said, her tone calmer and firmer than I had ever heard. "But first you need to lie down."

I didn't feel much inclined to argue with her. The pain was coming in steady waves, very little reprieve between them now.

With one hand she took my arm, and, sliding the other hand around me, she supported me up the stairs.

"I know it hurts an awful lot, madam, but you'll get through it. Women are sturdy creatures, and you're stronger than many I know." Her words were very sure, and I derived strength from this. I was about to endure an ordeal with which I had no experience, and the thought was terrifying.

"It's too early," I said, the worry that I had been trying to keep at the back of my mind coming to the surface.

"Not as early as all that," she said as we reached the bedroom. She pulled back the bedding and helped me ease myself onto the bed. "My sister Tansy was born a good six weeks early, and it was all as right as rain. She was a little mite, but she's very plump and pretty as can be now."

I didn't answer as another wave of pain washed over me. It seemed the length of time between these occurrences was still shortening. That meant the baby was coming soon, didn't it?

"You must ring for Dr. Jordan, Winnelda," I said through clenched teeth once the moment passed. "I don't think there's much time."

"I'll do it now," she said, turning toward the door. "I'll be right back. Just try to relax. Take deep breaths. I've done this plenty of times, and it's all going to be fine." Normally I was the one giving reassurances to Winnelda, but now it was she calming me with her words.

It was true that Winnelda had five younger sisters. It occurred to me that she had probably participated in childbirths before. It was a comforting thought. Especially since I was not at all sure the baby would wait until the doctor arrived.

The memories are a bit fuzzy after that point. It was all a haze of pain mingled with hope and despair. Though I would later learn that it had not been more than half an hour, the time seemed interminable. Winnelda, however, was an angel through it all. She was calm, patient, and very sure of herself. I don't know what I would have done without her, for it was so very frightening to stand on that threshold between life and death.

A thousand thoughts churned in my brain as the intensity of labor magnified. What if there was something wrong? What if the doctor didn't arrive in time? What if something happened to the baby? To me? To both of us? What would happen to Milo? I couldn't bear the thought of leaving him alone.

But Winnelda soothed and coached me as she bustled about and shouted orders to two of the upstairs maids who ran about doing her bidding, and, in the blissful but increasingly short lulls between bouts of agony, I found confidence that we would all survive this.

"You're almost there, madam," she said at last. "Just a bit more, and the baby will be here."

Everything went hazy again, my vision dimming at the corners, and then suddenly there was relief as a shrill little cry split the air.

Winnelda looked up at me, her face glowing. "Oh, madam! It's a girl."

IT FELT AS though I had slipped from a nightmare into the most blissful of dreams as I looked down at my daughter. My daughter. How strange the words were. I had known that I would soon be a mother, but it was so much different to hold this tiny person in my arms, to realize that she belonged to me, was my responsibility.

Winnelda had cleaned the baby and wrapped her tightly in a blanket before handing her to me, and now I felt as though I never wanted to let her go.

Her thick hair was the same jet black as Milo's. But her little rosebud mouth was mine, and her nose was mine, too. I felt a surge of love for her as I looked down at the tiny features. She was absolutely perfect, and I loved her more than words.

There was nothing for Dr. Jordan to do when he arrived. He examined me and the baby and gave a nod of approval.

"It looks like your maid has handled everything admirably," he said.

"She was a wonder," I replied, and Winnelda beamed.

"There was no difficulty?" he asked Winnelda.

"No, sir. It was all very natural."

I was surprised at the confidence in her tone, the quiet steadiness in her gaze as she looked from the doctor to me and back again.

I had a new appreciation for her strength. She could be counted on in a crisis, and that was most comforting to realize.

"Well, I suppose there's nothing much else for me to do. Fine thing for these young ladies to be taking jobs right from under the doctors' noses," he said with a wink at Winnelda.

"Mr. Ames?" I asked. "Is he here?"

"I sent Geoffrey to the Priory, madam, but he hasn't returned yet."

I wished someone might go now that the baby was here. I knew Milo would be worried when he heard I was in labor. Whatever reassurances he had given me, I knew there was a part of him that worried he would lose me as he had lost his mother.

"Will you send him up to me when he gets here?"

"Yes, madam."

"I'll be back to check on the both of you in the morning," Dr. Jordan said, "though I don't foresee there being much need of me then either. Congratulations, Mrs. Ames. She's a beauty."

"Thank you, doctor," I said, looking down at the bundle in my arms.

"I'll make you some tea, madam," Winnelda said. "You could do with a bit of sugar, I'm sure."

She followed the doctor out, and I was left alone with my precious daughter. I lost track of time looking at her angelic face as I fed her and then she fell into a contented sleep.

A short while later the door flew open and Milo came striding into the room. His eyes met mine, and for a moment we just looked at each other. There was some emotion in his gaze that I couldn't name, something I had never seen there before.

"Are you all right?" he asked at last.

"Yes. The doctor says everything is just fine."

"You're sure?"

"Yes. There were no difficulties."

He nodded. Though his expression changed little, I could sense the immense relief in him.

"It's a girl," I said softly.

And then there was another expression on his face that I had never seen there before. It took me a moment to realize that it was something akin to uncertainty. He was always so very sure of everything that he did, but this moment was entirely foreign to him.

"Do you want to come and see her?" I asked softly.

"Yes, of course." He came to the bedside and leaned over to look at her.

For a moment, he said nothing. I watched as his eyes took in every inch of her pretty little face, and I felt tears in my own eyes at the expression in them.

At last, he looked up at me. "She's beautiful. She looks just like you."

"I think she looks very much like both of us."

He sat down gently on the side of the bed, leaning in closer. "I knew it was going to be a girl."

We looked at each other, knowing that our lives had changed irrevocably for the better.

"My two beautiful darlings." He reached out to touch my face and dropped a kiss on my lips.

"What shall we call her?" I asked, fingering a lock of her hair.

He looked down at her again. "I don't suppose Delilah would do?"

I smiled. "Not if we ever want peace with my mother. Millicent?"

Milo shook his head. "It doesn't suit her."

A sudden thought occurred to me. "Your mother was called Dora. Was that short for Theodora?"

He looked up at me. "Yes, I believe it was."

"Let's call her after your mother."

He smiled. "Yes. I like Theodora very much. Theodora Rosamund."

I nodded. It seemed to fit her perfectly.

She stirred in my arms and opened her eyes then. They were a stormy blue, a mix of his bright blue and my gray. She moved her little mouth, and a dimple appeared in one cheek, like Darien's. Milo's father had passed something good along after all.

"Would you like to hold her?" I asked Milo.

"Yes," he replied without hesitation.

He took her easily into his arms and looked down at her. "Hello, Teddy. I'm your papa."

She looked up at him, her blue eyes locking on his, and tears sprang to my eyes. I felt a joy so immense that I thought my heart might burst with it.

"WOULD IT BE all right with you if Darien were to live with us for a while?" Milo asked me one afternoon a week or so after Theodora's birth. We were in the nursery, the bright spring sunlight shining through the windows. Below us, the gardens of Thornecrest were in bloom, the fragrance of primrose and wisteria floating on the warm breeze through an open window.

I was surprised at his request. Though they had begun to be on much better terms, I had assumed it would be preferable to both of them to set Darien up somewhere else, perhaps with a flat in London.

Milo seemed to guess what I was thinking. "I told him I'd help him if he was inclined to go elsewhere, but he says he wants to make up for lost time."

Looking at Milo, I suddenly had the impression that Darien wasn't the only one who wanted to do so.

"I think it would be lovely if he stayed with us," I said sincerely. Though Darien could be very trying at times, I was already growing fond of him.

"You're sure?" Milo asked.

"Yes, of course." After all, it wasn't as though Thornecrest was a small place. We wouldn't be bumping into each other at all hours.

Besides, it would be good for Milo and Darien to spend some more time together. Neither of them had grown up with a sibling, and they both had a lot to learn. It was a relief that it seemed that both of them were willing to do it.

I suspected things would not always be smooth between them. I knew the future likely held more escapades for Darien, as young men of that sort rarely learn their lesson the first time. But it would be better for him to have family to steer him than to send him out rudderless.

I was happy that they had found each other, happy that Anthony Ames had left each of his sons something they hadn't known they needed: a brother.

We had gained more family than we had expected this month, but I didn't regret it at all.

Although, as I looked down at my beautiful Theodora, I couldn't help but reflect on how glad I was that Milo had been right, that she was a girl; three Ames men might have been more than even I could handle.

ACKNOWLEDGMENTS

I count myself extremely fortunate to have had so many wonderful people accompany me along this book's journey. I am indebted:

To my excellent editor, Catherine Richards, for her insight and expertise.

To the fantastic Nettie Finn and to the team at Minotaur, for all their hard work on behalf of this book.

To Ann Collette, agent and friend, for always being just a phone call away.

To my marvelous mom, DeAnn Weaver, for everything she does.

To my entire family, for being fun, funny, and all-around amazing.

To Becky Farmer, for being my companion in travel adventures, brainstorming sessions, and celebrity spirals.

To Chalanda Wilson, for keeping me both sane and crazy every day as we work.

To my fellow Sleuths in Time authors, for their support and friendship.

And to the Book Wormz, for helping me maintain a nimble mind with Tuesday night trivia.

I am so deeply grateful for all of you!